THE OMEN TREE

FREDRICK NILES

FEVER GARDEN PUBLISHING

THE OMEN TREE

First edition. May 1, 2020.

ISBN: 978-1-950021-06-2

Fever Garden Publishing

Cover design Daniel Lloyd,

http://artonthedl.com

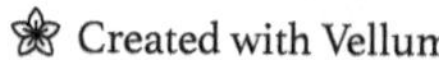 Created with Vellum

CONTENTS

PART I: OCTOBER, 2003

"The monsters of our childhood do not fade away,
neither are they ever wholly monstrous. But neither,
in my experience, do we ever reach a plane of
detachment regarding our parents, however wise and
old we may become. To pretend otherwise is to
cheat."

— JOHN LE CARRE

1
———

Ella Windthrope was soaring through the air.

On the back of the wind, beneath the bright and brittle stars that crackled overhead like lightning, each of them an entire world in itself. She was a bird. An angel. Huge and night-feathered, beating her wings against the tar-black darkness unobserved and unmolested. She was in a world of her own. She was free.

Lightning cracked and the stars flared, her small 13-year-old body reeling from the concussive blow.

"You want another?" her father bellowed. "Do you?" He grabbed a stack of magazines from the coffee table and flung them across the living room in what seemed like a flutter of paper wings.

It was one of those situations that Ella could barely even remember how she had ended up in. One moment she was sleeping and then the next she was arguing and yelling and the blows were raining down on her like fist-sized hail. Her father was furious, the small and cluttered house quaking around them in his anger.

Slumping against the side of the couch, Ella squeezed her

eyes shut, focusing on the rattle of the storm that had kicked up outside. The rain pelted the windows, the strong wind causing boards and nails to quake and squeal. Ella's head felt like those thin and shabby walls, threatening to break—screaming to let the world come crashing down.

THE RAIN HAD JUST STOPPED when Ella stepped out onto her porch a few hours later. At some point, her father had stomped off to bed while his daughter lay as small and unmoving as possible in a tight ball in the corner of the living room. Now there were thin wisps of sunlight reaching gently down toward the moist earth below and lifting up the rich aromas from the forest nearby. The air was thick with it. The sharp scent of pine poked out of the dull aroma of dead leaves like long fingernails on an otherwise soft hand.

Today was warmer than usual. The past week had been drizzly and overcast, but for the first time in a while, the sun had decided to creep out from behind its castle of dark grey clouds. Cold weather wasn't something unusual for Poplar, Wisconsin but Ella still had a hard time getting used to it when it finally reared up into the atmosphere from the ashes of an entirely too-brief summer. The sun was out though and she was determined to make the most of it.

She thought about her sleeping father inside. He had come back from a long and stressful shift in the morning's pre-dawn hours and was unable to find something he was looking for—a dish or mug or something—and had started slamming cupboard drawers, which had woken Ella from where she was sleeping on the couch. Lamenting the disorganized state of the house, most of which he was responsible for, the situation had spiraled almost instantly, Ella being the only person he could take his frustration out on.

Her father was a male nurse. His job was to assist the doctors and take care of patients' needs when the doctors weren't around. One would think that compassion was a prerequisite for a job like that but Ella knew better. About the time the sun began its early descent behind the hilly horizon her father would wake up hungry and angry and demand she cook something. She wasn't a particularly good cook but today was Thursday, and Thursday was steak night, which was easy enough. Butter, salt, and medium heat. What was there to screw up?

A lot, actually. Or at least a lot in his eyes. With a mother who had run off years ago and a brother who was living somewhere down South with some relatives she had never met, Ella was the sole target for her father's short-fuse temper. The bruises were easy to hide if for no other reason than nobody really looked. It wasn't so much the severity of the physical pain that was bad as much as its unpredictability. Ella's father worked long hours for a relatively decent amount of money, all of which he would spend on booze and illegally acquired pain pills. His life was a constant slog through chemical highs and emotional lows. She knew that the only thing he lived for was his fix, and even though he had a steady supplier somewhere in the clinic at the moment, that could all end in the blink of an eye. It would take practically nothing for the fragile peace they tried to maintain to go off the rails. If he lost his supplier he would start stealing. He would become paranoid and immensely more impatient. His sleep would decrease, the beatings would increase, and in no time at all, he would finally burst through that paper-thin veil that was hiding the truth of what his life actually was: worthless.

The day that Ella's father realized his lack of purpose, it would be *anything goes*. She knew he couldn't give any less of a shit about his own daughter and the moment she stepped too far in the wrong direction he would smite her off the face of the earth. Ella had learned that for an addict, there are no consequences, only inconveniences. And her life would be just as much of an inconvenience as life in prison.

The problem that Ella had was that she wouldn't know when that final tether between her father and his sanity had finally broken until it was too late. She'd be entering high school the next year, but four years was too long. Too uncertain. She had to figure a way out. She had to run. Run like her mother had.

Where though? She had little-to-no friends at school. No close relatives. The Northwoods wasn't exactly an ideal place to be homeless. Unlike urban areas, people around Poplar weren't used to vagrancy. She would make it about ten miles if she were lucky, and would then inevitably be hauled back to town in the backseat of Sheriff Anderson's car. Then there would be the questions and Ella had no doubt in her mind that her word wasn't worth shit. They would take her father's side in about one-second flat and then there'd be hell to pay.

With a huge effort, Ella pushed all of her fears aside. She didn't want to think about things if she couldn't change them, so that was how she found herself walking back to Poplar River. "River" was really a strong word for it when she thought about it. It was more like a thin thread of trickling water that made its way to Poplar Lake a few miles down. What would you call that? A creek? A stream? She wasn't sure. All she knew was that the river was her favorite place. She could sit down by its edge and watch the clear water constantly trundle up and over the earth. She couldn't say why she liked it exactly, other than the fact that —unlike her—there was nothing stationary about it. Not only was it headed toward Poplar Lake, but it could literally be headed anywhere. Maybe some of it would evaporate and make its way to the ocean, or perhaps it would one day become snow on the top of a mountain or the bottom of a deep valley. She didn't exactly have a strong grasp of weather patterns and how it affected the water before her, but she didn't want to know. She liked to sit there and dwell in the mystery of it. The possibilities.

The river was close now and she could hear the subtle noise of it rolling over itself, but that wasn't all she heard. She heard what sounded like the beating of wings.

Ducks maybe? Or geese? She knew it couldn't be an eagle or hawk; they were virtually silent in their movement. So, what then?

As Ella broke through a familiar stand of young pine trees she was brought to a sudden halt. Sitting barely thirty feet away was a giant bird. It looked like a swan, Ella thought. But not like any swan she had seen before. Every swan she had seen around here was white, yet this one was jet black, the color of liquid midnight.

Ella gasped as it rose in the water and beat its wings. The huge appendages seemed to conduct the very water before it, sending it in the opposite direction it had been flowing; then the bird stopped and the water resumed its course.

This was by far the most amazing thing she'd ever seen down here before, and she was careful not to disturb it. She watched it for what seemed like a mild and comfortable eternity as it preened itself. What was it doing with its wings though? Why was it beating the air like that? She had not the slightest clue.

"Why are you here?"

It took Ella a few seconds to realize that she had spoken aloud, and with that realization came the sudden panic that the bird would spook and fly away. She clenched her teeth.

Stupid. Stupid. Stupid.

But it didn't fly away. It stayed right where it was like some great monument to the unpredictable beauty of the world.

And then something happened. Something that Ella would

think about and turn over in her mind every day for the rest of her life. It turned and looked at her. Looked her right in the eyes.

And in those eyes, she saw the future in all of its horrible glory. She saw a tree growing from cracks in the Earth, snarled and terrible. She saw snakes and antlers and spiders and reaching tentacles. And then finally, she saw herself.

2

Rosaline Shuffer ran her fingers along the spines of the books in front of her. She had everything from the tiny mass-market paperbacks that had been worn out so much that the titles were barely visible anymore to the big and heavy leather-bound editions that always smelled musty and old, but in a comfortable way; as if they were aging rather than decomposing. Shelves full of valuable men and women, some of them wise and gentle, others bright and funny. The big ones even felt like they gained weight as they aged, which made her feel a little bit better about the weight *she* had gained in the last few years—as if her steamy romance novels and illustrious nature writing compendiums gained sympathy weight—but the heavy books didn't seem to agree too much with her arthritis, so if she happened upon an occasion that required her to open one, such as a cold and windy day in October, she'd just lay it down flat and read it that way rather than trying to prop it up on her knees while she reclined on the couch.

But what should she read tonight? You'd think that working in a library would have her burnt out on books by the time she got home but quite the contrary. Seeing all that literature around her all day made her long for it that much more. Not to mention the fact that she was actually an elementary and middle school librarian, which severely limited the content of her professional collection.

Well, at least her *publicly* professional collection. The school wasn't the only place she was a librarian, and the other place had a far more...*interesting* kind of books. Unfortunately, her other job didn't really pay the bills, no matter how unique and engaging it was, plus it had far fewer readers. Even the elders had slowly grown complacent in their comfortable lives, not seeing the need for the same level of vigilance that she upheld.

Enough about that though, Rosaline thought to herself. *No need to think about unpleasantries at the moment.*

After all, there hadn't been many occasions for her to put her obscure knowledge to the test, had there? Sure, there had been a few times but most of those had been false alarms. Regardless of the spiritual geography of the area, nothing had really...*come through.* So maybe she couldn't blame the elders for their lackadaisical attitudes. Maybe she should learn to relax like they seemed to be able to do.

Still though...

Rosaline picked out a worn copy of *Wuthering Heights* and lay down on the couch. She cracked it open to a random page and started reading.

Sacrilege, I know, she thought to herself. But she knew the book so well that at this point it was practically like flipping through the channels on TV and landing on a favorite movie. Which was perfect actually, seeing as she didn't own a television.

Some popcorn would be nice though...

She read and reread the lines in front of her, trying to stop thinking about popcorn. The last thing she needed was a hunch of empty calories, plus all that salt and butter would get the pages all greasy.

It would be so *good* though.

Finally, she succumbed to the temptation, dropped a thin and well-worn bookmark in between the pages she had open, and got up off of the couch. Striding into the kitchen, Rosaline wondered why anyone would eat microwave popcorn. Sure, stovetop wasn't as convenient and it technically took twice as long, if one could consider six minutes instead of three an inconvenience.

In virtually no time at all, Rosaline's kitchen was filled with the loud crackle of popping kernels and a sweet, buttery aroma. The tiny white pieces appeared to be pressing up against the stove pot's lid as it overflowed, but that was hardly unusual. It's not like a few more handfuls would make much of a difference. Plus, she could always just-

All of a sudden there came a loud *thump* from another room, like something heavy falling to the floor.

Maybe it's just Tony, Rosaline thought to herself. Tony was the lazy kid that she rented her second floor to. He was all right but could be careless at times like blaring his music or inviting... *unsavory* people over.

But even as she thought it, she knew she was wrong. The sound had come from her floor. Either the living room or her bedroom probably. Fumbling, Rosaline reached up and turned off the stove. The popcorn kept popping, but she had enough anyway.

"Hello?" she called. "Tony?"

With her hands trembling and her legs feeling a little bit like jelly, Rosaline walked slowly out of the kitchen and back into the living room. Maybe she had placed *Wuthering Heights* on the edge of the lamp stand without realizing it, and it had fallen off. That was probably it, actually. Working in a school library, she had grown quite accustomed to the sound of books being dropped on the ground.

As she thought about it, she felt a bit of her fear ebbing. She was just being paranoid. One would think that she would have gotten over that pretty early on in her life, seeing as she'd lived alone for the greater part of it, but here she was.

But no, *Wuthering Heights* was sitting right where she left it: light shining down from the lit lamp, bookmark poking out like an accusing finger. Rosaline felt a chill run up her spine.

Well, that only leaves the bedroom. Unless, of course, something she couldn't quite imagine had fallen over in her bathroom. She did have books in there as well. *Or maybe some kid threw a shoe at the door. Wouldn't be the first time.*

But Rosaline knew almost for certain now that the noise had come from the bedroom. Now that she was thinking about it and how it had sounded in the kitchen, that sounded right. The muffled sound of something hitting the carpet. The acoustics of how the sound had traveled. She had lived in this house for a long time now after all, and she felt like she knew every creak and bump this old thing was capable of uttering.

She walked to her bedroom. It was dark and the door was open, but the light switch was mercifully just inside the doorway. Still, as she reached in and flicked it on, there was that brief second where she imagined a pair of rough hands grabbing her before the switch was thrown. It was quick and fleeting, but something that her mind had done ever since childhood.

But it stuck with you, she thought. *That morbid imagination stuck with you, because you know the kind of things that lurk in the dark. The kind of monsters that only children nowadays have names for.*

The bulb sprang to life overhead, and in a split-second, the small and semi-orderly bedroom went from being the dark home of possible dragons to warmly lit sleeping quarters for a single woman who made her bed, did her laundry regularly, and quite obviously loved books.

These were her professional books though. The ones that she didn't want company to see when they came over. It was a weird thing sleeping in the same room with them. At times it felt daunting and frightening—as if they were watching her—but mostly they were comforting. She had had them for so long that they were like comfort items for young children. They exuded warmth and history and that wonderful old-book-smell.

But the moment Rosaline flipped on the lights, all of that comfort drained out of her. She kept the books in glass cases with small but sturdy locks on each of them. She had five in all: two on the left side of the room and three on the right. But now one of them was swung wide, the battered spines staring out at her with dusty eyes.

And a hole in the center where there shouldn't have been one.

Slowly, Rosaline approached the case. No need to try and find the missing book, it was lying right on the floor where it had dropped, likely making the sound that had drawn her in here in the first place. What concerned her was the case. It should have been closed—should have been *locked*. So why were the glass doors now hanging open like the arms of a reanimated corpse longing for an embrace?

For a short, middle-aged librarian, Rosaline checked the house astonishingly fast and thoroughly. In the end it took her two whole minutes to check her entire floor. She checked every closet and cupboard and lock and looked underneath her bed and all of her tables but there was nothing. No sign of anyone. No indentations of footprints on the carpeting that weren't hers. No faint whiffs of someone else's perfume or cologne. Nothing.

Feeling more secure now, she returned to the room and picked up the fallen book...

And felt her stomach flip.

This wasn't just some antiquated guide to the properties of local herbs or some vague dictionary about dreams. This was one of the big ones—one of the core texts. This book was one of the reasons her little secret society even existed in the first place.

It was an encyclopedia of sorts. One could even call it a field guide, though it was more thorough than any you might find in a local gift store on Northland birds or mammals; and it tended to meander a bit more as well. Still, it *did* have some pretty detailed illustrations.

The book had been lying face down when she had come in, and as she picked it up, Rosaline hesitantly turned the open pages up so that she could see what it had opened to. And not for the first time that night, she felt the blood drain from her face.

No.

There was a dry smack as she slapped the book closed. She ran her hand over the cover—navy blue with thinly etched lines of black—then she jammed it back into its place, hurriedly shut the glass doors, and then moved to her nightstand where she kept the keys.

When she tried to lock it however, the key wouldn't move. *C'mon you piece of...*Rosaline wiggled the key and tried to force it to lock but to no avail. What was more was that when she bent down to inspect the lock, she found a number of cracks spreading out from the tiny hole, as if it had been slowly and methodically forced apart.

Books like these often had a kind of aura around them. A mind and life of their own almost. But what was this one saying?

Rosaline dropped the key back into the drawer and let out a shaky sigh. She thought about the page she had seen—about the picture. The *creature*. Why? Was it just some fluke? Did the lock just crack after all these years? And did the doors manage to pull the shelf forward as they swung apart, causing a book to come tumbling out?

It sounded unlikely, but possible. At least, she hoped so because the alternative was unthinkable. Even the idea of someone sneaking in to steal it and then getting frightened and ditching out a window or something was better than the alternative.

The alternative was that the book had been warning her. An omen of sorts. The world as Rosaline knew it was knit closer together than most people realized, and occasionally certain events were preceded by tiny warning signals. They were often hard to observe and even harder to interpret correctly, but this seemed like a pretty big one if that was the case. And if it *was* the case, then the small town of Poplar, Wisconsin was about to get a lot more exciting.

Finding that she had lost her taste for both popcorn and reading for the night, Rosaline decided to skip any sort of real activity and just sat down on the couch to think. She knew that books had lives of their own sometimes—a sort of predestined path they followed from reader-to-reader—but these books were different. They were rooted in the deep black soil of a reality that most people didn't even know existed and they acted in ways that normal books didn't act. In fact, the more she thought about it, the more she thought she had just witnessed some sort of sign.

Signs were tough to understand though and easily misinterpreted. The meaning of the creature it had shown may have been clear enough but if she had a nickel for every person who thought they were some prophet of the future...No, she would just go to bed. She would let her subconscious work on it while she got some much-needed rest.

Rosaline's sleep was troubled however and at one point she awoke to find herself standing inches from the unlocked bookcase. The window in the room was wide open and a cold gust of air blew in through the screen, raising goosebumps on her skin.

She didn't sleep after that. After throwing on some clothes and quickly grabbing the book in question and chucking it into an old shopping bag, Rosaline got into her car and drove to the library. The *other* library. The one that wasn't at the school.

On her way there, she glanced down at the book in her passenger seat.

3
———————

Another night like the last, which wasn't necessarily a bad thing. Lilly Carlyle had gotten used to the routine. To tell the truth, her life had always been rooted in repetition: get up, go to school, do homework, hang out with friends if time allowed. It was comfortable, and it didn't wear on her the same way she saw it wear on others.

Lilly was young, skinny but not particularly athletic, and hadn't worn her maple-brown hair any longer than an inch from her shoulders since she was eight years old. She didn't smile a whole lot, but people seldom said she looked angry or unhappy. If anything, she gave off an air of defiant humor that was shot through with a streak of cynicism.

The chirpy sounds of *The Powerpuff Girls* were there to greet her as always when she walked in through the door to her parents' house, which she supposed was also her house at the moment.

"Aren't you a little old to be watching cartoons?" she asked her sister, Claire, as she hung her coat on the already overstuffed coat rack. Claire had become a perpetual figure in front of the television set recently, so much so that if Lilly had walked in and heard the news or sports or anything else she would have actually been concerned.

"Aren't you a little too old to be living in your parents' basement?" Claire replied monotonously. Even though they had this little back-and-forth every day, the comment still stung a bit. After all, Claire was the reason she was living in her parents' basement in the first place.

College had been pretty much exactly what she thought it would be. Late nights studying with friends. Ordering pizza five days in a row, then eating virtually nothing for two days after because her bank accounts ran temporarily dry. Lilly had a theory. It wasn't that college kids were necessarily poor; they just had no idea how to manage money. Or in her case, knew how to manage money but didn't really care.

One of Lilly's favorite things about school was that dating expectations were pretty much the same all across the board. You could hang out cheaply without *feeling* cheap. If for whatever reason you didn't want to hang out, homework was always an acceptable out. You could sleep around without worrying about an impending marriage. Lilly could do that now if she wanted but in a town like Poplar, Wisconsin, where she couldn't even eat a sandwich for lunch without everyone knowing what kind of cheese was on it, it didn't feel like a great idea. There were always eyes on her here and after experiencing the anonymity of a big college town, she was exceedingly aware of how everyone's expectations silently guided her everyday life.

After clunking down the stairs with her boots still on, she flicked on her bedroom light, revealing a gravely quiet tube-television, piles of clothes—some dirty, some not—and an empty and almost certainly cold bed.

Lilly thought back to Garret's room. It hadn't looked that much different than hers did now—random piles of clothes, beer bottles that could be hidden at a moment's notice, posters to cover the dents and cracks in the drywall. Maybe Garret's room had been a little smaller, but it had *Garret* in it.

It wasn't even that she liked him that much. Almost definitely didn't *love* him. But he was a warm body to sleep next to at night and if she was a little less wise, she would have married him on the spot if for no other reason than to solidify a promise of never being alone again.

God, that sounds sad, she thought to herself. *I mean it's not like I did ask him to marry me, I at least had that much sense.*

She felt achingly lonely and the worst part was that she couldn't tell if it was because it was the beginning of winter in Northern Wisconsin or if she had just grown tired of the small town she had called home for so long. She thought back to those lazy nights with Garret where, on a night like this, they would curl up under a bunch of blankets with a couple of mugs of hot tea and watch hazy romantic comedies on a TV screen the size of a piece of office paper.

The break-up had been pretty soft. He had secured an accounting job with his father's firm in Iowa that would start right after he graduated. Garret had followed a girl to UW-Oshkosh and when they broke up about two months into their freshman year, he had decided that he wouldn't be repeating that mistake. After a few weeks of dating, he had told Lilly this, and while she was already toying with the idea of following *him* back, it suddenly seemed childish.

She often wondered what Garret might be doing at that very moment—wondered how her life could have been different. Maybe she could have learned to love him. It's not like he was a bad guy or anything, he was just...

What? Boring? That was probably it. He was comfortable, but not once did he *excite* her. Lilly didn't think that she *herself* was particularly exciting but there had to be *some* kind of spark, right? You couldn't just love someone because they were warm and soft, could you?

Unfortunately, that was exactly what Lilly wanted at the moment: warm and soft.

Oh well, at least the dogs will be getting home soon with dad. They're pretty warm and soft.

Lilly had graduated with a degree in philosophy and a minor in literature, which was basically graduating with a degree in unemployment. But her major did benefit her in one way. She was acutely aware of her position in life: her home, her job, her friends...

And of the loneliness it caused her.

She heard the door burst open upstairs and a parade of stamping clawed feet shook the entire house. From the time she was born her father had always owned at least three Siberian Huskies. Sometimes, especially when she was trying to eat, she felt like she was literally being raised in a wolf den.

Lilly was able to distinguish one of the sets of paws clicking across the linoleum floor and down the wooden steps. She heard a snuffling at the bottom of the stairs and she whistled to get the dog's attention.

Numi trotted in and tilted her head. She was the prettiest of the three, Lilly thought. Her fur was so grey it was practically silver, and here-and-there she had small dark patches that seemed to shift in the light.

"Hey!" Lilly chirped playfully.

Numi gave a short, excited jump and a small whine then tilted her head again.

"Go for a walk?"

The wall of energy that the dog had been holding back burst forth and she jumped in circles, panting loudly; which, in Lilly's small room, was borderline catastrophic.

"Just let me get changed real quick."

Lilly had hoped that they had done the routine enough times that her favorite of the three dogs (and obviously the smartest) would have learned what she meant by "change my clothes," and go wait upstairs.

But she didn't and Numi just kept jumping around and knocking piles of laundry over while Lilly shrugged out of her work uniform and rooted around for some clean clothes, finally deciding on a pair of worn blue jeans and a mustard yellow sweater that her stepmother had bought her for Christmas a few of years ago. The color reminded her of pee and she was convinced that if she had worn it in front of anyone outside her family, they might mistake her for a shirtless Homer Simpson.

Back upstairs, she found Claire still sitting in front of the TV.

"Where'd Dad go?"

"He had to run back to church and drop something off."

"Do you know when he'll be back? I was going to take Numi for a walk and was wondering if he wanted to come with."

Claire didn't answer right away. Mojo Jojo was getting the shit kicked out of him on the television screen, and the 12-year-old girl gave the fight the attention one might reserve for a Breaking News bulletin.

"Claire?" Lilly said in a jilting tone, hoping it would be enough to pull her sister out of her reverie.

"Claire," Lilly barked. All three dogs snapped their heads up and looked at her. Claire slowly turned her head toward Lilly, then finally her eyes followed.

Lilly often forgot how cute her little sister was. With light blonde hair and a wardrobe that spoke of an intense naivety toward current fashion trends, Claire often felt to Lilly like a girl who had just been born.

She was only her half-sister, on her dad's side. When her father was 19 years old, he had spontaneously married a girl named April who he had only been dating for about four months. They were in love, her father had said, and things may have turned out differently if it hadn't been for the events that soon followed.

Her father didn't like talking about the accident specifically but he mentioned time and time again how miraculous of a day it was. It was, after all, the day that Lilly had been born. Her dad often referred to her as a "miracle child," though it was hard for her to feel the same when she could look around at all of her friends and their mothers that they undoubtedly took for granted.

Lilly never got to meet her real mother and she never would. When she was seven though, her father married a girl from his hometown in Wisconsin, and three years later, Claire was born. It was weird. Lilly's stepmom, Helen, had been in an abusive relationship until then but when Lilly and her father had come along, they gravitated toward each other. Three broken people stitched together into a family, and from that: Claire.

The fact that Claire had even been conceived was a miracle. Lilly's stepmom didn't talk about it a lot, but it didn't seem as if she had any sort of desire for a physical relationship. Obviously, they must have shared *some* sort of physical intimacy or Claire wouldn't have been born, but their relationship seemed to be devoid of all of the surprise grabs from behind or deep looks of longing that parents try to lob over their children's unobserving eyes. It didn't seem *bad*, Lilly thought. Her father simply gave Claire's mom a lot of space, and she seemed to appreciate it. And Claire never brought it up. It was all she had ever really known, after all. That was how parents *acted* in her eyes.

The ten-year age difference between the two sisters often felt like a deep valley they were on opposite sides of and when Lilly went to college she was afraid that they would drift apart in a way that would be hard to reconcile. Right after she graduated though, Claire got sick.

Really sick.

It's strange how something like leukemia can strengthen a family right before it tears it apart. And it would have too, Lilly had no doubt about that.

Lilly was sure that her father was going to have to face yet another family tragedy. Between the late-night prayer groups and relentless medical researching, the worry of losing his youngest daughter after he had already lost his first wife wore him down to a trembling and ragged version of his former self. He ate only the most minimal amount of food and slept roughly eight hours a week during that time. He was strong though and —he believed—faithful. Or at least his God was. After all, his first love was taken from him, but his daughter was miraculously spared in the process. Why would God save his daughter in such a fantastic way, only to take the other a few short years later? He had faith that God would deliver though. Lilly's father was a man seasoned with tragedy and calloused by sadness, but he was also warmed by the love of both his family and his friends.

Lilly had finished school, and instead of looking for a job like she had planned to, she moved back home to spend time with her sister while she was closely monitored within the confines of their house. Lilly picked up a job waitressing at Bee's Bustling Diner, a job she had worked the previous summer, and she resumed her life almost as if she had never even gone to college.

The two sisters' relationship hadn't been necessarily strong to begin with, but over the time they spent together, the sarcastic back-and-forths and sometimes surprisingly honest words of comfort strengthened their bond.

With the strength, however, also came the fear. If Claire didn't make it, it would be that much harder for Lilly. Lilly had always had a special bond with her father, but one thing she didn't share with him, was his faith. All she saw growing up was a man trying desperately to come to terms with the death of his first love, and with Lilly being spared in a seemingly miraculous manner, faith in a loving god was the closest thing he could latch onto.

He practically threw himself into it.

Lilly and her father were taken in by the church that was previously frequented by her mother. They were nice and generous people without a doubt—they sheltered them, fed them, and even employed her father—but Lilly could never *believe*. She just couldn't. It's not like she didn't try. She often thought that she had even tried harder than her father had. But when she called into the void...

Nothing.

It's not like an all-powerful God was impossible. She wasn't necessarily an atheist, but after twenty years of searching for an omniscient source of love, she never really managed to find what had only taken her father less than a year to devote himself to.

Lilly's dad was a warm and tender man behind the sadness that always hummed behind his smile, and people saw that. The church staff virtually *poured* opportunities onto him. He worked his way up, attended seminary two hours away, and became a full-time pastor when the old pastor stepped down. At times, Lilly almost wondered if her father was their...*project*. People resorted to strange things in the boredom of rural life.

Well, they had succeeded with him, but with Lilly? Not so much. And if Claire was taken away? That would be the end of it. If Claire died, whatever deeply buried coals of faith living inside Lilly would die also.

But she didn't.

In fact, Claire got better. *Way* better. It was expected among her father's congregation, but even among the doctors, the word "miracle" was being thrown around. Lilly was astonished. The second miracle child.

That was one month ago.

After bundling up and throwing a quick "be back in a while" at her sister, Lilly stepped out the door with Numi and observed the fresh snow that seemed to have come early this year. The air was cold but the sun cut through the chill and warmed her face. Numi trotted alongside her and the pair of them made their way out of the driveway and down the slushy gravel road, the newly snow-laden trees looming out of the ditch beside them like a wall between their world and some other new and strange world that only required a 90-degree turn and ten feet of walking to enter. She imagined herself stepping through the curtains of branches and out into some vast expanse of sparkling wilderness where all manner of magical creatures frolicked.

She didn't want to go *into* that world, obviously. Lilly had simply wanted to go on a nice walk with Numi, not on some mystical adventure. No, it was good enough to just pretend that *maybe* there was something special on the other side of those trees.

She moved further to the side of the road as a few teenagers in a beat-up Honda Civic slid around the corner, fish-tailed slightly, then finally regained control and continued their journey past a girl and her dog.

I wonder what they're up to today?

Lilly suddenly felt a small pang of loneliness and thought about turning around and heading back home. Her father would be back soon and they could start making dinner with the hopes of having it done by the time her stepmother arrived.

She thought about her dad. Despite the fact that his eyes were blue and hers were brown, people often said that she had her father's eyes. Whenever this happened, she felt an ache for the mother she never knew while also feeling a unique connection to the father she knew better than anyone.

Maybe that was why she couldn't find God. Maybe she didn't *need* God, because her father was God enough. He had always been there when no one else had. They were the only two that shared the painful loss of Lilly's mother—the mother whose parents had disowned her on account of her unplanned pregnancy and whose friends were never really there in the first place. The people at church acted sad but their awkwardly hushed tones and mournful faces felt almost obligatory. But not with her father. He felt it. She felt it.

But, just maybe, after this supposed miracle with Claire, she would look again. Maybe she would call into the void one more time for a God that hadn't answered back before. Apparently, she had been witness to not one but *two* miracles in her short life. Maybe that was sign enough.

Lilly blew out a foggy breath.

Something to think about, she supposed. Maybe one more way she and her father could grow closer. What she really needed right now though...

She thought back to Garret and his warm bed. The feeling of being with someone *real*. Tangible. Someone you could wrap your arms around.

Maybe I just need to get laid.

The thought made her snicker on the lonely road, and suddenly her mind was tired of thinking about God. Tired of wondering and hoping and worrying.

A gust of wind snaked by her and Lilly folded her arms, hugging herself among the swirls of snow that danced among her feet like the ghosts of children never conceived.

Tired of being alone.

They had been walking for almost 20 minutes and it was starting to get dark.

"C'mon girl." Lilly patted her side and pushed away every-thing she had been thinking about for the last hour.

"Let's go home and see dad."

SIX HOURS LATER, Claire looked at the clock for the hundredth time. Her mother was speaking hurriedly into the phone to her father who had returned and then some hours later, gone back out again to drive slowly up and down the snowy roads that wound around their neighborhood.

Lilly however, hadn't returned at all.

PART II: NOVEMBER, 2003

"What would an ocean be without a monster lurking in the dark? It would be like sleep without dreams."

— WERNER HERZOG

4

There were eight open spots left on the bus. Ella had counted. Not four. Not two. Not one last and lonely spot that would uncomfortably force a boy to sit next to a girl so that they could start talking and develop a budding friendship that blossomed into something more and then get torn apart by unforeseen circumstances and be the basis for a bestselling book written by a distant friend, followed by a semi-faithful movie adaption with two (only slightly related) sequels, the last one bombing at the box office so hard that all of the good qualities of the first film would be magnified tenfold and held in nostalgic reverence. No, definitely not *that* kind of seating arrangement. The thought of *that* kind of thing happening made Ella nauseous with repulsion. This was bad enough.

Eight. That's seven other spots Ian Whelan could have sat in. But no, he had to get on and walk almost all of the way to the back of the bus and sit down next to her. It's not that he smelled bad or chewed loudly or panted like a dog or anything. He was actually uncharacteristically quiet, but that wasn't the point.

The point was: Ella liked her space. She liked to stretch and sleep and put her backpack on the seat like it was the world's perfect boyfriend: silent and low maintenance. But she couldn't do any of that with Ian sitting next to her. If the bus wasn't constantly rattling like an airplane flying through a Category 5 hurricane, Ian may have even been able to hear her grinding her teeth.

They rode silently on the bus for half an hour before Ian broke the silence. And when he was done talking, Ella decided that she hated him.

———

IAN HAD NOT PLANNED on sitting next to Ella. After clunking up the too-big-steps of the bus, he looked down the aisle, saw the top of a single head with dark hair, and assumed that that head belonged to Ben Ryewheeler. It did not, however, because it was Thursday, and every Thursday morning Ben's mom dropped by Saving Grace Church to cook breakfast for the members of a local outreach program before they went about their daily activities. Since she drove right by the school, she usually dropped Ben off instead of making him ride the bus.

Absolutely none of that crossed Ian's mind though; there was only one thing rattling around in his 13-year-old brain and that was what he had seen the night before. The very idea of it was so heavy that he almost toppled over due to the weight of it. He thought that *that* might be half-imagined but that wasn't a line of thinking that he was willing to pursue.

Ian needed to tell someone, and he was so prepared to spill his guts that when he sat down next to Ella and not Ben, his heart almost stopped working.

He sat there. Staring. At the Seat. If someone were to ask him to relate the situation to another experience in his life, he would have told them about the time he was seven years old and the recess monitor wouldn't let him inside to pee because he had to learn to "hold it like everyone else." So he had stiff-leggedly walked around a corner and a couple of feet down a pathway that led to the front of the school.

There, on the side of the building, in front of the only highway running through town, he began to urinate. It was everything he dreamed of. And just like a dream, it was cut short. Mrs. Reynolds was her name. She had watched him walk around the side of the building and had a pretty good idea of what he was doing.

Years later, he would describe the incident as "entrapment." He would have kept peeing out of spite if it weren't for her ice-cold eyes that caused him to clench shut and pinch the flow.

Ella had those same eyes and right now they were doing the exact same thing: pinching his flow. But he had held it in for too long and finally it came bursting out in a torrent of borderline nonsense.

"Hey Ella, so last night me and my mom and my dad sat down to watch TV and my mom wanted to watch the X-Files and my dad said that it might scare me and I told them that it wouldn't because I'm 13 now and those things used to scare me but they don't anymore so they let me watch it and I was okay at the beginning but then I saw this old woman go into an attic and she got attacked by some creature so I said that I was tired and that I was going to bed but I couldn't sleep because I was so scared and then I walked around my room and checked under my bed and in my closet and in my toy box which is empty, I don't play with toys anymore by the way..."

In the midst of his rambling, Ian began to get light-headed, and somewhere in the back of his head he realized that he needed to breathe.

He stopped. Took a deep breath.

Ella began turning away.

"Anyway so I checked my bed and closet and toy box and then I checked out my window and I saw this-"

Ella moved her head almost imperceptibly. *Yes?*

"It was a-" Ian's voice croaked. "A hell beast."

There was a pause. Ian thought that maybe—*just maybe*—she cared.

She did not.

Ella grabbed her backpack and tossed it into the seat adjacent to them, climbed awkwardly over a still petrified and emotionally exhausted Ian, and stomped briskly away as if he carried some sort of transmittable disease.

Well. Ian's face felt hot and he was overcome with the same feeling of shame as when Mrs. Reynolds saw him relieving himself on the school. *Ben would have understood.*

BEN DID NOT UNDERSTAND. Ian was beginning to think that *no one* was going to understand. Come to think of it, did he even understand?

"I don't-" Ben reached up and rubbed the back of his neck. "Are you sure it wasn't like, an owl? Or a deer?"

"I know what deer look like, Ben." Frustration had begun to permeate Ian's voice. "I've seen about 100,000 deer. This thing stood upright and was taller than that big fiberglass hummingbird feeder in my backyard. You know how tall that thing is, right? It's huge!"

"Maybe a bear then?"

"If it was a bear it would have stopped at the hummingbird feeder and smashed it. We've had a bear doing that for years. Plus, have you ever seen a bear run on two legs? It's like a toddler taking its first steps. I don't think they even have knees."

"Sorry Ian." Ben started walking down the hall toward Art, his first class, and Ian followed along. "I just—like, a *hell beast*?

What even is that? I'm pretty sure you just heard that word for the first time yesterday, and now you're imagining things."

"I swear, Ben. I swear on-" Ian glanced down and thought for a moment, then his head shot back up. "My badges! In Pokémon Red! I have all of them *and* I've beaten the Elite Four."

Ben stopped and turned around. "Well, I wouldn't really know what those are, would I? Considering that whenever you play Pokémon, I just have to sit there and watch and listen to you explain what's going on. Do you think I enjoy that man? Do you think that's *fun* for me?"

He was on the verge of being in Ian's face. He backed off a bit.

"Still." Ben tilted his head and looked away for a second. "That's pretty serious."

The pace of the other kids in the hall picked up a bit and Ian could feel the tension mounting as people began to hurry to their morning classes. Ben looked up at the clock and said, "C'mon, we better to get Art."

"I'm not in Art, Ben. I have Resource this hour."

"Yeah, and today you will be resourcefully learning Art. C'mon."

Even with Ian's uncultivated sense of aesthetics, Mr. Tadler's art room often felt like it was an example of what not to do in art. The paintings on the wall looked like they were hung at random; some were too close together while others were too far apart. There were a lot of self-portraits, which was strange because Mr. Tadler was not a particularly striking man and the paintings themselves didn't seem to capture any real-life aspect of his personality.

The walls also felt cold and sterile. This was to be expected in a public building, but Mr. Tadler's walls felt the *most* sterile.

Ian often felt like he was in a hospital. Maybe even a hospital for art, where all of the sick paintings came to hang on the walls. Perhaps other paintings that were the product of the same oils and brushes would come with flowers and shake their heads and whisper about the futility of it all. Why do some art supplies end up in the hands of great artists while others are forged at the hands of ignorant fools? Ian did not know, nor would he ever, he thought.

He thought these things very often, but not right now. Right now he was trying to figure out if he was crazy. Had he really seen what he thought he had? Maybe he was just imagining things. Maybe he was just scared from the X-files episode.

Maybe I should stop being such a baby and actually make it through a whole X-files episode.

One day. Maybe.

Ian squirmed in his seat and looked over at Ben. They had planned to sit by each other, but as luck would have it, there were only two seats left and they were not the least bit next to each other. The room was filled with three-by-six foot tables and at each table was a pair of chairs that faced the front of the class-room. Ben had gone to his normal seat in the back-left corner, while Ian grudgingly walked over to the only other open seat in the back-right corner. The chair on the right side of the table was empty and seemingly clear of anyone's sweatshirt or books that might indicate their returning.

The chair that Ian was sitting in was hard and cold from a long night of buttless-ness, but what made him feel *real* uncom-fortable was the person in the seat to his left.

He glanced at Ella. She was glaring at him with her dead brown eyes while simultaneously sketching something in her notebook.

Ian cleared his throat. "Whatcha drawing?"

Before she could answer—though she probably wouldn't

have—he leaned over and peered at a crude drawing of himself being murdered.

"Good." He coughed. "Life-like."

It was clear that Ian would not be talking to Ben this hour, and come to think of it, there was no real reason why he should be here in the first place. It's not like Ella would listen to him. But as he was getting up, Mr. Tadler walked in and flipped on some lights that were previously turned off. The reason they were turned off was that there were far too many lights in—not only this classroom—but every classroom except for Mrs. Lionel's room, which was pretty close to being pitch-black.

After turning on the lights to a chorus of shocked groans from blinded students he began writing on the board. Drawing, actually. Once Ian was sure that he was drawing and not writing, he immediately knew that he was drawing a picture of himself. Mr. Tadler always drew himself in some form or another.

Despite all of Mr. Tadler's self-focus, Ian did have to acknowledge the fact that he almost always knew what was happening in the classroom, so when Ella folded up a piece of paper and slid it across the table in a manner that could hardly be considered discreet, the middle-aged teacher's head snapped around and fixed on Ian.

"Are we passing notes over there?" He used one hand to slick back his thinning grey hair while the other adjusted an ill-fitting baby blue sports blazer. His hard, round belly jerked back and forth as he stomped back to the last row of tables.

Ian was sure that Ella, embarrassed, would quickly hide the piece of paper, or maybe tear it up and eat it so no one could ever accuse her of premeditated murder somewhere down the line. She did not, however. She just sat there and watched while Mr. Tadler wheezed over to where they were sitting, picked up the piece of paper, and gave it a good hard look.

"Ella? Ian? Why are we passing pictures of what appears to

be-" he adjusted his small-framed glasses for a better look, "–a young man being shot to death by a young woman?"

Neither of them answered.

"Well." He crumpled up the piece of artwork. "It does have a certain sort of primitive brutality to it, I'll give you that. But if you are trying to express rage or anger, you might want to try giving her a knife or a hammer. Firearms often evoke a coldness or disconnection in the subjects that can contradict the intended mood."

Mr. Tadler shot the piece of paper like a basketball toward a wastebasket about ten feet away, where it then proceeded to bounce off the wall behind it and land in an already massive pile of paper balls that circled the basket like fallen leaves around a tree.

There was a pause. All eyes were on them. "Did either of you understand a single word I just said?"

Before Ian thought about it, he blurted "I did!" It wasn't often that he was able to show off—at least what he perceived to be—a pretty fair vocabulary. But when he glanced over at Ella it was clear that, while she may have understood the gist of what was being said, she didn't fully comprehend the language. From what Ian knew of Ella, she was definitely more of a movie person than an academic.

"And Ian-" he began dramatically, placing both hands on his hips. "You're not even supposed to be-"

"What's with all of that trash?" Ella interrupted loudly. Her face was bright red but wore a sneer. "I know that the janitor empties that every morning, so why is there a ton of shit around the garbage can?"

"Young Lady, I-"

"Don't you always arrive late? All stammering and..." Ella waved her hands, searching for the right word.

"Disheveled," Ian ventured.

She turned on him with a downright bloodthirsty look, then turned back to the teacher before he could gather the words to throw her out.

"I'll tell you why." She stood up suddenly and grabbed her notebook. "It's because you come here and draw and paint all morning because you don't have any art supplies of your own, because you're a piece of human fucking garbage that can barely afford to feed yourself. But all of your paintings suck 'cause you're a horse-shit artist so you throw them all away."

Mr. Tadler made a face like he had just drunk out of a milk carton he had found in a ditch along the highway.

"But you suck at sports too so you can't make a free throw to save your life."

The now sputtering teacher was verging on volcanic. "You get-"

But she cut him off. "And then, you leave ten minutes before we get here so you can walk in late and make us think you're some sort of John Keating!"

Everything seemed to freeze for a second until Ella snarled, "I'm sorry, did you even understand a single word of that?"

Like an escaped zoo animal, she got up, bolted, and dodged a frantic lunge from Mr. Tadler before she lurched out the door and down the hallway. A few seconds of shocked silenced passed before she stomped back into the room, tore down one of Tadler's portraits and ran out again with it fluttering behind her.

Everyone was quiet until Ben snorted and spoke across the room to Ian. "See? Way better than Resource."

5

—————

Ella hadn't known how easily she could be overwhelmed until all those eyes were on her. First Ian had to come and sit next to her *again,* as if sitting next to her the first time around had gone so well that he wanted seconds. The idea that he might have a crush on her flashed through her mind but she quickly snubbed it out. Not after that, he didn't.

It was about three miles back to her house but she was content to walk it by herself. The snow was melting so there were giant puddles all along the side of the highway. Some of them were so giant that she had to go far out of her way to avoid them.

Still, she would much rather be out here on a gorgeous fall day than be cooped up inside of a classroom where a teacher could tell all of his students exactly how to become a washed-up failure like himself. So what if he knew all those giant words? Let's see those words get him a well-paying job that can keep his family fed. They obviously hadn't or he would *have* a family, she thought bitterly.

Ella didn't actually know if Mr. Tadler had a family. He had never spoken of one, but that didn't mean that he didn't have six little life-ruining rascals at home. Why would anyone put themselves through that? Why put the world through that?

As she was walking, a beat-up brown pick-up truck slowed a little and slid on by her.

Suddenly she felt like there were a thousand eyes on her. It was something that she hadn't noticed before but thinking back she now felt like she had been watched ever since she had stormed out of the school without a word to anyone.

A newspaper article that her father had been reading flashed through her mind. What was it? Some young woman had gone out walking last month and never returned. Ella didn't know her —couldn't remember the name, something sappy but still kinda pretty—but she knew her sister, Claire. Claire was one year below Ella and had been shocked to silence for about two weeks after the incident. Eventually, she had begun talking to people again, but it still felt like there was something missing in her— something Ella felt like she could oddly connect with.

Gossip wasn't really one of Ella's pastimes, but Claire's story had been interesting enough that it passed through the school like a burning wind, and soon enough, everyone had heard about "miracle girl." Everyone knew that she had been sick. People started avoiding her in the hallways. Most stopped talking to her except for the occasional awkward sympathy. People disconnected from her like she was a weak link.

But then she was fine. Better than fine. A "medical miracle" some were calling it. And all of those people who had pulled away from her suddenly came rushing back. Ella thought that *that* had probably been the moment when Claire stopped talking to people. She had probably wanted everything to go back to normal, but when it did, all she could remember was how her friends had acted when she was sick.

Then her sister disappeared. In fact, she disappeared so fast after Claire's recovery, that some of the more superstitious people in town had suspected some sort of pact with the Devil. Claire's father was a priest or pastor or whatever, so she guessed that if anyone had contact with the Devil it would be him.

A brisk wind swept up and ruffled some of the dead leaves that had been recently exposed. November was a strange time for weather in Wisconsin, and they had just gone through a surprising warm patch that had melted a bunch of the snow. It was still a cold day, however, and Ella definitely wasn't dressed to walk home. All she wore was a pair of tattered Nike sneakers; a pair of jeans that had once been a dark grey but were now closer to white; and a light hooded sweatshirt over one of her father's old AC/DC shirts.

She hadn't decided if she liked her father's music or not. There was something about it that appealed to her, but she wasn't sure what. Perhaps it was like their shared love of movies. All bad things aside, she still liked watching movies with her father. It was the one thing that hadn't been corrupted.

Ella wondered what would happen if she suddenly disappeared off of the road like that other girl had, or got sick and died: would anyone talk about it the way they talked about Claire? Would anyone even ask? Or would her teachers just wonder where she was for a bit, but eventually write her off as a drop-out?

No, Ella thought. *I'll never end up like that.*

Her eyes swept the road vigilantly and saw nothing that alarmed her. But still, that feeling...

ELLA'S HOUSE was a single floor with brown siding and gnawed-up, white trim. It was pretty crappy looking, but to see it one would have first had to make their way down the winding, brush-bullied driveway. It was actually a pretty large chunk of land, which was cool, even though they had trouble paying for it. Her father had missed the last two payments and they had been selling stuff off ever since her mom left. *Mom...*

Ella couldn't see any lights on inside as she approached the crumbling front step, but that didn't mean anything. Her father's old 1988 Buick LeSabre sat in the driveway, so chances were good she was going to get an earful. It wasn't that her father cared if she was in school. She could be out hooking in front of Mary Tart's Fudge Shop for all he cared, as long as she wasn't at the house. Between her day schedule and his night schedule, they only saw each other for about three hours every day, and that was more than enough.

When her mother had left six years ago, Ella's father got stuck with parenting duties. He wasn't a big fan of her in the first place, and as soon as all of the responsibility of raising a child got dumped on him, he gladly dumped it right out back with his busted stair-climber, a dilapidated couch, and his ambitions of being a "rock star" one day.

Beatings were regular, but not bad. Well, not too bad. It usually only took one good smack for him to vent his frustration. A good smack from a grown man was a lot though when dealt to a child, and sometimes she would be black and blue for days. If the bruises were on her face, she'd skip school until they were gone, but most of the time the slaps were upside her head or on her arms or midsection, and those could be hidden by clothing.

When Ella entered her house, she was greeted by the familiar smell of sweat and onions. No matter what they cooked or cleaned or sprayed that was always the smell: sweat and onions. It was like living in a bad diner that shared a space with a gym. There was actually a place exactly like that in town. It was called Pain n' Gain, (the gym was called Frank's) and walking inside either of them felt like stepping inside her house, so she steered clear of both.

"Ella?" Her father didn't sound too drowsy, so he probably hadn't gone to bed yet. Still, there were virtually no lights on in the house and if she had never been there before she would have probably fallen down the stairway that stood gaping about four feet from the doorway. An incredibly bad design.

"It's me," Ella said as she dropped her notebook down on the table. "Got out early today."

"How'd you get home," he asked as he stepped out of the bedroom.

He looked horrible. Sporting a pair of worn, post-white underpants and a muscle shirt of matching color, Ella's father stood in the hallway and scratched his right leg, then ran the same hand through his thinning brown hair.

"You look like hammered shit," she said by way of greeting.

"Yeah." He glanced around drowsily. "Trying to get some sleep." His eyes were glazed.

"Okay, well I'm going fishing. God knows there's nothing to do in this heap." She moved to go grab one of her father's heavier coats that was lying in a pile by the door.

"Yup." He turned in a lazy circle and began walking back toward the bedroom.

Ella grabbed the coat, threw it on, and walked outside.

The image of her father's glazed eyes gnawed at her slightly. He was almost certainly high on something, which explained why he took the comment about looking like hammered shit so lightly. Whatever. She didn't care. They were more like roommates than father and daughter, and he could be selling meth out of his bedroom for all she cared. In fact, if he did that, maybe he would be able to make a house payment on time for once. She'd run the idea by him when she got back.

EVEN THOUGH ELLA had a hard time admitting that she liked anything to anyone, she truly loved the woods and river behind her house. She felt safe there among the trees that stood taller and stronger than any person could hope to. It wasn't particularly quiet—the birds were always chirping and squawking away—but it was peaceful. If she could spend her life back here, she thought she would.

Then there was the river itself.

POPLAR RIVER WAS ABOUT ten feet wide and four feet deep at its deepest. Still, if you fished along the weedy spots you could often pull out a couple of northerns.

Northern pike were long, slimy fish that were overly aggressive and often too skinny to eat. Weighing in at about 100 pounds, Ella often thought the same of herself. She smiled at the idea. That wouldn't be a bad life: just hang out in shallow pools all day, catching the occasional bluegill while snaking in and out of the weeds. *Mmm, the life of a fish.* Fun until a bigger northern came along and ripped you apart for no other reason than you just happened to be there.

Ella carried an old Shimano rod and reel with ten-pound fishing line tied to the end of a leader that was clipped onto an old silver spoon lure. The spoon was about five inches long with a treble hook on the end, and even though it was heavy and snagged on logs all the time, it was effective. She didn't need $50 lures or scented fish eggs or whatever. She just needed something that was flashy and sharp. They'd hit it every time.

After 45 minutes of casting, Ella had dragged in three pike between 14 and 16 inches and had gotten snagged seven times. Whenever the hook got caught on a rock or a piece of wood, the water was shallow enough for her to tip-toe in and free it by hand. Having not quite frozen over yet, the river was ice-cold and the water felt like fire on her skin. She would leave her shoes and socks behind on the shore and then quickly retrieve them and put them on. The process worked okay, but she couldn't do it for very long or too often or she'd get frostbite.

Most people would have never even considered the idea, but Ella had tested her own limits over the years and figured out what she could and could not take. Thankfully, she was in one of the shallower parts, and if she reeled fast enough, she could keep the spoon close to the surface. That way, it would only get snagged in about a foot-and-a-half of water, and she could just hop in and out. Then she would wipe her feet on the hoodie she had replaced with the coat and use it like a doormat to some fancy home. Sometimes she would even take the whole log with her if it was light enough, and just unhook it on the shore.

Despite the short amount of time she had to spend in the water each time she dashed in, her feet were still almost numb with cold. She stood on top of the old hoodie and shivered.

One more cast.

She hooked her right finger around the line at the base of the reel, opened the bail, reached back, and snapped the lure into the middle of the river. Immediately, she started reeling. Not too fast where it would break the surface, but not too slow where it would drag on the bottom.

Snag. *Dammit.* She needed to get one of those weedless lures: the ones with the wires that guarded the hook from getting caught on things. Oh well, she'd wade out quick, unhook it, and then head home. Despite the warm day, it was still too cold to be out here.

Ella sucked in a quick breath. *Quick. Like a deer.* She wiggled her toes in anticipation. *Go!*

The water was definitely the coldest the first time she dashed in but she was by no means used to it. It felt like she was being burned with every step. The distance was short though, and she quickly found the log the lure was caught on.

At first, she tried lifting the log, but it was either too heavy or was rooted into the ground. *Burning precious seconds.* She was about to reach under it and try to pry the lure loose when she saw something glide along the top of the water to her right.

A small muskellunge by the look of its dark back, disturbed from her splashing around in the water. They were usually pretty hard to find just by looking but occasionally she would see one linger near the surface with its long back poking up and out of the water like a snake. But why would this one stay here when she was just feet away? Injured probably, or maybe it was slow and groggy from the cold water? Ella didn't actually know much about fish or how their bodies worked in cold water versus warm, but it seemed plausible.

Forgetting the numbing cold for a second, Ella gave way to her curiosity and reached out to touch the long fish. With a gentle prod, she lightly touched its back with the pad of her index finger. It gave too easily and wasn't nearly slimy enough.

Any cold that she felt from the frigid water was suddenly forced to the back of her mind. Everything was wrong. Wrong species. Wrong region. Wrong time of year. The thing in front of her didn't just look like a snake. It was a snake. Long and obsid-ian-colored and shockingly out of place. But there it was, as real as everything.

Ella drew back slightly...

Then the world exploded in front of her.

6

At school, in the hallways, amongst all of the other kids, convincing Ben of the monster's existence was just as hard as convincing Ella, but by the time they were on the bus ride home Ian thought he could see Ben's interest beginning to blossom.

"You said it was big? Like a bear?"

"Not like a bear," Ian explained. "No knees remember?

"Pretty sure bears have knees, Ian..."

"Whatever," Ian shifted in the brown pseudo-leather bus seat to face his friend. "What I'm saying is that this thing definitely had long legs." He paused and thought for a second. "And long arms. And long everything."

Ben smirked and began to say something but Ian cut him off.

"I'M SERIOUS. This thing was big and-" he groped for the right words. "-lanky." Ian tried to think of a good comparison, then said,

"Ben, do you remember Welch Rataster?"

Ben furrowed his brow. "You mean back-of-bus Welch?" He jabbed a thumb behind him.

"Yeah, remember how he kind of walked with his shoulders and hands swinging, like a skinny bigfoot? That's what this thing was like. It was like Welch, but, ya know, from Hell."

"Welch is a gross name," Ben said nodding.

"Welch was a gross guy. Remember how he used to blow his nose in his hands and wipe them on the bus seats?"

They both looked down at the bus seat and squirmed uncomfortably.

"But yeah," Ian said getting back on track. "This thing was tall and lanky, and its skin was rough looking, like big scales or something."

Ben still looked skeptical. "I don't know man. Maybe we should like, look for tracks or something when we get off."

Ian brightened. "Yeah! Yeah, yeah, let's do that! I bet that thing had monster feet."

"And you know what monster feet means," Ben said with a grin.

They both said it at once: "long *every*thing."

THEY COULDN'T FIND any tracks. It's not that there weren't any, they just weren't entirely sure what they were looking at. To someone else, the nearly perfect circle that centered on a big maple tree in the middle of the yard may have looked like definite proof that something abnormal was happening out back, but the reality was that Ian's dog, Robin, had a long chain that connected to a cable that looped around the trunk of the tree, and when the big yellow Labrador had to go to the bathroom or got too rowdy inside, he could be tied-up to run around the center like a pencil on a mechanical compass. Since Robin had to go out roughly 35 times a day, the prime monster-tracking landscape provided by Father Winter had been scratched, ripped, and pounded into one big circle of paw prints and poop piles.

Robin had probably been let out countless times since Ian had seen his monster, and the whole area had been made anew by being thoroughly tread upon and shamelessly baptized in dog feces.

"Man, I can't tell shit from shoe-prints out here," Ben said. The two boys had gotten off the bus at the Wilmer Street stop so Ben could join Ian in the hunt for monster tracks.

"Yeah, this isn't working." Ian stood up from a patch of ground he was examining and brushed the dirty snow off of his jeans. "Let's go check in the woods, maybe it left some there."

Ben, beginning to lose faith again, rolled his eyes and half-heartedly walked beside Ian toward the edge of the yard.

Ian's house was surrounded on three sides by houses: Ben's to the back, the Schilling family to the left, and Mr. Rutledge to the right, but between each house was a good 30 to 100 feet of trees depending on the yard.

"I think it ran from the Schillings' toward Mr. Rutledge's," Ian said.

"Man, if we're going to go over near Mr. Rutledge's place then we're going to need to be careful," Ben cautioned.

Ian understood Ben's hesitancy. Not too long ago, Ben had snuck back behind Mr. Rutledge's woodpile to shoot squirrels from his bird feeder (all squirrels and chipmunks already knew not to go toward Ben's and Ian's houses) and he saw a pileated woodpecker land on the edge of Mr. Rutledge's roof. Being a young boy with a pellet gun, the big red head was hard to resist. Long story short: Mr. Rutledge had just opened his sliding glass door to shoo Ben away when the majestic bird fell twisting and flapping at his feet, its head punctured obscenely.

It set something off in the old man. He didn't yell or scream or stomp, he just looked up at the young boy with tears in his eyes and said, "If you ever step back on this lawn again, you'll be fertilizing it."

Ben said he didn't get it at first—not for a while actually—but the tone of the man's voice told him all he needed to hear. When he finally *did* get it, he was in science class and they were talking about the lifecycle of plants and trees. He said he almost peed his pants right then and there.

While facing north from Ian's yard, Mr. Rutledge's house was visible through the woods, so they decided not to approach it directly. Instead, they approached from the east and—placing Mr. Rutledge's woodpile between them and his sliding glass door—moved in slowly.

It was during this time of cautious focus that Ian noticed something: the birds weren't singing. The wind was rustling some branches and a few sticks snapped as Ian kneeled down behind his neighbor's woodpile, but there weren't any of the usual whistling bird sounds or chipmunk scuttlings that he was used to. In movies and books, that usually meant there was something foul in the area, and maybe the main hero would say something like "we're being watched, I can feel it."

Ian stopped. "Do you feel someone watching us?"

Ben didn't answer right away, and Ian had been Ben's friend long enough to know that he didn't feel anything but was afraid that if he were to admit it, it would be like admitting some weakness of senses. Ian knew because he would have thought the exact same thing.

So, no one felt anything. Either they weren't being watched, or the movies were full of shit. Both probably. And when Ian thought about the lack of forest sounds that usually accompanied a bright winter day like this one, he realized that they hadn't stopped, but simply hadn't been there all day. "Where are all of the birds?" Ben asked, echoing his thoughts.

"I don't know, maybe you killed them all with your pellet gun."

"Yeah, like you haven't dropped your fair share of songbirds."

Ian spun to face Ben and hissed "I only pump the gun five times, which is only enough to knock them unconscious."

"Not when you're using pointed pellets and they go right through their heads."

"That doesn't happen!" Ian's voice was getting louder. "They just get knocked out!"

"Yeah! They get knocked out of the tree, because they're *dead*." Ben was starting to smile.

"They're unconscious." Ian made a motion with his hand to signify the end of the conversation, but Ben kept going.

"They're unconscious because they're dead."

"You can't be unconscious *and* dead, Ben."

"Oh what, so they're *conscious* and dead."

Ian squeezed his hands and was about punch Ben in the arm when a big hand landed on his shoulder and wheeled him around.

"Aw man," Ben said, eyes going wide. Before Mr. Rutledge could grab him too, he spun and bolted. Over his shoulder, he yelled, "Sorry Ian!"

Ian gulped.

"You know you're being so loud I can hear you kids from my living room, right? The windows aren't even open." His voice was low but lacked the anger Ian had expected. "You here to kill more birds, or put more holes in my lawn?"

"I only pump the gun five times, which isn't enough to—holes?" Ian was confused.

Mr. Rutledge pointed a finger at Ian and then slowly pointed down toward his feet. Sure enough, all around the woodpile were holes of varying size; some were barely an inch wide while others stretched to at least four.

Ian glanced at the woodpile. "I think you've got a big squirrel problem." He almost said that he and Ben could take care of it for him but squashed the words before they came out of his mouth.

"When you say I have a 'big squirrel problem' do you mean that the problem is big or the squirrels are big?"

Ian didn't understand until a smile slowly crept over the man's wrinkled face. It wasn't cruel like Ian had expected, but warm. Mr. Rutledge gave Ian a hearty slap on the shoulder. "I'm just pullin' your leg, kiddo. I know you didn't make those holes," his smile suddenly dropped into a frown, "but if you kill any more animals in my yard..."

This, Ian did understand, and he made sure that he nodded hard enough to let his neighbor know that. Mr. Rutledge was a big man with broad shoulders, salty-black hair, and a confidence about him that commanded immediate compliance.

"So what are you kids doing back here anyway? I don't see any guns, and your friend seemed to abandon you in a pretty big hurry."

"Well," Ian cleared his throat. He wasn't quite sure how to explain to an old man that he had seen a monster running toward his yard. "I uh—I think someone was in my yard last night, and I thought I saw him run over here. Did you see anyone last night?"

Mr. Rutledge's eyes flicked to the left and then refocused on Ian. "Like, a person?" His expression was soft and inquisitive, and there was something almost childlike in his eyes.

"No, like-" Ian gritted his teeth and was already hating himself for what he was about to say. "Like, a bear."

"Oh, yeah." The old man stretched and stood up straight. "His name is Hamburger. He likes to come in here and knock over the bird feeders once in a while or root around in the garbage cans. He ain't hurting anyone; he just kinda wanders around going about his business. That's what all these animals are doing, you know? They all got stories of their own, and my yard is part of it. So when you start killing them over here..."

Mr. Rutledge blabbed on for about five minutes about the bear and the birds and the squirrels and the raccoons. He had named them all, which was kinda weird, Ian thought. Eventually, the old man ran out of air.

"Yeah, don't worry about that ole boy. He's a big softie..." It finally looked like he was going to let Ian go, but then he turned to him one more time. "You said 'someone' though. You thought you saw *someone* running toward my yard?"

"No." Ian shook his head. "Sorry, I meant 'something.'"

"Okay..." a look of skepticism flashed over his face. "Well, you better run along. That friend of yours probably thinks you're fertilizer by now. Oh, and if you ever want to come over here tracking some critter, or even if you just want to have some tea and watch the birds or something, could you please knock on the front door?"

He smiled and Ian smiled back.

"Sure thing."

"Where the hell were you?" After Ian had left Mr. Rutledge's house, he had walked back down Wilmer Street toward home, where Ben intercepted him. He had thought that Ian was—as Rutledge had said—fertilizer.

"Just talk'n to him. He's kinda cool actually. I think he's a bit lonely though. He names all of the animals that come into his yard. Which, by the way, I think you killed one of his best friends when you killed that woodpecker."

Ben was shaking his head. "Guy's pretty weird..."

"A bit." Ian actually kind of liked him. He even thought about joining him for tea and bird-watching some time.

"So, did you see anything?"

Ian was confused for a second and his face must have shown it.

"*Tracks* man? Did you see any tracks?"

There would be countless times when Ian would think back to this moment. He would think about how different everything could have been. An endless number of scenarios playing through his mind, if only he had said something different.

"Yes," he lied. He couldn't let the trail go cold. He couldn't let Ben's interest die. Someone *had* to believe him. "Yeah, something weird around the woodpile where we were sitting."

And many years later, Ian would often wonder how many people's lives would have been different. Or longer.

7

The two boys determined that the monster's point of interest must have been the woodpile. Maybe it had hidden something under it. Maybe it *lived* under it? Who knew? Ben's interest was hooked, and Ian's lie fed it like a dry forest feeds a rapidly expanding fire.

It wasn't totally a lie—or at least, that's what Ian would tell himself for a little while—he had seen all of those holes. If he probed that line of thinking for even a few seconds though it would immediately crumble. He knew that rodents loved woodpiles and he also knew that rodents liked to dig holes.

It didn't matter. Ian *had* to convince Ben that what he saw was real. If they went through their lives, Ben thinking that Ian had just gone crazy for a few days, then—well, who knew? Who knew what that could mean? Ian had this massive fear that Ben would never respect him again—that Ian would always just be a tag-along. A follower. Someone who never initiated anything and made up weird stories for attention.

That simply wasn't an option. Ian couldn't bare the possibility of falling back behind Ben as some...embellisher.

So he pushed on. The two boys planned what they would do

next: the what, when, where, and how. They tried to anticipate what they would need to get the job done: a reason to be out behind the woodpile, first of all. In addition, they would also need some sort of weapon. This thing was a *monster* after all. They didn't just want to find it. They were two young boys that had grown up on action movies and were deeply entrenched in a culture of glorified heroism and monster slaying.

They had to kill it.

The problem was, what could they use? Everyone in the Northwoods had guns, but they were almost always locked up; most of the time in a safe, with a trigger lock, and separate from the ammunition.

A bow was always an option. Both Ben and Ian's dads bow hunted, but the last time Ian had curiously and mischievously snuck down into the basement when his parents weren't home and dug the bow out from its case, he couldn't pull the string back more than a few inches. Ben was a bit stronger but he doubted he could pull it back much further.

So what did that leave? Kitchen knives, sharp sticks, pellet guns; all of them were either too unwieldy or too weak. This thing was bigger than a person. It was *tall,* and it probably had claws on the end of its long fingers. Ian couldn't be sure of that though. It was possible that that was something his mind had added later.

"Do you remember the story that Josh told us at the lunch table?" Ben asked suddenly.

"The one about Preston's birthday?"

Ian did remember, with surprising clarity actually. He remembered the day that they were all huddled around the table during their lunch period. The pungent odor of greasy burgers mingled with the smell of a hundred kids sitting in one room. The bright lights reflecting off of the not-quite-white tiled floor. The deafening roar of everyone yelling because they were trying to be heard over everyone yelling. It was a typical day in the cafeteria and what would a typical day in the lunchroom be without an outrageous story?

Joshua Davis was the kind of kid that snapped girls' bra straps and threw sand in people's faces. If you were having a good day he was determined to change that. Ian remembered a time when he spat in an old math teacher's face. The teacher had been so mad that he had spat back, and then been forced to resign later that year, which was too bad. Most people liked him better than Josh.

Despite everyone's growing impatience with the future fugitive, most of his stories were something to be treasured. He always gave it his all. He always made big hand motions and used large words and long phrases like he had written it down and practiced it in front of a mirror. The one he told about Preston's birthday party was especially enjoyable because for once, it had the faintest possibility of being true. Ian had even been there but hadn't witnessed the entire scene. But the proximity of it made him feel larger somehow. Important.

"Okay, listen here guys." He almost always started that way. "This last weekend I was at Preston's birthday. It started off pretty tame. Preston's brother bought a cake, and we got him presents. We mostly just watched *Jurassic Park*, played *Goldeneye* on his N64, traded Pokémon cards; you know, the usual."

Ian nodded along. He knew most of this already. But this was the first time he was able to hear one of his own experiences transformed into living mythology as it passed through Joshua's genius mind.

"All was going well until his father came home. Now as you might guess, he was already drunk and thoroughly relieved of the heavy burden of good judgment. However, as we all know, Tony,

Preston's 20-year-old brother, was not inclined to obey his father, nor did he advocate any sort of tolerance *of* him, from anyone, anywhere, ever. The resulting clash of these two forces was broken glass, drawn blood, and a vocabulary of coarse language that all but desensitized us to the wildest profanities ever contrived."

Josh then stood up in proper story-telling fashion.

"Being roughly a thousand miles out in the boonies, down a hopelessly complex maze of dirt roads and trails, the attendees of this birthday party—me included—began frantically and unsuccessfully searching for a quick and easy ride home. We were looking for old bicycles, trying to hot-wire ATVs, Kimmy Stewart even found a key to Tony's snowmobile, but as it turned out, the engine block had been replaced by a thriving family of mice."

"By this time, Tony and his dad were yelling at each other so loud that we were hoping someone a few miles away would hear it and call the police. We would have done so ourselves, had a tree not fallen over in their yard and clipped the telephone wires a few weeks back. Apparently, some guys had come out to fix it, but ya see, Preston's dad has a pretty substantial fear of the government and had in fact been planning to clip the wires himself in an attempt to go "off-grid." But being a lazy piece of shit, he hadn't quite gotten around to it yet. Legend has it, he murdered the first guy who came out there and buried him in the woods out back, but that's a story for a different day."

"Anyway, the tension eventually came to a sky-scraping climax when Preston's brother stomped into his room, only to return thirty-seconds later, toting two monstrous handguns."

Josh jumped up on the lunch table and cocked his fingers like a pair of pistols.

"He had one in each tightly-clenched fist, and waved them around like a trailer park version of Laura Croft: Tomb Raider."

"His old man then starts yelling 'Do it! It's 'bout time you become a man!'"

"Ready to avenge his pride, Tony pointed one wobbly cannon at his old man."

"BAM!"

Josh stomped his foot on Ian's lunch tray, obliterating his hamburger. A teacher was starting to come over now, her expression already exhausted.

"Thankfully for the boys' father, Tony was better at buying guns than he was at shooting them. What Tony failed to comprehend was the importance of the right kind of ammunition. So when the hammer of the .50 pistol hit the primer of the .44 caliber round, his hope for a fatherless life exploded in his hands. Literally." Josh had now caught sight of the teacher that was making a beeline toward the table and started speaking faster.

"One might say that the birthday party had officially ended at the point in which Tony was rolling around on the floor, clutching his shrapnel-shredded face, with his powder-pulverized hand." Josh loved alliteration. "However, this did not signify the end of our stay at the now blood-splattered household. First, we had to watch Tony do some on-the-spot doctoring to his hand and face, which was basically just him pouring cheap whiskey on his wounds and then screaming for what seemed like an entire solar cycle."

'AHHHHH! AHHHHHHH! AHHHHH!'

"Then we got to watch Preston try and figure out if his father was dead or alive, for he had collapsed when the gun exploded. The shattered television told us that the bullet had missed and we eventually concluded that the surprise of the rupturing gun barrel caused him to fall back and knock himself unconscious on the now-broken N64."

The teacher, who had just reached the table, grabbed Josh by the collar, but he kept going.

"Still shaking and wincing in pain, Tony sat us down and told us not to tell anyone about the events of the birthday party. He explained to us that attempted murder meant jail and he had no desire to go back. So after a barrage of scare tactics that were laced with-" The teacher was tugging on his shirt and telling him to get down, but Josh's feet were firmly planted. "-with the kind of skewed wisdom that could only be accepted by a group of children, the small hand on the clock finally hit 7 p.m. and the parents showed up and took their gravely silent children back home."

And with that, Josh swished his hands back and forth, which apparently signified the end of the story. He then went willingly to the principal's office, a look of triumph and satisfaction on his face.

"MAN, JOSH IS CRAZY," Ian said shaking his head. "And there is no *way* he doesn't write those stories out and edit them while looking at a thesaurus."

"I'm pretty sure he researches them too," Ben said. "No way he knew about the bullet thing; how the smaller one would blow up in the wrong kind of gun."

"So," Ian started, getting back on track. "Are you saying we-" he moved his head in a circle with a question mark on his face, "ask Tony...for a gun?"

Ben nodded in satisfaction. "Almost. We could ask him for one, but if I know Tony, he won't just give it to us. I'm thinking, we *buy* a gun from him."

Ian was sure that Ben did not actually—as he had said —"*know* Tony," but it didn't sound too far-fetched. Tony was stupid. And he would probably sell a gun to two middle schoolers. The problem was: what if they got caught? They were buying a *gun* after all. If either Ben or Ian's parents found out, a monster in their neighbor's backyard would be the last thing they would have to worry about.

It had to be done though. Ian knew that if he set Ben on this track, he would go all the way and do whatever it took. If they crossed this line there was no turning back.

AFTER THE BIRTHDAY INCIDENT, Tony had moved out of his dad's house and into a place of his own, and since then, Ian had driven by it every Saturday morning as his mom drove him to the local community center for swimming lessons.

Tony's place was no palace, but it certainly looked better than his old house. His dad must have had at least six cars in their yard that he planned on restoring in the future. But considering his motivation level, they were doomed to become habitats for birds, rodents, and the occasional beehive. Ian distinctly remembered them having a lawn but no actual grass. It was mostly just dirt, dog crap, and cigarette butts.

Tony's new place was the second level of a duplex. It was a strange choice for him because the bottom level was occupied by Ms. Shuffer, the school librarian. Ian wasn't entirely sure how Tony spent his free time, which he certainly had a lot of, but he didn't seem like someone who would cherish the idea of being in close proximity to any sort of school staff. Ben assured him however that—unknown to most of the people at school, students or staff—Tony actually had a uniquely positive relationship with the librarian.

Ms. Shuffer was an extremely mild-mannered woman who moved a lot when she walked but didn't actually get anywhere very fast. It wasn't because she was overweight, which she was a bit, but more like she didn't learn to walk right when she was a child. She kind of swung her arms back and forth like she was wading through a ball pit. A nice lady for sure, and Ian had to laugh every time he caught her reading what looked like racy romance novels. Not that there was anything wrong with that, but whenever someone saw her with one of her small paperback secrets, her face reddened with embarrassment and her speech patterns derailed into a jumbled mess of throat-clearing and neck-rubbing.

Apparently, when Tony had been in school, a lot of his teachers gave up trying to teach him and would send him down to the library to "study." In actuality, he could have gone and snorted cocaine in the basement for all they cared, just so long as he was out of the classroom. So most of his days, he sat back behind the counter chit-chatting with Ms. Shuffer and spinning in circles in an office chair. He had actually aspired to be a librarian for a short time, at least until he found out that you had to go to college for that.

The house was a beige paint-peeled thing with a centered front door on the first level and a stairway leading up the back to the second level. Thankfully for Ben and Ian, it was only about four blocks south of the school, so instead of taking the bus home, they hiked down the slushy sidewalks to what they hoped was the answer to their "home defense" problem.

Ian had never been there but apparently Ben had. Every once in a while, Tony would invite a bunch of people over to play Goldeneye and drink cheap beer, and occasionally his little brother Preston was allowed to do the same. So after drinking said beer and playing said Goldeneye, Ben had told Ian that beer tasted like piss, but Goldeneye was greatly enhanced when everyone you were playing against was hammered.

Despite the vague association with Tony through Preston, Ian was still quite nervous about approaching Tony and asking him for a gun. He was so worried in fact, that he couldn't even think of what could go wrong. Would cops bust down the door and haul them away for gun-running? Would Tony go crazy and shoot them like he did his father? It wasn't even that there was a clear danger, it was that Tony was unpredictable, and they were about to do something pretty serious. Ian had heard all sorts of crazy horror stories about kids messing around with guns and accidentally blowing each other away. He considered himself smarter than all of those kids, but surely they had thought the same thing.

The stairs to the second level were snowy, more than half-rotten, and looked like they had been nailed together by a six-year-old: everywhere someone could pound a nail there was one. In fact, he was pretty sure that the staircase was more metal than wood at this point, which would have been more encouraging if nails could somehow fasten themselves to each other. As it was though, the monument to tetanus looked as if it could fall apart at any second, and being surrounded by nails as you fell couldn't exactly enhance the situation, Ian thought.

"Do you suppose he walks up this thing every *day*," Ian asked as they slowly ascended.

"Have you seen him? He's like 5' 10" and 95 pounds. He's like one of those mummies they find buried in tombs that are all tough and dehydrated like a piece of old fruit."

For the briefest of seconds, Ian believed that Tony actually *was* a mummy and that they were going to leave the house with what they wanted, but under the penalty of some wretched curse.

"Here we go." Ben took a deep breath and knocked once, then two more times.

Nothing. They could hear the sounds of machine guns coming through the small TV's speakers inside, but it was possible that he was one of those people that left their TVs on all day, every day; like it was some electronic Atlas: baring the weight of Tony's singular taste in movies and video games for the rest of eternity.

It had been maybe two seconds before Ben decided to turn around and try heading back down the stairs, but before he could take a step, the door creaked open and Tony's pale face peaked out.

"Tommy!" Tony's voice was as screechy as his stairs and his face had about as much metal in it.

"Tony!" Ben said, unconsciously mimicking Tony's voice.

For whatever reason, Tony thought Ben's name was Tommy, and he also thought it was really cool that both of their names sounded alike. Ben had apparently corrected him a number of times, but Tony's mind was like one of those waterfalls that goes down a hole in the ground and no one knows where it goes or comes out. You could talk to him all day and just watch the words you were saying get sucked into nothing.

"What can I do ya for?" He still only had the door cracked and when Ian shifted his weight, Tony noticed him for the first time and gave a little jump. "Who's this?"

"This is Ian." Ben waited a second, then added: "he's cool."

Ian *was* cool actually. Tony's skittishness reminded him of a squirrel trying to figure out if it's okay to eat from someone's hand or not, and the thought made Ian's worries dissipate a little.

Ben gave a so-here's-the-deal-man nod and said, "We talk to ya inside about a possible...transaction?"

Tony's face was impenetrably blank, but after a second he nodded and said, "For sure man."

When they got inside Ian started taking off his shoes, but Tony laughed and said, "Don't have to worry about that. This place is a shit-hole."

Ian took a look around and concluded that Tony was correct. The air smelled like skunk and gym class, but if he was being totally honest with himself, Ian had seen worse. Some things were actually neat and straight underneath the piles of junk. It looked more like two organized people had moved into separate rooms, and then one of those rooms had been dropped on top of the other. Plus, Tony had the same scales Ian had used in science class, so he began developing this idea that Tony was more like one of those frantic doctors you see in movies: someone who was too busy with his work to clean. It was the only logical conclusion he could come up with, because as far as Ian knew, Tony didn't have a job anywhere in town so he must have worked out of the home.

"So what's up?" Tony asked, nodding the whole time.

"Not much," Ben said. It looked like he was still trying to figure out the right words. "We were wondering, is there any chance we could buy..." he reached down and fished for some bills he had stuffed in his pocket. Getting the money hadn't been that hard; Ian had been saving up for a PlayStation 2, so he had to dig into his piggy bank a bit. Ben, on the other hand, had a jar full of small bills that his parents had foolishly trusted him with. Now it looked like he was going to have to score a scholarship if he wanted to make it to college.

"Whoa, whoa guys! I know you're almost in middle school, but you're still a bit young. I mostly just deal with high schoolers. If the cops found out I was dealing to you guys they'd put my nuts in a vice. And if Ms. Shuffer found out..." He looked genuinely afraid.

"Come on, man," Ben blurted. "I know our parents wouldn't approve, but they wouldn't understand!"

Tony's eyes moved back and forth between Ben and Ian, then finally settled on the wad of bills.

"Well, I guess..." he said with a shrug as he bent down to grab something out from under the TV. But as he was reaching there was a hard knock on the door. Not the door that they had come through, Ian realized, but another one that was on the opposite side of the room. Tony glanced at the two boys and then yanked the bills from Ben's hand and replaced it with a baggy full of what looked like densely packed lawn-mulch.

Tony was whispering excitedly now. "This is worth a little more than what you gave me, so just keep that in mind for next time, yeah?"

Ben tried to object but there was another hard knock from what had to be Ms. Shuffer's balled-up fist; and suddenly Tony was pushing them across the room, out the door, and shooing them down the outside steps. Ian spun around as soon as he finished stumbling onto the old stairs but the door had already slammed behind them.

Ben looked at the bag in his hands and sighed. "Well, do you suppose I can use *this* to pay for college?"

8

R ichard Carlyle was a man in conflict. He had long ago shed the belief that the good things in life were rewards from God while the bad things were punishment. In his experience, bad things often happened to good people and vice versa; what people deserved never really factored into it. However, a month after his daughter's disappearance, Pastor Carlyle found himself staring at the ceiling and wondering why.

This wasn't the first time he had found himself in this situation. When his wife April had died years before, Lilly was there to soften the blow. Now that Lilly was missing, his other daughter, Claire, had been inexplicably healed from her disease—a disease that he had prayed to God to cure. A prayer that he had not expected to be answered. Or at least, he hadn't expected a "yes."

Helen, Richard's current wife, lay softly snoring beside him. Her face was delicate. Her hair fine and lightly golden. How easily she could be swept away. Like Lilly. Like April.

April still held a place in his heart that he couldn't quite get at. No matter how much he tried he couldn't let her go and maybe that was because he didn't want to let her go. Not really. He loved Helen and she held her own place inside of him, but it was separate from April. Richard had always thought that once you loved someone, you couldn't love anyone else—that one would replace the other—that that special someone would fill you up and if you loved them—truly loved them—nothing else could get in. So when Helen came into his life he was surprised by the chemistry between them. Both of them had experienced tragedy in their lives, but it wasn't just that—it wasn't just what they had in common. Helen was fierce in conversation where Richard was a little more laid back. She was strong, opinionated, and stubborn. Something about that appealed to Richard. Her strength was a comfort to him.

But now, even with her lying next to him, Richard couldn't sleep. He hadn't been able to since Lilly had vanished, and every aspect of his life was suffering because of it. His sermons were weak and uninspired, he would often forget appointments and people's names; he felt like he was falling apart.

Careful not to wake his sleeping wife, he swung his legs out of bed and quietly planted his feet on their soft bedroom carpet. Now that he was up he didn't want to move. Helen was sleeping so peacefully, and with all of the work she had been doing to find Lilly, he felt like waking her up might literally shatter her; like she was a fine vase filled with liquid worry.

She wasn't related to Lilly by blood, but she had—for all intents and purposes—been her mother for a good deal of her life. She had poured herself into her family and when Lilly had gone missing she had reacted far worse than Richard had. Or at least far more demonstratively. She had organized search parties, called and interrogated almost everyone they knew, and hosted group prayer meetings both at the church and in their home. The organizer, the planner, the *doer* was firing on all cylinders. She wholly devoted herself to finding Lilly which would have been an all-around good thing, if it hadn't been for Claire.

Richard eased himself out of the bed and quietly exited the dark room. Barely able to see, he patrolled the house. Claire slept with the door cracked, so he was able to peer in and see her curled up warmly in bed. Before he left, he made sure he could see the gentle rise and fall of her breathing.

Claire was missing her sister, but she was also just a kid. She was a 12-year-old girl who had been brought back from the brink of death, and within a few short weeks, her victory was squashed. Snubbed out. The bright flame of her recovery fell under the impossibly heavy shadow of her older sister's disappearance and she became sad, confused, and angry. She didn't say any of these things. She probably couldn't even articulate what she was feeling. But as her father, Richard felt it nonetheless.

As he walked down the hall and into the living room, he heard something stir off to his left. Debbie and DeVille, the two remaining dogs, reminded Richard that his daughter wasn't the only one missing. Numi had disappeared as well and though it had seemed for a while that there was no room for any more despair, Richard suddenly felt the loss of the dog get heaped on with the rest of his sadness.

He had planned to go downstairs and scope things out—all the dark corners of the house were empty—but when he hit the third step—the step that creaked, the creak that he had heard every time his daughter stomped down the stairs toward her room—he stopped.

A soft yellow light from outside hovered on the steps like a golden fog and if he had put more weight in the idea of omens, he might have taken it as a good sign. But he knew it was just the light from outside and the shadow that he cast downwards made his path ahead seem that much more uncertain.

The unlikely pairing of miracles and tragedies had happened twice now in his life and while others might view it as a sign that there was no God, Richard couldn't help but see an author's hand in it. The question was: why?

A wave of despair so strong it was almost physical washed over him, hitting him so hard that he actually wavered and became unsteady. A sick, tingling feeling crept down his left arm and suddenly he thought he might even be having a heart attack. Wouldn't that be the icing on the cake? What would Helen and Claire do then? No sister. No father.

But no, the feeling was passing. Strength was coming back into him, even though he felt as if he had just lost a pint of blood and had it replaced with something toxic and terrible. He placed his hand on the door handle and an idea came to him so suddenly that it was as if he had simply heard it spoken by someone else.

Staring out into the unfathomable darkness that permeated the outside world, Richard knew two things: he wasn't going to find answers here and as long as that was the case he could not sleep in this house. Family or no family he had to be alone.

9

—————

Four days. No one called, no one asked, and no one cared.

When Ella returned home it was like she had never left. Her father barely looked away from the TV when she squelched in and across the floor in her now almost totally disintegrated Nikes. She hardly expected a tearful reunion, but this? Ella looked down at her clothing and thought she looked like she had just dug herself out of a grave she had spent the last four years rotting in.

Her father wasn't the only one that barely noticed her return. When she attended school the next day there was no "welcome back Ella," or even a "where have you been?" She was completely ignored. Invisible.

But was that their fault or hers? After all, she was the one who skipped school, who avoided talking to people, who came and went as she pleased. She had done this to herself, hadn't she? How could she expect someone to care for someone they barely even knew?

She had heard as much in her time out in the woods. She had heard...a lot of things.

"Ella? Hello?"

Whoa. Where am I again? School. Right.

"Mmmm?" Ella looked up and it was at that moment she realized that she didn't even know who she was talking to. She had attended the class before, but she had been there so infrequently that, not only did she not know who the teacher was, she didn't even know what the class was. The teacher repeated the question and Ella added the answer to the growing list of things that she didn't know.

She finally just ended up mumbling something and shrugging her shoulders, only to be met by a stern stare.

It went on like that for most of the day. She drifted through the hallways and classrooms like a tourist on the opposite side of the world, surrounded by people she didn't know—people saying words she didn't understand the meanings of. She even got lost once.

What the hell was she doing here? She didn't belong in this school. She didn't even belong in this *world.*

When Ella looked around at the fast-paced cliques—the kids running around giggling and lying and leaving early to make out beneath the bleachers—she observed that the massive torrent of bodies was like the river she fished in, except she regarded it more as a giant foaming serpent.

She shook her head. She couldn't let go of the idea of snakes no matter how hard she tried. That's what the school was though. It was a giant snake, racing through the dirt, and if she tried to touch it?

It would strike her.

When Ella got home she found her father passed out face-down on the couch, and as she gazed upon him in that filthy house on the brink of foreclosure, she was disgusted. One of his arms was all bruised up from puncture wounds, which meant he had probably run out of pills and had to switch to the other stuff —the kind of stuff that stupid kids made in sheds out in the woods. And if he was black and blue, then he had been drunk as well. Maybe even fighting, which was the last thing she needed. Before he had been like a partner in a science lab project: she didn't get along with him, but she didn't really have a choice.

Things were different now and she realized it for the first time. She was done with him. Done taking his shit. Done cleaning up after him, just to have him knock her to the floor whenever he felt like it.

Ella was stronger now. Maybe not physically, but mentally. Emotionally. She had just spent four days in a virtual Hell, and she'd be damned if this fat sack of shit would have control over her.

"No," she breathed. "Never again."

She was still by the doorway and the basement stood gaping up at her like some filter-feeding sea mammal. Next to the open basement door was a box of old CDs and VHS tapes that her father had hoped to sell. *Like anyone would pay for a dusty copy of Delta Force III.*

She kicked it down the stairs.

If she were to guess by the explosive noises it made as it bounced down the steps, she would have said that every single item in the box was broken by the time it hit the dirt basement floor at the bottom.

Her father looked like someone had just hooked a car battery up to his belly button. Writhing up and off the couch, there was nothing he could do but fall to the ground. He came sputtering up like he had just been dunked in a lake.

"What the fuck," he yelled. He was still wearing his work shoes and they slapped across the floor as he stalked toward her.

At first, Ella thought that he might strike her open-handed like normal, but as he used his whole body to swing at her, his fingers closed into a fist. Ella didn't have time to think, didn't have time to block or dodge.

She didn't have to.

Her father reeked of alcohol and was still feeling the effects of his morning's liquid breakfast. By the time he was actually swinging, he was almost right on top of her and his fist sailed passed her and through the screen in the door behind them. The momentum of the swing was extreme and with Ella being right there, his sweaty body hit her like a brandy-soaked F-150 and they both went tumbling out into the neglected snow-streaked front yard.

Her father was bigger and stronger. By a lot. But they weren't fighting on the same level. He had been rudely woken up and was fighting like an annoyed wild animal. He wanted to sleep. He wanted quiet. He wanted to *make* her quiet. He wanted to beat the quiet into her, or rather, the noise out of her.

Since hitting the ground, Ella no longer wanted to fight her father. Like in the classroom: something clicked off inside of her. She wanted to kill him.

On the ground a few feet away was a broken branch that had been blown there by a high-wind and heavy-rain summer storm. That was almost a year ago and the stick was now dry and hard.

As her father rolled onto his back and moaned like a bear waking up from hibernation, Ella walked over and picked up the stick. It was about four feet long until she broke it in half and snapped the small protruding twigs off against her leg in one raking motion. Now the branch looked less like a branch and more like a gnarled rapier.

She had nothing in her mind as she strode forward. It wasn't like something came over her, more like something left her. For a moment she was just a machine.

At the last minute, finally starting to realize something was seriously wrong, her father struggled to one knee, raised his hands, and brought his head and right shoulder together in a protective motion that probably saved his life.

Instead of going into his neck like she had planned, Ella stabbed diagonally through her father's left cheek and into his tongue.

The noise he made was like a trumpet being blown underwater, and in its strangeness, Ella finally came to the realization of what she was doing.

She stopped, and stood, and stared and it was exactly the wrong time because her father absolutely exploded. He hit her so hard in the side that she lifted off the ground and landed by the front door. She tried to get up, but fueled by pain and rage, the big man moved at an almost superhuman speed. He leaped over, picked her up by the shirt, and held her in his hands for the last time.

Ella was a doll. A toy. Just another piece of her father's garbage and like her father's garbage she sailed through the air, hit the stairs, and then tumbled downwards into oblivion.

SHE AWOKE some time later in the pitch black. The basement door didn't have to be tested for her to know it was locked. Her father was gone, she thought. If he hadn't have left then he would have killed her.

She had never thought of him as someone who could kill somebody, but at that moment, she knew it in her heart. He had a choice: kill her, bury her, and stay; or leave. Leave everything. Forever. Whether that meant packing up and driving off or going and sticking a gun in his mouth, she couldn't say. But even if he stayed in Poplar she doubted that she would ever see him again unless by accident.

Sleep started to crawl over her again but then the pain came. It covered her like a blanket. She ached as if someone had just crushed her underneath the weight of ten lifetimes but as she tried to push herself up the pain suddenly receded. It wasn't gone, but it had been pushed into the background by an ever-powerful sense of realization. She couldn't get up just yet. She had to think.

Ella sat and put the pieces together in her mind about the last four days—those terrible days that felt like an eternity—that she could never tell anyone about. In the woods, they had said that she would find the answers she was looking for beneath her feet. The answer to a question that, over last few years, she had not had the courage to ask.

What could that mean? What did *this* mean? She sat there and thought about it and as she did, she slowly—almost unconsciously—made tiny circular motions with her index finger around the inside gap of one of the many, very deep, holes that speckled her basement floor. Each one ranging between one and four inches.

And one in the middle that was over a foot wide.

10

———

I t was a few days later that Ben and Ian found out what happened at Tony's. Apparently, Ms. Shuffer had a "no selling drugs to children," policy. It sounded weird—you'd think that she would have a "no selling drugs to *anyone*" policy, but apparently Tony and she had an understanding.

She liked Tony. She knew what he was about and decided that if he was going to be dealing, she wanted to be able to have some sort of say in the matter. He could live above her with discounted rent and someone to vouch for him, as long as he didn't sell to anyone younger than 14, didn't *murder* anyone, and stuck strictly to marijuana.

None of these were a problem. Tony found most people under the age of 14 to be fickle and tedious customers. He wasn't particularly prone to violence aside from the attempted *patricide* of his earlier years. And as far as he was concerned, dealing anything harder than pot was just too much of a drag.

Still, even with all of these stipulations, neither Ben nor Ian was entirely convinced. After some prodding, Tony mentioned nonchalantly that Ms. Shuffer *may* have had a pretty bad case of rheumatoid arthritis and *may* have self-medicated via Tony's product.

Somewhat satisfied, the two young boys dropped the subject.

"I also feel like I should tell you guys," Tony began. They were up in his apartment again, and this time Ms. Shuffer had been assured that they were there strictly to play video games and hang out. No transactions. "When you handed me that wad of cash, I kinda assumed that uh-"

Tony tilted his head to the side and pursed his lips.

"What?" The way Ben said it sounded more like a command than a question. He was somewhat less amused with the situation than Ian had been. "Spit it out."

"Well, I assumed that there was uh-" he reached back and scratched his neck. "More than just singles."

A flash of anger crossed Ben's face but he held it together. "We weren't here to buy pot man. We were here to buy a *gun*."

Tony looked confused for a second. First, he looked at Ian, then at Ben, then back to Ian. Finally, after an uncomfortable silence, he leaned back with a sigh that may or may not have been a laugh.

"I SWEAR I'm going to beat the piss out of Josh the next time I see him." Ben was fuming as they stomped down Tony's stairs. Structural integrity be-damned.

"What are you going to tell him? 'Say, Josh, we tried to buy a gun from Tony, and as it turns *out...*'"

As it turned out, Tony had never owned a gun in his life. What he did own, however, was a *cap* gun. A cap gun was a device that, when the trigger was pulled, allowed the hammer to fall on a small deposit of gunpowder which, like a real gun, exploded. *Un*like a real gun, the amount of gun powder was barely enough to cover the eraser of a pencil, and when detonated, did nothing more than make a loud pop.

When Tony came out of his room on the now-infamous date of Preston's birthday party, he thought that it would be funny to fire a cap gun right next to his drunk dad's ear. For maybe the only time in his life, Tony was right: it was funny. His dad flipped out, stumbled, and fell through a coffee table. When he woke up many hours later and wondered why he looked like a cartoon character that had tried to jump out of the TV screen and failed tragically, Tony just told him that he had been drunk and passed out standing up. Satisfied with the answer, his dad apparently lifted himself out of the wreckage, suffering only minor cuts and bruises, and stumbled off to his bedroom.

"Man, I thought you were there. Didn't you see what happened?" Ben asked.

"I was outside at the time," Ian said defensively. "I didn't want to be anywhere *near* that man. I was the one trying to figure out a way to get a snowmobile with no engine to run."

"Well shit, you should have at least seen *something*."

"Someone should tell Josh that the real story is a much better one," Ian said.

"I think he'd disagree. He likes his own versions of the truth way more and apparently, so does everyone else."

Ben looked sullen, and not for the first time, Ian wondered when this had become more important to Ben than to himself. He knew it was going to happen of course—had known as soon as he had told the lie about finding tracks in Mr. Rutledge's yard.

Ben was the kind of person that—once he set his mind to something—couldn't stop. He would obsess about it and beat it to death until he either conquered the task or it conquered him. And with this acknowledgment, Ian felt the rising nausea of guilt.

As they walked down the sidewalk back toward home, they

passed by the town cemetery and Ian stopped next to the fence to tie his shoe. He didn't actually need to tie his shoe, but he had a thing about the cemetery. He liked to stop and look at the graves and imagine all of the past lives of its inhabitants. What was their day-to-day life like? Did they have to cook using wood? Did any of them serve in World War II? Who were they? How did they get there? Stuff like that.

A gust of wind kicked up and the branches of the trees in the cemetery clattered together like the clapping of hands, a sort of dry sound that might be made by an audience of skeletons.

"You thinking about dead people again?" Ben asked as Ian got up.

"Yeah," he admitted. "It's just interesting you know. Almost comfortable. Like—maybe someday someone will walk by my grave and do the same thing."

Ben looked over the fence at the grey stones jutting out of the ground in all sorts of shapes and sizes. The day was cold but there wasn't much snow on the ground. A thin layer of frost covered the whole cemetery and made the place seem like a world all its own.

"I don't feel very comfortable right now," Ben said, shifting where he stood.

Ian wanted to argue with him but as he took a good hard look into Poplar's small burial ground he suddenly felt something in him sour. Something about it seemed different but he couldn't quite put his finger on it.

"I don't know, maybe you're right," he finally said. "I guess it doesn't feel very comforting today, does it?" And even as he spoke, he continued to search for why that might be. But after another couple seconds of silence, he couldn't identify anything other than a vague feeling of rot and foreboding emanating from the cemetery. Maybe it was just the fact that they were currently searching for a monster and the idea of being anywhere near a cemetery carried with it certain associations.

"So, what should we do?" Ian finally asked. He turned toward Ben, trying to remove that cloying sense of unease that had crept up inside of him over the last minute.

Ben seemed to be having a similar reaction and he was finally able to tear his gaze away from the lumpy field of head-stones. "I have an idea," he said. "I'll show you when we get back to my place."

IT CERTAINLY WAS "AN IDEA," Ian thought, but whether it was a good one or not, he wasn't entirely sure. It was obvious that this wasn't something that Ben had thought up on the spot though, because when the two boys walked into Ben's dad's workshop out behind his house, Ian could tell that his friend was already thoroughly into the project.

"I'm not entirely sure that this is going to work," Ian said hesitantly. *Although*, he thought, *there have certainly been worse ideas*.

In his hands, Ian held the foot-long wooden grip of a two-handed broadsword that Ben had made out of a long, straight, sharpened stick. He had then fastened two shorter and more flexible sticks perpendicular to the first one and tied them so as to make a cross-guard. After that, Ben had taken a few pieces of thin, triangular scrap lumber from his dad's scrap pile and secured them parallel to either side of the main shaft for greater width. Finally, he had covered the entire thing in silver duct tape. Ben said it was for security, but also, Ian thought, because it looked like metal. All in all, it felt to Ian like a real sword and grasping it firmly with both hands gave him that much more confidence in the idea.

Ian wanted to remain skeptical of Ben's tools of war, but to tell the truth: it was hard. After all, who doesn't want to hold a massive broadsword and go to war with it against a creature that was almost surely pure evil?

Maybe...Just maybe...

11

I an's mother was a semi-stern woman with dishwater blonde hair and a sort of midwestern thickness that was common among Poplar's population. She wasn't prone to yelling very much but she had a certain severity to her that spoke volumes and instilled immediate respect.

When Ian walked in the door that night he immediately felt his mother's attention latch onto him. He figured there was something that he was either going to be asked to do or had already been asked to do and forgotten about. Rather than trying to guess what this was though, he slowly and quietly slipped off his boots at the door and began tip-toeing toward his bedroom.

"You're going to want to put those back on." His mother was sitting on the couch, the evening news mumbling gently in front of her.

Ian simply stopped and began walking back toward the door. She would surely explain herself.

"Aren't you going to ask why?" She was smiling now and shaking her head.

Ian stood for a second and weighed his options. Then he

spoke up and asked, "Was there something I forgot to do?" He tried to sound as innocent as possible.

"Gosh, you don't have to sound so guilty." His mother laughed. "I saw Mr. Rutledge while I was getting the mail today and he mentioned that he could use some help shoveling his driveway. He hasn't really been able to manage it since the last snow so I volunteered your assistance."

"Cool. Thanks mom. Glad you did that."

"No need to get snippy." Her voice had an edge now. "Would you make that poor man break his back just trying to clear his own driveway?"

"He's not *that* old. He's like 60 or something."

"Well, he's not that young either and I think you could learn something by helping him out a little bit."

Ian wasn't quite sure what he could learn but he knew that it was useless fighting with his mother. He slipped his boots back on and walked the short distance down the road to his neighbor's house.

SHOVELING MR. RUTLEDGE's driveway didn't take quite as long as Ian had expected, but occasionally he would get an extra heavy shovelful of wet snow and strain to lift it up and hurl it off to the side. He was dressed lightly in his boots, coat, and his favorite floppy winter hat, but before long he was sweating hard beneath them.

When he was done, he knocked on Mr. Rutledge's door.

"You should be all set. I made sure not to pile the snow on the ends so you can still see down the road when you're pulling out."

"That's great." Mr. Rutledge said happily. He pulled out his wallet, opened it up, and peeled a couple of ten-dollar bills out and handed them to Ian. "Fine work, son." Though he hadn't really looked at any of Ian's work yet.

"No problem." Ian began to turn away.

"I talked to your mother," Mr. Rutledge said. She said you could have dinner here if you'd like. I could fry up some steaks, plus I have some apple pie for afterward.

Ian stopped turning. *Apple pie...*

THE INSIDE of the old man's house wasn't like the inside of any old man's house Ian had ever seen before. On the few occasions that Ian had been inside of single elderly men's houses or apartments, he had always found the same thing: piles of dishes, dirty clothes, a bag of golf clubs that could be picked up and carried out at a moment's notice, and somewhere between two and twenty-two dogs.

Old guys loved dogs. One time Ian's family had to be part of an intervention for one of his uncles because he was quite literally collecting dogs. After hours of denial, then yelling, then finally tears, his uncle's pack of dogs were split up within the family, thus resulting in a new addition to the Whelan household in the form of a yellow Labrador named Robin.

A surprising lack of dog hoarding here. Ian's thoughts rambled as he walked through Mr. Rutledge's house toward the dining room. *Lots of books though.*

Ian was a big fan of books. When he was young he would often read the choose-your-own-adventure stories along with the *Goosebumps* and *Animorphs* books. When he got a little older he began reading the *Harry Potter* series and eventually pushed forward into classics like *Frankenstein* and *Dracula*. When asked, he would tell people that Frankenstein was his favorite book of all time, though he hadn't quite decided why. He had even read tried to read some F. Scott Fitzgerald. The parts of *The Great*

Gatsby he had read were good he guessed, but it was mostly just good that it was short.

Ian now found some of these same books along the shelves that lined Mr. Rutledge's living room and dining room. Lots of times Ian would go over to other people's houses and see their bookshelves and be immediately excited, only to find out as he got closer that they were occupied with sequential, annual releases of the Webster's dictionary or technical manuals or the predictable collection of Study Bibles. Every time this happened, Ian felt cheated. He felt the same way when he opened a big box on Christmas and found patterned sweaters or a bulk pack of underwear. For one of the first times though, Ian was not let down.

In addition to a bunch of classics, some of which he recognized and a bunch that he didn't, there was also an assortment of small paperbacks by authors like Nevada Barr and Sandra Brown. Upon seeing these, Ian suddenly felt affirmed in his love for *fun* reading.

"I don't know a lot of people with bookshelves in their dining room," Ian said as Mr. Rutledge cut open a package of steaks.

"Good conversation starter," Rutledge said. "That, and I'm running out of room to put them."

Ian wanted to keep the conversation going. On the shelves, there was a small book with the words "Les Miserables" printed down the spine, and right next to it was a significantly larger book with the same title and a dark yellow bookmark poking out of the top somewhere near the beginning. Next to it was a copy of *Tales of the Jazz Age* by Fitzgerald and Ian decided on that as a topic of conversation.

"I've read Gatsby," he started, sounding maybe a little too casual. "How's that one?" He pointed toward the book.

"Fantastic. When it comes to Fitzgerald, the shorter the story the better. As far as I'm concerned at least." He dropped the steaks on a plate and began grinding some pepper on them while Ian sat down at the table. "That there is a collection of short stories." He stopped for a fraction of a second, then continued seasoning. "You can borrow it if you want."

"I'd love to," Ian said enthusiastically, though he wasn't sure how much he'd actually enjoy the book. It looked a little too...civil.

"All of these books tell the truth." Mr. Rutledge waved the small bottle of seasoning at the packed shelves. "They may be fiction, but the stories they tell are more real than anything you'll find in a manual."

Ian nodded his head, though he wasn't quite following.

"Everything has a story." The way he said it sounded like he was beginning to lapse into a conversation with himself. "Even these steaks here." He patted the slabs of meat with a bare hand.

"The animals that provided this meat were born to mothers who cared for them. They probably felt comfort the first time they were nursed and fear during their first thunderstorm. But their stories are like anyone else's: they have to come to an end." The old man leaned over and knocked on the table for emphasis.

Mr. Rutledge turned solemnly toward Ian. "Can you do me a favor son? Every time you eat meat of any kind, I want you to think about the animal it came from. I don't expect you to switch to fruits and veggies—we were given the ability to eat meat, and that is part of *our* story—but it is important that we don't forget the sacrifice that is made for us to live."

Ian was thoroughly weirded out. Thankfully, all that was required of him was an agreeable nod of the head.

Mr. Rutledge worked quietly over the stove as he fried the meat and boiled some spinach, a detail he had conveniently left out of the original proposal. When the food was done, the old man poured some whole milk for Ian and himself, dished out the food, and they began to eat.

"Seen Hamburger lately," Rutledge asked.

Ian sat looking at his steak for a second, confused. *Was he regretting his choice of meat or.....*

"Ya know, the black bear?"

A light clicked on in Ian's head. "Oh! Um, no, not really."

"He's a sneaky one, I tell you what. You know, sometimes he comes right up to that window over there and peers in with his nose pressed up against the glass. One morning I came out and..."

Ian nodded dutifully as Rutledge continued. To tell the truth, he didn't really care, but he wanted to *seem* like he cared. He just couldn't though, because somewhere back toward the front of the house, Ian thought that he had seen a basement door. He didn't think about it much at the time but he was thinking about it now. He was thinking about it because, even though Mr. Rutledge was prattling on and on and the fan over the stove was running and somewhere down below he could occasionally hear the *clank* of a pants button hitting the inside of a dryer as it tumbled around, he could also hear something else.

Ian thought about the tall creature that he had seen running through his yard and tried again to remember what its hands had looked like. He still wasn't sure, but the more he thought about it, the more he seemed to remember that it had had claws.

Yes, big dragging ones. He could see it now: two knife-tipped hands swinging alongside its lumbering form as it strode quickly into the woods. He grappled with this detail as a growing feverishness overtook him, causing the blood to rise in his face and sweat to bead on his forehead. He sat totally still, honing in on the noise he heard coming from that closed door some 20 yards away.

Over all the racket of the kitchen and conversation, Ian thought he could hear the distinct sound of claws scratching on wood.

12

———

They were set to go. They had armed themselves, they had a location, and now they had a decent idea of the monster's lair.

"It has to be underground," Ben said. "There must be some sort of trap door under the woodpile that connects to the basement."

"Do you think Mr. Rutledge knows?" Ian was nervous and fidgety. There was definitely an element of fear but he was also feeling the enchanting haze of adventure that seemed to throw everything into fast forward and at the same time slow everything down. "He seemed pretty okay. And why would it let him live?"

"I don't know." Ben was tapping out a rhythm on his desk. This time Ben was the one to dodge out of his morning class to join Ian in Resource. Mr. Tadler would surely mark him absent, but Ms. Shuffer hadn't seemed to notice him yet. Leaning back in her chair, the librarian/resource teacher/apparent landlord to good ole drug-dealing Tony seemed to be quite absorbed in whatever risqué romance novel she had hidden below the front desk counter.

"There's another thing," Ian said. "So...what? Does the monster have to move a bunch of logs when he wants to get in or..."

"I don't know," Ben repeated. His foot was tapping now too. If he kept it up, Ian thought, he was liable to break into a drum solo at any time.

"Maybe it has something to do with those holes," Ian said it almost to himself.

Ben stopped tapping. "Holes?"

Right. Ian hadn't told Ben about the holes. He had just said he had found tracks.

"Yeah, that's right. I forgot to tell you." Ian's gaze shifted to the floor. "There were all of these holes around the woodpile."

Ben spread his hands in a gesture of *and you were going to tell me this...*

Ian pushed on. "Yeah, there were all these holes around the pile. Like this-" He held his fingers in an O-shape for Ben to see.

Ben looked skeptical and Ian suddenly felt the entire thing waver. He wanted to go: "look, Ben, there were no tracks." He wanted to find the monster and slay it but he also wanted to come clean with his friend. If they were about to charge into the mouth of Hell, then he didn't want to do it based on a lie. He wanted to tell Ben everything, he really did.

But he didn't, because almost out of nowhere, Ella was there, grabbing an empty desk and placing it so it was facing both Ben and Ian. She practically fell into it, arms plunking down on the top of the backrest.

"Tell me about this thing you saw." She was dead-serious but neither Ben nor Ian could focus on what she was saying.

"Geez Ella, you look like you fell down a mountain," Ben said, and Ian agreed. Covered in dirt and bruises, Ella looked like she might be more at-home in a coal mine rather than a library.

"I did," she said without missing a beat. "Now tell me about this thing you saw."

First turning to Ben, Ian hesitantly began to fill her in. After all, he had already told her once, hadn't he? Not like it was any secret anymore.

He told her about the thing's tall and lanky figure—about how they tracked it to Mr. Rutledge's and the woodpile and how it was scratching on Mr. Rutledge's basement door. Then he laid out their rough plan to raid the monster's lair, complete with possibly-exaggerated descriptions of their homemade armament.

She looked skeptical. "Did you see any holes?"

Ian perked up and Ben blinked a few times.

"Yeah!" Ian was stammering in excitement. "A bunch of them, by the tracks we found by the woodpile!"

Ella leaned back in her chair and seemed to turn her gaze inward. "OK, we'll go there tomorrow night. After dark. Right now, we need to get some information."

Ben and Ian looked at each other. They hadn't really thought of that.

Ben spoke up first: "What do you mean 'information?' I mean we can't exactly go look up 'big tall skinny shadow monster' in the dictionary now, can we?"

Ella stood up out of her desk. "The church has a big library in the basement. We'll start there. C'mon."

Ian felt suddenly nervous again. "What, you mean *now*? We're in school."

"Fuck school," she said a little too loudly. Everyone in the room turned to look at her, including Ms. Shuffer.

Visibly wrenching herself out of whatever she was currently enthralled in, the librarian leaned forward and called, "Ms. Windthrope, I do believe there are a few students in here who would like to at least *pretend* to study-" at this she knowingly eyed Ian, "-without their thoughts being interrupted by shouts of profanity."

"Sorry," Ella said. "There won't be any more disruptions."

Ms. Shuffer nodded approvingly and returned to her reading.

"Wow," Ben said, looking at Ella. "I didn't know you knew how to use the word 'sorry' in a complete sentence."

"Shove it, Ryewheeler. I'm just trying to get out of here as fast as possible."

"Hey, can't argue with that," Ben replied. "Let's go."

SAVING GRACE CHURCH WAS A SMALL, wooden building with modern, square architecture. The sanctuary could seat a couple hundred people and the lobby could hold about fifty if everyone straightened their arms by their sides and pressed in on each other like matches in a matchbox.

Ella, Ben, and Ian had left school without being stopped and had proceeded to walk the two empty miles that lay between them and the church. With Ella out in front, they walked at a pace that Ian would have felt more comfortable jogging at. No words were said between any of them and in under thirty minutes they were stepping through the unlocked doors of Saving Grace.

The building wasn't empty if the cars out in the parking lot were any indication, but the staff were most likely nestled away in their offices doing whatever they did. Ian had little idea of what made a church run and he wasn't particularly interested at that very moment. All he wanted to do was find the basement.

"How do you know they have a big library?" Ben asked. "I've been going here for years, and I've only been down there twice."

"Ella?" Ben's tone was persistent but she didn't seem to be paying any attention.

After failing to receive an answer for a second time, Ian made the mistake of placing a hand on Ella's shoulder. She immediately whirled around and backhanded Ian across the left side of his face.

"Ow! Son of -" Ian's eyes flicked around at the inside of the building. "Ow..."

"My mom brought me here when I was a kid. Now where the hell is the basement?"

They had only been in the building for a few seconds but after glancing around, the only immediately visible doors were to the sanctuary, the offices, the kitchen and dining area, and the bathrooms.

No one said anything for a moment, but after shooting an unpleasant glance at Ella, Ben motioned with his hand. "This way. It's at the back of the sanctuary."

As Ella plotted forward Ian fell back to talk to Ben. "Were you just not going to tell us?"

Ben gritted his teeth so loud it sounded like there was a miniature rockslide in his mouth. "I don't know man. Breaking into a church? With her? Just look at her."

Ella had reached the door and was now throttling the knob like she was trying to wring the neck of a live chicken. After a few seconds she gave up, twisted the handle as far as she could to the right and threw her shoulder into it once—twice—and on a third time the door banged open with a loud crack. She strode hastily through.

"The door sticks," Ben muttered. "All she needed to do was push her foot against the right corner and it would have opened just fine." Ian waited a few seconds to let him return to the conversation. "That's what I mean though. She doesn't *belong* here."

"You seemed fine with it at school," Ian offered.

Ben threw up his hand and made a sour face, then picked up

his pace to follow Ella down the steps. "I know." He seemed to contemplate for a couple of seconds. "I was just excited, I guess."

Ian knew what he meant. When you were talking about it everything was merely a possibility, a chance for adventure. But when it actually came down to buying guns, breaking into churches, and ditching school it suddenly felt like a whole lot more than just some fun game they had been imagining in their head.

There was a short hallway through the door that led to what looked like a broom closet on the right and a staircase on the left. It struck Ian that if the staircase had been right on the other side of the door, Ella might have simply crashed down the steps all the way to the bottom. Ben's analysis of the situation was beginning to feel more and more accurate.

All thoughts of Ella were extinguished however when the two boys reached the bottom of the steps and took in the library. For some reason, Ian had pictured the scene in *Beauty and the Beast* where Belle steps into a massive room with vaulted ceilings and endless shelves of books lining the wall. What he encountered, however, was a lot less...romantic.

A few harsh lightbulbs illuminated a massive square room that was packed with rows and rows of metal shelving; each shelf overflowing to the point where the books had begun accumulating on the floor, creating something like a big, dusty obstacle course.

It was at this moment that Ian suddenly realized he had no idea what he was actually looking for. Ben stood at his side with an expression that mirrored Ian's while Ella ran her finger along the spines of the top shelf of books and—her lips silently moving—read the titles to herself.

"So do we just look for books about...evil? Or monsters?" Ben's voice was incredulous and his words flowed over Ian's mind like ice water being dumped on a dreaming man.

If there was any doubt before it was gone now: this was a stupid idea. What had they expected? For the *Demons and Monsters of North America Field Guide* to fall off a shelf and open to a picture of a scraggly, black roamer of the night; complete with weight, height, and diet?

"Let's get out of here." Ian's voice betrayed both his irritation and sense of defeat.

But as they turned to leave, they heard a voice ask, "Can I help you?"

All three of them whirled toward the center of the room where the voice had come from. Out from behind a shelf; a gruff-looking, unshaven man stepped out and leveled his gaze at the young girl standing only about five feet away from him. He then turned to observe Ben and Ian at the foot of the steps.

At first, Ian had no idea who the man was. He was wearing tattered jeans and a drab bunched-up dark blue hoodie. It looked like the man hadn't showered or changed clothes in some time, his eyes giving off a desperate look that Ian had seen before in various wild animals that had been cornered. For a second, he thought that maybe this man lived down here without permission—that he had broken in one night and made a nest out of torn book pages like a rat.

It was the voice that cast doubt though. Ian had heard it before and it carried with it an air of authority. In the seconds it took for Ian to realize that the man standing before them was in fact, Pastor Carlyle, Ben had already begun weaving his apology.

"Sorry sir, we were just looking for some books and we thought maybe they'd be down here but there was no one to ask and we needed them but, like, they're not that important so— I'm sorry, we'll just—I'm sorry." Ben spun to make his hasty retreat, his face so red from embarrassment and the harsh lights overhead that he looked like a tomato.

"Hey, hey, hey," the pastor spread his hands apart. "No need to leave. I was just wondering." The wildness had gone from his eyes and been replaced with the practiced calm he wore every Wednesday, Saturday, and Sunday up on the pulpit. "I can help you find whatever you're looking for. We obviously have-" he waved his hands "-a *lot* of books down here."

Ian's mind raced, trying to think of a plausible explanation. He had heard the word "Calvinism," a few times before, and even though he didn't actually know what the word meant, he had just made up his mind to ask for a book on it when Ella interrupted.

"We were looking for books on demons actually—or various creatures of the Bible. Or from anything, really. We're doing a project for English class." She didn't speak with a patronizing kid's tone one, but in a flat voice that—if Ian closed his eyes—could have come from an adult woman. "We're studying mythology."

"God's not a *myth*, Ella," Ben scolded.

"Actually," the pastor broke in before an argument could develop, "a lot of people consider mythology to exist outside of fact and fiction. Some people believe that, when most of the Bible was written, we were in a period where we didn't even concern ourselves with what actually happened and didn't happen. It's just not how we thought about things at that point. Everything was so obscured and unknowable back then that people simply told stories to convey truth, and that if the myth concerned itself with some sort of revelatory wisdom, it didn't matter if it had happened historically or not. All that mattered was the wisdom."

"And what do you believe?" Ian asked.

"What?"

"You said 'some people' believe that, so what do you believe?"

A smile flitted across the pastor's face. It looked like he was about to say something, but his body seemed suddenly frozen, as if the question had hit an off-switch. A few uncomfortable seconds passed before he finally straightened up and said, "I believe, that we should have what you're looking for around here somewhere."

Fifteen minutes later, all three of the children had about four or five dusty books in their hands. Ian had expected them to be leather-bound and perhaps written in human blood but most were regular old hardcover books that had had their dust jackets taken off.

"Why are there so many books down here?" Ben asked as he tried to figure out a comfortable way to carry his stack. "Most churches don't have libraries like this, do they?"

"Well, Mr. Ryewheeler, you know Ms. Shuffer who works at your school as the librarian?"

Yeah, Ian thought. *It's her class we ditched today to come here.*

Ben nodded.

"She is also the *church* librarian. She's been collecting books for Saving Grace almost as long as I've been alive. She's been doing it since she was a little girl."

"I didn't even know we had a library," Ben said.

"Yeah well, it might surprise you to hear, but unfortunately most of the church-goers would rather go to church than bring it home with them, if you know what I mean."

It was clear by the expression on Ben's face that he didn't. He glanced over at Ian who was just as lost but after a few seconds it was clear that the tired-looking man who seemed to have run out of book recommendations wasn't going to elaborate.

In fact, as he guided them silently back through the maze of books toward the stairs, Ian wondered if the man he had hardly recognized down here beneath the buzzing lights wasn't quickly running out of words to say in general, whether from the pulpit on Sunday mornings or to anyone else who cared to listen.

EVER SINCE THE restless night Richard had spent pacing the dark hallways of his house, he had opted to start sleeping in the basement of Saving Grace Church. It was dark and damp down here, which meant that there weren't a lot of people who would come down to bother him. Sure, the church elders seemed a bit worried, but this was a sanctuary after all, wasn't it? And what good was a sanctuary if the pastor himself couldn't seek solace and shelter here?

Still, there had been some growing concern about Richard's half-hearted sermons, canceled counseling sessions, and increasingly dissolved appearance. Did they actually know he was sleeping here or did they just think he was spending a lot of time down in the virtually unused library?

Rosaline Shuffer would have known for sure—the cot back in the corner of the basement had been strategically placed behind a huge pile of books, but nothing happened in Rosaline's library that she didn't know about—but Richard doubted she'd be inclined to rat on him. He was a grieving father for gosh-sake. Who would rat on someone like that?

Are you really grieving though? Do you know she's dead or is she just missing? Maybe you should be out there looking, hitting the back roads and beating on doors. But you won't, will you? She's probably out there somewhere waiting for help, but you won't come. You're too cowardly. Too lazy. She's better off dead than with a father like you.

This wasn't the first time thoughts like these had slithered through Richard's head; it did feel like they were becoming more frequent though.

What do you expect? You're down here in a dirty hole with nothing to do but dwell on your failures.

But Richard didn't have any other choice at this point. Claire would hardly talk to him. Helen tried, but the last time they had seen each other after a Sunday service she was visibly afraid of him. How long until she stopped speaking to him altogether? How long until that bitch Rosaline ratted on him and the church had to kick him out? What then?

The elders might let him stay, but all of that would depend on how it looked from the outside. If they could spin it as the church offering help to someone in need, then Richard would probably be ok. But if he seemed even the least bit dangerous or unpredictable, they would very quietly shoo him out into the streets like a stray dog. The idea was ugly, but then again, so was this place, wasn't it? This cramped and overflowing room full of bizarre books. He was glad those kids came and took some away. He hoped Rosaline would be furious. What were they doing again? An English project? That sounded thin, but in reality, what they decided to do with those books was about the last thing he cared about.

Richard lay down on the cot, the springs squeaking angrily. He stared restlessly at the grey drop-tile ceiling for a few seconds before turning over on his side and looking at the big stack of books that hid his new sleeping quarters. Not only did it block the line of sight from the basement entrance, but all of those books lying there with their covers opened and pages pointed upward soothed him for some reason. They looked dead and at peace, like plucked lilies floating down a river.

13

———

From the church, they went right to Ian's house. Originally they'd planned to go to Ella's since it was almost certainly empty—she explained about the fight she had with her father and how he was probably too chicken-shit to ever come back so long as he thought there was a possibility he had killed his own daughter—a fact that remained somewhat dubious in the ears of both Ben and Ian. But as they walked and talked it over they realized that they needed to stop by Ben's house anyway for the swords, plus it'd be quicker to move on the "Gateway"—as they'd begun to call Mr. Rutledge's woodpile—from either Ben or Ian's house. Ella fought with them vehemently on this but as she did she began to wear down. After all, her house was another mile-and-a-half down the road from Ben and Ian's neighborhood; not to mention the fact that, in the northern winter cycle, the sun was already beginning to set, and they'd need all the time they could get to pour over some of the literature.

Ella's stomach turned at the thought of voluntarily doing homework. She had some idea of what they were up against— more than Ben and Ian at least—but the information she had received in her time in the woods was vague and cryptic at best. She even briefly considered revealing all that she knew to her two new companions but she dismissed the idea almost immediately. There was no way they'd believe her, and even if they did, what good would it do her? Sure, they'd be more aware of the danger at hand, but to what end? From what she'd seen of them so far, there was a 50/50 chance that they'd ditch the instant things went sideways, and Ella wasn't so sure she could outrun the two of them. She could probably beat Ian in a race, but he knew the specific area better than she did. And Ben— well, he was almost certainly faster than her. How many times had she seen him out at recess in elementary school playing football and basketball with the other kids? Racing up and down the courts and across the fields with ease. No, he was a natural athlete. Ella might be a bit hardier, but with what they were likely to come up against, it wouldn't do her a lot of good. She had to play this smart and to do so meant keeping the other two in the dark.

———

IAN TRIED to page through the books but the writing was dense, even for his reading level. The paragraphs seemed to run on for ages and most of them contained words he couldn't quite discern the meaning of like "acquiesce," "firmament," and "leviathan." The pictures were often crude and spare, and even if the books were easier to read, he'd still have had a hard time focusing.

Ben hadn't even bothered to make a show of trying to read the books they had gotten from Pastor Carlyle and had instead chosen to practice fake sword maneuvers on invisible foes. The three of them had arrived at Ian's house at almost the exact time they would have if they had taken the bus home and Ben went immediately through the woods to his house where he rolled the wooden swords and some other supplies into a blanket before heading back to Ian's.

Meanwhile, Ian and Ella stood awkwardly apart from one another as Ian's parents winked and made thinly veiled remarks about what was sure to be the children's immediate marriage to one another. They asked a few pointed questions about how they had met (school) and what they had planned for the night (homework) and then quickly rushed out of the room as if the two were about to consummate their love on the living room floor. Just as Ian's mom slunk out, Ben flung open the back door without knocking and trundled passed her with his bundle of supplies.

"Oh, hi sweetie," Ian's mom said reflexively as she passed, her face twitching ever so slightly at what she probably regarded as a threat to her son's budding new relationship.

"Got the stuff," Ben said breathlessly as he plopped down in his spot on the living room couch. He unwrapped the blue, threadbare blanket he had procured from his house and spilled the contents onto the floor. "I got the swords," he declared, as if they weren't immediately visible. "We only have two, and I figured we didn't have time to make another one so I grabbed you this," and with that, he popped off the couch and shoved a shiny, chrome gun into Ella's hand.

She stared down at it for an uncomfortable second.

"This is a staple gun," she said blankly.

The three of them glanced wordlessly at each other, and finally, Ian spoke up. "Well, staples *do hurt.* They could even be fatal if the staples are old and rusty and you don't have your tetanus shot."

Ella hefted the staple gun in her hand, lifted it to eye-level, and then fired it at Ian's head. The staple zipped about four feet through the air, bounced off of his forehead, and landed in the carpet where it would be lost for days until his dad finally stepped on it with his bare feet.

"*Geez*, don't *do* that," Ian said, flushing red. "That could have hit me in the eye and *blinded* me. Or *worse*. Do you even know what tetanus does to people? Their bodies slowly seize up until they're finally frozen in place and their lungs stop working and they *die*. Are you trying to *kill* me?"

Ella gritted her teeth.

"Tell ya what," she said. "How about you look through those books and see if you can't figure out what we're going to be going up against tonight, yeah?"

Ben snorted a laugh and then went about swinging the sword in the living room.

Sulking, Ian picked up a book and started to read.

FOR FIVE HOURS they tried to suppress their excitement for the coming night. Ian's parents stopped back into the living room after a while and drilled them about what their night looked like. They explained that they had to do some homework for their English class that involved both a book report—they gestured at the books in front of them—and also a somewhat more bizarre assignment where they had to go outside and watch the stars. Improvising, Ben explained how they were to try and see if they could discern any shapes, and if so, what they were and why they might be important. Ian's dad wasn't quite grasping it so he asked what the overall point of it was. After a few moments of silence, the three students just shrugged, and Ian's dad went downstairs muttering about "taxpayer dollars" and the "broken education system."

Ian's mom ordered pizza and all three kids dug in hungrily as soon as it arrived. In all of the excitement, they realized they had missed lunch, and the pizza was like water to a person lost in the desert.

Taking a few slices for herself, Ian's mom began walking downstairs to join her husband. "We're watching *Casablanca*," she said excitedly, stopping on the stairs. "Has anyone seen it besides Ian?"

Ian rolled his eyes, even though he secretly loved the movie.

"Isn't that a kind of cheese?" Ben ventured. "Like, for chips?"

"Oh, you kids," Mrs. Whelan said laughing, and with that she turned and thumped down the stairs to join her husband, leaving Ben thoroughly confused.

THE HOURS DRAGGED on as their anticipation mounted. Ian thought that maybe they should come up with some sort of plan —some kind of exit strategy if things went south. But in the end, they opted to just wing it. If things got bad they would just run. Ian's house was the best option in terms of somewhere to flee to, but Ben's backyard lights were on as well and visible through the woods.

"If something happens," Ian finally said, "just run toward the lights. Both houses have people in them and it's not going to matter how stupid you sound as long as you're safe."

Ella seemed to accept this while Ben nodded distractedly. He had fiddled with the cross guards on one of the swords too long, and now it had come loose and he was trying to fix it with a roll of masking tape he had brought.

In addition to the swords, tape, and staple gun; Ben had also brought five bags of potato chips.

"You planning on having dinner with the monster too?" Ella asked.

"Hey, we got no idea how long we'll be out there," Ben said.

"What if we get lost? Or we get trapped somewhere? Then what?"

"Well, I'll tell you one thing," Ella said, "I'm not about to have whatever's out there hear us coming the minute we step out the door because you're crinkling a bag of Lay's."

Ben opened his mouth to speak but then shut it. Finally, he got up and went over to the kitchen table where the boxes of pizza were sitting. He looked down at the leftovers for a few seconds, and then defiantly shoved two full triangle slices into the front pockets of his jeans.

"You're ridiculous," Ella said.

"Here," Ian said getting up, "I'll at least get you some sandwich bags."

WHEN THE TIME finally came for them to leave, the last few hours seemed suddenly all-too-short. They had done little else but bicker with each other and had formed no real strategy, but as soon as they closed the back door quietly behind them, they all felt instinctually unified in their goal. For better or worse, they'd have to have each other's backs, so any disagreements they had were either squashed or left back in the living room.

The night was brisk and cloudless and the moon and stars reflected off of the snow in a blue, luminescent glow. The three kids stood at the edge of Ian's backyard as if it was some sort of enchanted pool they were hesitant to step into.

"Won't your Dad wonder why we didn't turn the backyard light off? If we're going to look up at the stars, I mean?" Ben asked, his breath puffing white into the winter air.

Ian thought about that.

"They're probably passed out downstairs with the shopping network on," Ian replied. "I bet they'll stumble off to bed even later than we will."

Of course, that's if we even make *it back to our bed's tonight,* Ian thought grimly.

The three of them stood for a second more, and then Ella finally stepped forward and picked up a long stick that had fallen off of the maple tree that stood in the center of the yard. She gave it a once over, and then methodically snapped all of the smaller twigs and branches off of the main shaft before she finally set the tip on the ground and stomped on it about a half-of-a-foot up, leaving a sharp and jagged end.

"Guess that'll have to do," she said reluctantly.

"Sounded like it worked just fine on your father's face," Ben said helpfully. Ella had explained the confrontation with her father to them, and while it looked like she might argue the point, she then reassessed the long stick and seemed to decide it was a worthy weapon after all. And with that, the three of them set off across the yard.

Their figures stood out starkly against the iridescent land-scape, and to some observers, they could have passed for three upright adventurers on their way to distant lands and certain peril. All of them held their "swords" aloft and as they entered the black shield of darkness that stretched around the forest, the only one of them that looked back was Ian, and in that moment he felt that regardless of what was waiting for them, he was about to cross a line he couldn't come back from.

THE DISTANCE to Mr. Rutledge's house was relatively short, but the forbidding night that seemed to thrum around them made it feel infinitely farther. Nothing moved in the woods around them as they walked, the silence pressing in on them like a suffocating pillow. At last though, they made it to the edge of the woodpile that rose in the night like some dark pyramid.

Once they were all crouched and settled beside it, they

looked around and verified that they could still see the backyard lights of both Ben and Ian's houses.

"What now?" Ian asked.

"Now we look for an entrance or something," Ben said. "Ella, you keep watch while Ian and I start pulling logs out."

"Wait, you think it's actually *in* the woodpile?" Ella asked incredulously.

"This is where we found the holes," Ben said. "Ian said they were all around here, so this is the best place to start."

Ella scoffed, but after what appeared to be some great inner struggle she finally spat out a "fine" and spun around. "Just let me know when you're ready to move on."

Suddenly regretting the fact that they hadn't gone over what their plan was, Ian began to dig. At first, the logs were hard to dislodge without making a considerable amount of noise. A thin layer of snow had settled on them, but a few of them were still somewhat loose.

"These have been moved recently," Ben whispered.

"How do you know that?" Ian asked.

"Because we have a woodpile out back too, and the thing is frozen solid. You couldn't move the logs on there unless you had a pickaxe or something. These, on the other hand, come right off." As he said this he wrenched one off of the pile with a dull snap.

Ian nodded slowly and looked around, then he too began pulling pieces of wood off and setting them behind him.

The holes were still there but they had been partially filled in with snow. He poked his finger inside one and found he couldn't reach the bottom. What had made these, he thought. Could it have just been squirrels like he had joked about with Mr. Rutledge? How much did he actually have to go on? Ben was still under the impression that there had been tracks, and Ian was thankful that he hadn't brought the point up again, but in the end, Ian had no real reason to believe they were doing anything but trespassing and disassembling an old man's woodpile.

Except for Ella.

That's right, he thought. Ella had come to them talking about the holes too, and Ian hadn't even told Ben about that, so if she were playing some sort of joke or something, how could she have known? In fact, what *does* she know? She had been quite stringent in terms of information so far. Ian had been so caught up in his own validation that he hadn't thought to question it, but now that they were out here the whole thing seemed odd. What did she know? Why hadn't they drilled her for answers? It's as if, as soon as there was a monster to hunt, they could think of nothing but trying to slay it. They had done almost zero prep-work beyond making wooden swords and pretending to read books they couldn't understand, and now that it was time to face the thing, three kids with sticks began to seem like a rather ill-equipped force to handle a *monster*.

Ian was suddenly struck with the memory of the thing striding across his backyard in the dead of night, its long loping steps and the inhuman speed that it seemed to travel with. A shiver ran up his spine and suddenly he wanted to stop digging.

"Jesus, are you two done yet? I want to check out the house," Ella hissed.

"No we're not *done* yet," Ian whispered angrily.

"And no, we're not *checking out his house*," Ian added, shocked at the idea of breaking and entering.

"Look, you two can stack wood all you want, but if you're not done in five minutes, I'm putting a rock through that asshole's sliding glass door and walking in."

"What the *fuck*?" Ben blurted, raising his voice. "Are you insane? This is *Wisconsin*. People who break into other people's houses around here get cut in half by buckshot."

"I'm not here to piss around and play with toy swords you dumb, pig-headed, hick-town, asshole," Ella spat. "There's something here that I need to get answers from, and if you two aren't going to help then I'm going in alone."

"Whoa, whoa, whoa," Ian said. "What answers? What's here?"

"Yeah, Ella," Ben chimed in. "Why exactly are you here, anyway? What's in it for you?"

Even in the dim moonlight, Ian could see Ella's face contort and flush.

"Look," she said finally. "I don't have to tell you why I'm here. All you need to know is that bad shit is happening, and I'm here to help you stop it. Come to think of it, I'm not even sure why I thought you'd be good candidates for this. The police definitely wouldn't believe me. My father wouldn't do shit, and he's the whole reason I'm even in this mess. I guess I just heard you two talking and thought *well there's a couple of people who are at least aware of whatever's happening. No way they could be as dumb as I thought they were.* Well, it looks like I was wrong. It looks like all you want to do here is dig for nuts in the backyard of some stranger's house like a couple of goddam squirrels."

"And what were *you* planning on doing?" Ian asked, his anger rising. "You didn't even have a *stick* before today. What, did you just plan on stomping around until you ran into some big, tall monster and then just bitch him out?"

At this Ella rocketed up and flew at Ian. His wooden sword was on the ground next to him, but in the dark, he suddenly couldn't find it. He lurched up to defend himself, but as he did he stepped back and onto one of the newly exposed logs behind him.

Ella hit him in the chest with her shoulder and the two of them hit the woodpile as Ben scrambled backward. Ian flailed as Ella balled up her fists and began pummeling him, and as he tried to make his retreat, the log he was standing on began to roll.

And then the one on top of that one began to roll. And then another and another.

"Watch out!" Ben yelled, abandoning all pretense of quiet. And as he did the whole woodpile came rolling down and Ella and Ian were just barely able to clamber away without being buried underneath. One of the logs hit Ella's ankle and she lurched away with a yell. Another one landed squarely on Ian's foot and he hopped back and fell into the snow.

At that moment, all the lights came on in Mr. Rutledge's backyard. The three of them froze where they were, and if they had been positioned anywhere else they may have tried to run back home. Or perhaps they would have hidden and laid low for the next long minute that passed. And then, after the initial jolt of fear that would have certainly surged through them at the sound of the front door of the house being flung open, they would have then been able to savor the sweet relief that came with the sound of Mr. Rutledge's car door opening and slamming shut, followed by the turning over of his engine and the dry squeal of tires on snow as the old man peeled out of his driveway with nothing but the clothes on his back.

But they weren't anywhere else. They were behind the woodpile, and in their fear and amazement, they barely acknowledged the fleeing of Mr. Rutledge. Instead, they stared into the cold eyes of the figure in front of them. The shape that loomed halfway out of the stack of cut firewood like a buried statue. Its skin was pale white with a tint of blue, and it half-crouched there in a pose that could only be described as unnatural.

"What are we going to do?" Ben finally choked out.

But Ian couldn't find the words to answer. All he knew in that moment was the horrible face in front of him.

It was a face he had seen before in assemblies back when he

was in middle school. Or in the grocery store when he went shopping with his mom. It was the face that had stared at him across the table from the front page of the newspaper as his dad read the sports section, or from the signs that clung to telephone poles and community cork boards. It was the face of Lilly Carlyle.

And she was dead.

14

The search for Mr. Rutledge was in many ways identical to the search for Lilly Carlyle. It was fevered and intense at first: children were kept home from school until well after Christmas vacation, flyers of Mr. Rutledge's face were plastered all over town, and the local news was awash in numerous details that detectives and reporters had dug up in the course of their investigation. Where it differed, however, was the certainty with which the town regarded the guilt of Rutledge in contrast to the skepticism that surrounded Lilly's disappearance. The same people that claimed to know all along that "Rutledge had something off about him," were in many cases the same people that voiced several alternative opinions about the young Ms. Carlyle's disappearance.

At first, no one could find a motive for the murder. Except for blunt trauma to the back of the skull, there had been no other signs of assault. The murder appeared to be both premeditated and methodically executed. Investigators theorized that Lilly's routine walking of Numi, her Siberian Husky who had been found alive and well in Rutledge's basement, had been observed by her killer for weeks. There was a shaded stretch of road along their walking route that saw little traffic, and due to an eyewitness report by a few local teenagers that placed her a half-a-mile down the road from it near the time of her death and no such reports by drivers afterward, it was reasonable to assume that she had been ambushed and killed somewhere along that unobserved distance.

As time passed though, and Rutledge continued to evade capture, the slow and deliberate machine that was the American justice system began to unearth an unnerving wealth of facts about his past that was ripe for yielding the wildest of conjectures.

Though he was a Poplar native, Rutledge had moved a great number of times in his life, always unmarried and always alone, and every town he went to saw a low but noticeable spike in missing persons. No one was ever able to pin anything on him, or for that matter, even begin to suspect him of foul play, but every town he inhabited over his lifespan saw a marked increase in disappeared persons at about the rate of one every year or two.

"In larger cities, these numbers would have gone virtually unnoticed," explained the town sheriff, "but for whatever reason, it appears as if Mr. Rutledge prefers smaller communities as his hunting grounds."

33-year-old Sheriff Anderson had been in office in Poplar, Wisconsin for just under a year after his landslide victory against the town's previous sheriff, Trent Wilkinson. Trent had undergone a scandal in which rumors arose that he had slept with a number of key witnesses in various cases ranging in importance from assault and battery to money laundering. He fervently denied the allegations, but with Poplar being the small and traditional town that it was, Sheriff Wilkinson was promptly voted out in the next election cycle and replaced by the younger and noticeably more handsome Wick Anderson, who had recently returned from over a decade of military service. Anderson had been deputized by Wilkinson on his return, and in the few months before he started to run for sheriff he rapidly gained a reputation of being kind-hearted but fair in terms of enforcing the law. A Poplar native, he knew the people and was a natural in diplomacy. However, on the morning following the discovery of the body of Lilly Carlyle, Anderson couldn't have known the far-reaching effect his words would have when he inadvertently told his hometown that they now inhabited the "hunting ground" of a possible serial killer.

An increase in accidental firearm-related accidents plagued the town for over three months. Granted, the increased vigilance of the townspeople saw a dramatic decrease in home burglaries and auto thefts, likely due in part to both an increased tendency for people to actually lock their doors, and on the burglars' part, what could only be described as an understandable fear of being shot during a home invasion, which was something that most local thieves were already wary of.

Regardless, Sheriff Anderson noted the effect of his words and humbly accepted it as a mistake.

"Our town is still safe," Anderson declared in a later press meeting. "We've had no long-term disappearances since Rutledge has gone missing and it is very likely that he has moved on. However, we must still remain vigilant and watchful. If you see something that feels off say something, don't be afraid to look stupid. Better stupid than dead."

These statements also had unintended consequences, as Anderson soon realized. If he had thought the phone lines were busy before those remarks, then what they were now defied any description. The new sheriff had to approve overtime just for answering calls, recording tips, and responding to false alarms.

There might be a killer in my town, Anderson thought to

himself one night. *And with tensions running as high as they are, I'll be lucky if he's the only one who racks up a body count.*

———

AFTER WILDLY BURSTING BACK through the door to Ian's house that night and blasting his parents in a confusing stream of hysteria about a dead body in their neighbor's backyard, the two adults had eventually yielded and decided that Ian's dad would go over to check it out for himself. He didn't walk through the woods as the children had, but instead opted to drive the fifty feet down the road to Rutledge's house and knock. After a series of barrages against the old man's front door, followed by observing the recent departure of the Dodge Durango that had until now sat perpetually in the house's driveway, Mr. Whelan's curiosity got the better of him, and before he knew it he was creeping behind the empty house into the still-lit backyard.

Mr. Whelan saw the body immediately, so different was its blue hue from the scattered wood that surrounded it. Stumbling backward, much in the same way his son had, the startled man raced back to his car, fumbled his keys into the ignition, and fled back toward home.

Ian's mother was so surprised by the explosive manner in which her husband flung the front door open that she yelped like a small dog that had had its foot stepped on. Disregarding his wife and the small gaggle of children that immediately launched into their unceasing onslaught of questions and declarations, Mr. Whelan stomped immediately toward the landline, his boots squeaking and squelching as they tracked water all over the floor.

From there, the entire thing seemed to Ian like a dream. As soon as the task of convincing his parents was over, the series of events that followed over the next few days was almost wholly out of his hands.

At first they were questioned rigorously by the police. "Why were you over there?" they asked. Of course, the three children hadn't thought to come up with a reasonable excuse for tearing apart their neighbor's woodpile, so none of their stories really matched up. Ben had said they had gone over there to observe the stars for a school project and that the lights that surrounded Ben and Ian's house were too bright to get a good look at the night sky. When asked what class the assignment had been for, Ben immediately realized the flaw in his plan and broke down crying. When his parents arrived later they were so mad that their son had been questioned without them that they threatened to sue every single person they laid their eyes on.

Ben ended up being walked out of the Whelan's house exhausted and tear-streaked. His attitude was only slightly bolstered when he remembered the now-squashed slices of pizza he had stuffed in his pockets. They were cold and mashed into a pulp, but he took comfort in every bite as he finally sat quiet and alone in the security of his own bedroom.

Ella, on the other hand, refused to say anything beyond single-word answers. When they asked why the three of them had been there she just shrugged and said, "camping." After the officers informed her that she couldn't camp on other people's property she shrugged again and simply told them she was sorry.

When Ian was finally questioned—each of his parents on either side of him—he began with a story similar to Ben's that involved them trying to find a good place to look up at the stars. Where it deviated was when he began to explain how he started feeling that something was *off* about the old Rutledge place and that he had then convinced the other two to go check it out. He threw in that they had also seen something,

something *tall* and *monstrous* stalking through the woods and that he thought it was hunting them. Eventually, his tale became so fantastic that the investigators ceased their line of questioning and resolved to acquire the times at which notable events had occurred, like when they had left the house and at about what time they had discovered the body. Ian had intended to plant the seed for a full-scale investigation into the monster he thought he had seen stalking through the neighborhood, but he was equally relieved at the idea that he had likely been absolved by what one of the officers had detailed in his notebook as a "naive and whimsical nature, prone to digression and exaggeration."

A DETAIL that was initially overlooked, but later on began to trouble the authorities, was the fact of Ella's absent parents. As the investigation continued and Ella's mother and father refused to show, it became quite evident to the police that she had no real home with any sort of adult supervision. The night of the discovery, Ella was up so late being questioned that she ended up sleeping on the Whelans' couch with Ian curled up in a sleeping bag on the floor.

Mrs. Whelan gave her a ride to school the next day, and as the trio's classmates began bombarding them with questions, Ella found it easier to stick close to Ben and Ian, and when it came time for the two boys to get off of the bus, Ella spontaneously decided to get off with them.

For all of her apparent hardness, when it got right down to it Ella just didn't feel safe at home. For one, she had to admit that there always was the possibility that her father would show up and she'd have to deal with him, not to mention the fact that he was the least dangerous thing that might show up looking for her. She had remained somewhat safe up until now, but she was well aware of a certain danger that might pursue her.

Plus, there's the other thing.

Ella immediately pushed that out of her head. She had a lot on her plate at the moment, and everything was so confusing that there was no way she could be sure of what she was thinking. In fact, she was almost definitely wrong. She had to be.

So that was how, two weeks after venturing into the dark woods with Ben and Ian at her side, Ella found herself being moved into the Whelans' guest bedroom. The police said that her living situation would have to be addressed eventually, but they were gracious enough to let that fact fly under the radar for the moment. Ella seemed to be getting on well with Ian's family, and at the very mention of "foster care," Ella virtually exploded. The police had been conducting another round of questions at the Whelans' kitchen table a couple of days after the incident, this time with Mr. and Mrs. Whelan present during Ella's questioning, and it was observed that their presence saw somewhat of a marked improvement in a willingness for Ella to talk about the events that had taken place two days prior.

At first, she gave the same single word answers, but as Mr. and Mrs. Whelan began filling in some of the spaces, Ella began to elaborate somewhat on what they said. When she maintained her story that they'd been "camping," Mrs. Whelan said that actually, they had gone to do a homework assignment that involved looking at the stars. And for reasons she couldn't quite explain, Ella felt the need to contradict her.

"Actually, there was no assignment," she said, after which followed a long silence. Then Ella continued by saying, "Ben and Ian lied to you."

Another silence.

"Don't you mean Ben, Ian, and *you* lied to us?" Mrs. Whelan finally asked.

Mr. Whelan shifted uncomfortably as the officer began writing in his notebook.

"Ian said he saw something run through your yard a few nights ago. They said that they wanted to go look for it."

"...and?" Mrs. Whelan prodded.

Ella sighed, then said, "And I guess I wanted to go with them. I don't know."

"Can you describe this—*thing,* that your friend saw?" asked the officer.

Ella winced as he said the word "friend." She just shrugged and said, "Ask him."

From there the questioning followed a similar path. They asked if she had known Lilly or Mr. Rutledge. They asked why they were digging under the woodpile. They asked if she knew what the three of them would find under it. Through the slow, prying process of the investigation, the officers finally concluded that it had probably been Mr. Rutledge that Ian had seen that night from his bedroom window, and that he had been returning to his house from the back for reasons unknown. The children had noticed signs of activity around the woodpile and their curiosity led them to start dislodging the loosened pieces of wood that had been recently disturbed. When the stack of logs became unsteady and collapsed, the commotion caused Mr. Rutledge to panic and flee the premises.

The whole thing sounded somewhat farfetched and poorly strung together to Ella, but she wasn't one to contest their theories. It wasn't until they moved to the topic of foster care that Ella became exceptionally vocal.

"I'm not going to live with some strangers," Ella said, acid dripping from her voice.

"From what I can tell," the officer said, "the *Whelans* are practically strangers."

Ella didn't reply.

"She's been staying here for the last few nights," Mrs. Whelan ventured. "She hasn't told us much about her living situation, but it doesn't sound like she really has anyone to go back to at the moment. Is that right dear?"

Ella nodded.

"Do you have any extended family in the area?" asked the officer.

Ella shook her head so vigorously that the loose strands of dark brown hair fluttered back and forth in front of her face like stringy tree branches in a heavy storm.

The look on the officer's face clearly showed that he was less than convinced.

"Look," he said, "if you don't have any extended family to stay with, we need to look into finding you a proper place to live. If the Whelans would like to provide that place in an official manner then we can talk about that, but if you think you can just bounce back and forth between your friend's couches and guest rooms for the next five years then you're quite mistaken. We have to have a home address for you on file and know that you're *safe*. *Especially* now. Do you understand?"

For a brief second, it looked like Ella was going to relent, but suddenly her face flushed scarlet and she sprung up from the table and knocked her chair over backward.

The officer was on his feet in a heartbeat but didn't make a move toward her.

"Just calm down," he said, raising his hand. "We'll get this all sorted out. We just have to go through a certain process, do you understand?"

"Yeah, I understand perfectly," Ella said, yelling now. "I understand you're going to sell me off to some pedophile in South Carolina who already has fifteen fucking kids chained up in his basement. But as long as they're off the streets, right? As long as it's not *your* problem, right? I think *you* need to understand, officer shit-head, every adult I've ever known besides my mom has been some sort of version of Mr. Rutledge, and he's probably been killing people for the last five decades without you even getting a whiff of him. Why aren't you out there *right fuckn' now* looking for him?"

"That's the whole reason we're-"

"Oh, cut that shit!" Ella snarled. "You're not gonna find him and you know it. You didn't find Lilly, did you? No, three *kids* had to do that. You're just here to ask questions and cover up the mess. If you care about my safety, where were you when my father was giving me these?" Ella gestured at the bruises on her face and arms. "You were sitting at your desks doing speeding tickets or some shit."

The officer standing across from her looked like he was about to say something but held his tongue.

"You don't do shit for the people around here except take their money when they drive too fast and bust kids smoking dope. When was the last time you found a missing person? Or caught a murderer? Why are you even here?" Ella was in tears now and she was barely able to get the last words out. "Where were you-" She choked on the words. "Where's my—where's-"

But she couldn't say it. She couldn't get the words out, because to say them would be to give them life. To give them truth. Instead, she spun and booted one of the legs of the upturned chair so hard that there was a splintering noise as it spun around in a circle and came to a stop. Loose nails jutted out of the chair's leg joint.

After stomping out of the room and pounding down the hall to the bathroom and slamming the door behind her, the three adults let a moment of silence pass.

"You want her to stay with *us*?" Mr. Whelan finally asked his wife.

15

———

Ten miles away from the Whelan household sat a cabin owned by 67-year-old Peter Crawshank. Habitually messy and unorganized, Crawshank's cabin was full of counter-spaces and tables that were piled high with old junk mail, accumulated fishing gear, and pornographic magazines that acted almost like the rings of a tree: each undisturbed layer denoting a different place in time. Crawshank had never cleaned the cabin—had never really needed to. This was the place he came to escape his soul-crushing job and vampiric family members. Unmarried and childless, he had built the cozy single-room structure out on a small plot of land he had inadvertently inherited from his father when he had passed suddenly of a heart attack nearly 40 years ago. The only reason he even knew about it in the first place was that, as a child, he had been out here deer hunting on rare occasions with his father and stepbrother.

Which was why he was startled when he heard a firm knock on the door.

He had been reading a 23-year-old issue of Outdoor Life while a fire crackled away in the ancient wood stove next to his chair, but he stopped and lowered the dingy old magazine at the sound of the rapping. At first, he didn't respond, opting instead to freeze and remain silent like a spooked deer. The knocking repeated.

"Who is it?" The question came out hoarsely and more insecure than he would have liked. No answer.

The knocking repeated for a third time and at this, Crawshank flung down the magazine in a flutter of pages and stomped toward the door, throwing it open wide to reveal his stepbrother, Marshall Rutledge.

Before he could do anything, Rutledge rushed in to embrace him. No words. No greetings. Just an unexpected warmth deep down in his belly.

———

ON THE NIGHT a body had been discovered in his backyard, Rutledge had not known that Crawshank would actually be at his cabin—had, in fact, counted on him *not* being there. All the same, Rutledge wasn't a man prone to be caught off his guard, so however unexpected his stepbrother's presence had been, it wasn't so unexpected that Rutledge hadn't prepared for it.

"Good evening Peter," he had said drunkenly; and he *did* feel drunk. Drunk on something. On the open sky that watched him voyeuristically from above. "It's good to see you again after all these years." The words had barely even needed to be whispered, so close was Rutledge to his stepbrother's ear. The two men held each other awkwardly on the foot of the doorstep like the lost kin that they were, Rutledge's stainless-steel hunting blade buried deep in the right side of Peter's soft and voluminous belly.

Or maybe it was something else, Rutledge thought. Maybe it was the electric thrill at having been found out. As soon as he had heard the collapsing woodpile outside his house and thrown the lights on to see people scrambling around back there, he knew that this was it. That he had been found. Finally.

The thought of it was so nauseating it gave him an erection.

"I suppose you'd have to call it night though, not evening," Rutledge said, almost in a moan. "Even though "good night" has always been a phrase for departure, not greeting."

Peter groaned and clutched his brother's back.

"And you can be sure dear Peter, that this is a greeting—a welcoming, into the story—into *my* story. Lord knows you didn't want to be a part of it when we were children." Rutledge twisted the blade slowly, like the turning of a doorknob. "But now we're here, at the end of everything, with no one but each other."

Rutledge continued to turn the knife. Slowly. *Slowly.* Like pushing open the door to his parent's room, so as not to wake them. His father was a light sleeper, but his stepmother wasn't, and if she woke up then the whole house would be up in less than a second.

Peter tried to move—tried to turn his head to look at the man who held the knife inside of him.

"Shhhh, don't look at me Peter. Look out there. Look at the night—at the stars. You'll be there soon. Another pinprick of light looking down on me as I forge my way in this lonely world. Who else is there, Peter? Who else's story could you possibly be a part of but mine?"

Rutledge gripped the warm, leather knife handle even tighter, remembering how the creaking of his parent's door was so quiet and how he had hoped it wouldn't be enough to wake them. But he had been wrong. Both his stepmother and his father were already awake, grinding over each other in the dank summer heat like a couple of wild animals, and when the thin slit of light fell upon his father's face and that lone pupil swiveled in its socket to fix itself on the little boy of 11 years old staring in through the crack, Rutledge had slammed the door shut and run down the hall. Back to his room. Back to the piss-soaked bed that he had soiled in the night—back to wait for his father to blow open his bedroom door and show him what happened to pussies who pissed their beds.

Even then. Even at age 11. He had still been plagued with nightmares—nightmares of creatures in the woods, under the bed, in the cellar. Creatures everywhere. Tall and short and plump and lanky. They lurked in every shadow of his mind, and when they closed their wet jaws around him and sucked his body like kids suck their thumbs, the urine would always leak right out of him.

But that had been then. That was back before he was a part of other people's stories—back when the only story he was a part of was his own lucid, waking, fucking nightmare. With no one to embrace him but the dark. No one to hear him. No one to see him.

"They see me now, brother. They *all* see me." Rutledge could begin to feel the warmth of Peter's tears soaking his shoulder and he cherished it. "Soon they'll find the others too. Soon they'll find all the girls and boys and men and women."

Rutledge clasped his eyes shut and imagined himself at his parent's door once again—imagined himself twisting the knob, and as he did, Peter began to sob.

"Do you think they see me Peter? Do you think mom and dad see me?"

In a final, desperate act; Peter tried to lunge away, but his brother was too strong. For the first time in his life, his brother was too strong to push away, to hit, to knockdown.

"They do see me, Peter. And if not, I'll *make* them see."

And with that, Marshall Rutledge pushed wide the door to his parents' room. Light bathed their shocked faces—their wet and glistening eyes peering out from the dark. They opened their mouths to scream and Marshall let them. He let the warmth spread out below his waistline and soak his jeans. He welcomed it this time. But this time it wasn't urine.

It was his brother's steaming guts.

MARSHALL RUTLEDGE STOOD out in the cool, dark night with no lights but the stars above him. He had dragged his brother a couple hundred feet back into the woods and left his body uncovered for the scavengers. He couldn't hear anything moving around at the moment except for the night insects and the roar of frogs that inhabited a pond down the road, but he knew that between the raccoons, coyotes, bears, and a plethora of other creatures, the body should gradually disappear over the next week or so until there was nothing but scattered bones.

There was so much to do, Marshall thought, but he couldn't quite start yet. The hunt for him would be absolutely manic and although the cabin was pretty well secluded and out of the way, there were still a few people left alive that could put the pieces together and figure out where he was hiding. They'd have to do some digging, but it wouldn't be impossible. Thankfully, Peter's presence in town was so sporadic and unobserved that by the time he would be missed everything would be all over.

Marshall shivered at the thought of it. He was old now, but not too old—not so old that he couldn't do what he had to do. He could feel the tension already rising in him. It had been less than an hour since he had killed Peter, but even so, he felt like he needed another one, which was strange. He could usually go a whole year without killing anyone—he had even gone four once—but now was different. Now everything was different.

He was exposed.

His secret had been revealed and he had been uprooted. After seeing the people in his yard, it had taken him less than a minute to grab the pre-packed bag he had prepared for just such an occasion, exit the house, and drive away. He was somewhat regretful that he didn't spend more time saying goodbye to the old place, those walls had their own stories to tell about him— they had been there to watch him eat and sleep and go about his daily activities, as well as his *other* activities. He hadn't even been able to say goodbye to Pauline. Marshall knew the dog's name was Numi from the time he had been watching Lilly, but she was his dog now, and because of that she had needed a new name.

They had only had a short time together, but Marshall felt he loved that dog and that she loved him. Dogs were different that way. They were more forgiving than people. More willing to accept.

Getting the two into the car had been easy. There had been some uncertainty as to whether or not the dog would react poorly once her owner had gone down, but in his old age, Marshall was finally starting to embrace the thrill of the uncertainty. This last time he felt that he was possibly being downright reckless, taking Lilly in the day like that. But it had given him a thrill—a rush that now, near the end of his life, he had never really known. Before, the thrill came from the methodology. The slow and painstaking hunt over the course of about six months. The photography and the tracking of movements. The tension would be a slow-burning flame in the bottom of his gut until the day he finally let it out in a quick and destructive burst. One blow to the back of the head was usually all it took. One blow and they'd go down twitching.

Rutledge had pulled up next to her on the road and asked if she knew how to replace the coolant in these new cars. His Dodge Durango was only a few years old and he spun a story about how he had meant to learn how earlier but had forgotten, and now the temperature gauge was getting dangerously high.

The key had been to find an excuse to interact with her

without making her get in the car. There was no real good way to get people to voluntarily enter your vehicle that wasn't suspicious, Marshall had learned that long ago. No, what the situation called for with Lilly was a semi-plausible excuse, fast-talking so as not to get her dwelling on it too much, and after popping the hood where the crowbar had been fastened to the top he would take her down with one good swing.

The only real problem he had run into was that in his haste he had used the wrong side of the bar, and as she flinched away at the last second, he had hit her square in the temple with the hook-end and pierced her skull.

The reaction was almost instant, she convulsed and dropped to the ground and began to twitch like lots of the others had. In a way, he was lucky: some of them had even gotten back up and walked around slurring their speech and acting erratically, half of their brain crushed and showing. The thing that complicated things for Rutledge was all the blood. He had even flattened out the end of the crowbar somewhat so that he could cave the skull in without breaking the skin. Of course, the skin *did* still break most of the time, but not enough to cause such an immediate amount of blood. When Lilly went down though there was literally a *spray* of blood. Then as she fell it all came gushing out into the snow. He had to pick her up and hoist her into the back of his vehicle almost immediately so as not to create a huge "Someone Died Here" sign on the side of the road, all while Pauline paced and whined anxiously. He was just glad that she didn't immediately attack him like he had seen dogs do in movies. Instead, she just seemed concerned and confused.

After he had closed the trunk of his car, he had quickly thrown a bunch of snow over the top of the blood pool in an attempt to hide it. It was somewhat difficult due to the fact that the snow had been half-slush at the time; but being grey and dirt-streaked, it confused the coloring of the area enough to where you'd have to be standing right over it to really see anything.

Even so, Rutledge had been sweating bullets that night. He knew there'd be people out looking for her and he knew that they knew where she walked. It would be so easy for them to find that bloodspot if they just looked for signs of a commotion.

But he had been saved by good fortune. Snow had begun to fall and by the time people were out looking for Lilly the sun had set and the heavy flakes had accumulated. No one had ever found a thing.

Which led Rutledge to wonder about how someone had found her now. He didn't even know who *they* were. Probably just bad luck. Probably just Ben or Ian trying to shoot more of his goddam squirrels out of his goddam backyard. He'd have to listen to the radio tomorrow. He had driven his vehicle around behind the cabin as soon as he had finished with Peter, and he thought he should be able to hop back in the next morning and tune into the local radio news and make sure that he had actually been found out. He'd feel stupid if they hadn't dislodged enough to find the body or if he had successfully scared them away just by turning on the lights.

Mmm, Ian, that was something he'd have to think about. The boy was a good candidate—a perfect candidate almost. From the brief times he had seen Ian or heard about him from his parents or neighbors, Rutledge knew that he had a great imagination. A wild and even dangerous one perhaps. In all likelihood, the boy had the same kind of imagination that Marshall had had as a child: uncontrollable and nearly all-consuming. It was the kind of imagination that, somewhere buried deep, understood the vast unknowableness of the world and the monsters that inhabited it. Sure, there were the threats that were immediately at-hand—natural disasters and dangerous people—but what about the things you could never even conjure in your mind?

Rutledge always imagined dying in a prison cell or by lethal injection—maybe even being gunned down in a blaze of glory—but when all was said and done, he had no idea how he was going to die. For all he knew, some great and alien hand would reach up from the ground and tear him apart at any moment with zero warning. After all, who had seen the world beyond this thin pane of visible space? Who knew what was really out there?

That was part of the reason why he was doing what he was doing—had *been* doing for decades now. It was to see the space beyond. To crack the seal and see what came through. He didn't know exactly what was going to happen, but if the book he had read was correct, it wouldn't be pretty. Still though, he had no clue what was on the other side.

The thought was frightening and, Rutledge supposed, the very reason he had constructed his reality in the way that he had. By making it *his* story, he had control of it. All the monsters were of *his* making. Everyone had their own stories, but from his point of view, his story was the only one that mattered, and by inviting people into it, he was making them *worth* something.

Taking Ian would be an entirely new experience. Everyone he'd ever killed had only seen it coming in those last precious seconds, and it was in those moments he became the most important thing to them: the brutal punctuation mark at the end of their lives. But this time his victim—even if he didn't exactly expect Rutledge to pursue him—will have at least imagined it happening.

Marshall considered this for a second, but in the end he realized that the final result was virtually the same: the boy would die and it would be Rutledge that killed him—it would be Rutledge that became the last great figure in his short life.

Maybe Ian's anticipation would even sweeten it. Rutledge had always enjoyed the ambiguity of how his victims felt toward him: perhaps they wanted it, maybe they were even *glad* that this was how it would end. No rape or torture. Just...lights out. He would often find himself spinning tale-after-tale about how the characters might feel about their deaths in the grand scheme of things.

But not this time. This time he was rather certain that his victim did not want to die. When the moment finally came, he would have probably dwelt on it so long that it was his greatest and most tangible fear.

Ultimately, it didn't matter. The chance that Rutledge would be around long enough to begin weaving new fantasies was rather slim. Right now he had to focus on something bigger—he had to focus on *the* fantasy: his legacy. Every victim he had ever taken bore a mark carved into the bone of the right heel: a five-point-pentagram. The Summoning Star.

My stars in the sky, watching down on me. Rutledge closed his eyes and breathed in deeply, the frigid air scorching his throat like liquor.

Once they found the next body the pattern would be apparent. They'd be finding bodies for *decades* with stars on them and every time they did it would point right back to him. It would revive him in a way. In the memory of the world, Rutledge would be undying.

They'd truly begin to panic when he took the boy. Adults were one thing, but once parents knew—*really knew* that *their* children were vulnerable—well...

...then the shit would really hit the fan.

Not yet though, he was getting ahead of himself. He had to do the other one first. The woman.

Rutledge laughed to himself. *The woman*. Didn't he mean *the* woman? As in the most beautiful woman he had ever met in his life? The woman of his dreams? His wild rose who rode the same fantasies that he had as a child? Who rafted down the river with Huckleberry Finn the same time he had? Who feared the lurking and misunderstood monster created by Victor Frankenstein and had mourned the doomed fate of Heathcliff and Elizabeth at the same time he had? Yes, she was the one. At times, she was the *only* one for him. And soon, he'd be the only one for her too. He'd be the frost on her red petals, the cold that wrapped its white-gloved hands around her thorns and squeezed until she was just a memory.

His memory.

Marshall Rutledge turned around to go back inside. He kicked his boots a few times on the frame beside the door, knocking the bloody slush off that had accumulated from standing in the place where Peter had died, and then he stepped into the warm cabin nestled deep in the black heart of the wilderness, the wood stove glowing demonically in the corner.

Let them find the blood, he thought. *Let them find it all. It'll be too late anyway. It's* already *too late.*

PART III: MARCH, 2004

"But how could you live and have no story to tell?"

— Fyodor Dostoevsky, *White Nights*

16

———

When Richard Carlyle opened his front door, the last person he had expected to see was Rosaline Shuffer. He had maybe expected the police to continue their endless line of questioning, or perhaps some well-wishers to drop off more flowers or casseroles—some delusional part of him even expected Lilly to show up and wake him from this nightmare he seemed to have fallen into.

But that would never happen. Not now. He had seen the body, the cool blue tissue of her skin that was both her and not her, like some poor sketch.

"We need to talk," Rosaline said, shifting her weight from her left side to her right. "I think something's happening."

"WHAT DO you mean you don't have it?" Rosaline said incredulously. They had sat down at the kitchen table and the librarian had immediately begun asking questions about the books.

"I mean I don't have it," Richard said. "Some kids came asking for books on old myths or whatever, so I just grabbed some and handed 'em to them. And by the sound of your description—blue with black lines on it? Leather?" The librarian nodded. Richard let out a sigh. "Yeah, I handed them one that looked a bit like that."

"Look Rosie," Richard splayed his hands. "I don't really have time for this at the moment."

"You just gave it to some kids? For a school project? Do you have any idea how valuable those are?"

Richard thought about defending himself—thought about why a poor church in Northern Wisconsin would have 'valuable' books just rotting in a basement that was easier to break into than a jar of pickles. But he didn't have the energy—not for any of it. So he just sighed and shrugged his shoulders.

Ever since Lilly had been found, his life had been catapulted out of the wallowing hell he had been living in for some time. He had reluctantly moved back in with Helen—a point she had insisted on, arguing that what they needed was to be together—and since then he had felt something inside himself shift. The tension and uncertainty were gone. He had started sleeping again. Sleeping and planning.

"Who has the books?"

Richard motioned to answer when, seemingly out of nowhere, it struck him.

Rosaline saw the expression change on his face and asked again, this time more eagerly. "Who has the books, Richard?"

"The same three kids that found my daughter."

Richard slapped his hand down on the table. Of course, he had seen them that very day, hadn't he? With everything that had happened, he had totally forgotten. The officers hadn't told him the names of the children, but Claire had mentioned it one night as Richard had tried to work up the will to eat his dinner. Apparently, word had gotten out at school that Ben, Ian, and some other girl that Richard had never heard of had found Lilly when they were snooping around their neighbor's house.

Rosaline's face darkened, her age-worn lines deepening like the shadows in valleys at sunset. "Richard," she said carefully. "We need those books back."

"How am I supposed to get them back?" he asked. "I haven't preached a sermon in weeks. I-"

"Richard, do you remember what we told you when you were hired?"

Richard stared at her without comprehension. All he could remember about the day he was hired was the feeling of elation—of purpose.

"Do you remember what we told you about the town's politics?" She raised an eyebrow meaningfully. "About its...history?"

Richard directed his eyes toward the ceiling, trying to think. "Well, I remember that it was, uh...sensitive, and that there were some bad things that happened a long time ago. But-"

"Well, they're happening again," Rosaline interrupted. "And 'sensitive' is possibly the mildest adjective you could use. Now I'm not going to get into all of that right now, Richard. You have a lot on your mind and I am so sorry about Lilly. But you should know that not only is her death likely a direct result of this thing, but that your position is now more important than ever. You must be a barrier between good and evil, because right now it's at the door and it's twisting the knob."

STANDING on his snow-laden front porch, Richard gave a curt wave to Rosaline as she pulled out of the driveway and then he walked back in and quietly closed the door, so as not to wake Helen and Claire.

The idea that he needed to get some books back from some kids at a time like this was nothing short of absurd. He knew that Rosaline was a librarian by both occupation and nature, but this was ridiculous. And what was all of this about the town's history or—what was it she had said? Sensitivity?

He tried to think more about his induction into the church back when he was hired, and now that he thought about it he did seem to recall some strangeness in the way the job had been described, but at the time he just perceived it as over-spiritual-ized language. Still though, there had definitely been more talk about "encroaching darkness" and "the shifting landscape of the underworld."

For one panicked moment, Richard thought about the possi-bility that he had joined a cult but dismissed it almost immedi-ately. There were, of course, people that viewed all of Christianity as a cult, just as much as there were a fair amount of Christians that treated it like one, but that wasn't what defined Richard's faith. Richard's God was a perfect ideal that he tried to pursue in every facet of his daily life, rather than a rigid pursuit of blindly accepted traditions and routines. To him, God was everything that was good, and to follow Him was to allow him to transform him daily into a better person. God was the sacrifice of self for the world, and in that sacrifice there existed the immortality of Christ's Kingdom come to Earth.

Okay, so maybe when he described it like that it did sound a bit like a cult, but what worldview didn't that wasn't like: "you live, you die, you rot"? Whatever his beliefs were, he didn't think they were destructive, and he certainly didn't think some books from the church library could be somehow tied to the death of his daughter.

Thinking about it again was like a fresh blow to the gut. He had had that merciful distraction of whatever nonsense Rosaline was spouting, but now it was gone and the grim reality of losing Lilly was back to hurl wave-after-wave of despair at him.

She was gone. Both Lilly and April were gone. Richard

remembered what it had been like as a 19-year-old when he had heard that he was going to be a father. April had been nervous and uncertain, and for good reason considering her parents had kicked her out of the house almost immediately and refused to speak to her, but Richard had been excited. At that point in his life it had felt like he was tripping over good fortune and falling face-first into even better; so great were his blessings. He hadn't even believed in God at that point, but even then he felt like he had been afforded some great provision.

Then April died, their unborn child still inside her. Richard was devastated. He felt like he had been given life abundantly and had somehow destroyed the whole thing within less than a year. He remembered the delirium of the accident—how it felt like he had been talking to April and was suddenly swiveling his head around, trying to remember where he was and what had happened. When he described it to people, he typically said that it felt like waking up out of the pleasant dream that his life had been and into some harsh reality he had inhabited for the rest of his waking moments—as if he was living his life, and suddenly slipped through a crack in reality and fallen into somebody else's.

It had been nothing short of a waking nightmare—an existence of loss and suffering that had arrived without sign or warning to completely blindside him and destroy his whole world. He remembered laying in the hospital bed and thinking to himself, *I can't believe I'm here. Yesterday at this time I had absolutely no idea that I'd be where I am right now.*

But there had been Lilly. That shining beacon of redemption —the child that he was all but certain he had lost as soon as he looked over into his new bride's lifeless eyes, one ruptured red and staring blankly past him, as if there was something mildly amusing going on over his shoulder.

The doctors said that April had died almost instantly when

they had gone off of the road. Richard had been driving and—well, he still had no idea what had happened. The police report theorized a patch of black ice but he had remembered none of it.

All he remembered was the drunken state of semi-consciousness immediately following the crash, the searing pain of his broken ribs the next day that flared like lightning as he sobbed over April, and that unlikely feeling of reverence for whatever divine miracle-worker had saved his daughter.

Amongst all the feelings of guilt and anger and despair, her mere existence was like a soft warm light that didn't dull the pain necessarily but made it easier to bear. She was his grace. She was his miracle.

And now she was gone.

After Claire had been diagnosed with her illness and made a miraculous recovery of her own, Richard thought that he was done with all of it—that there was a threshold for how many times you could hit either rock bottom or soaring heights. But he had been wrong. Lord knows he had been praying for that third miracle.

A part of him didn't even believe the police when they had called. No. Not Lilly. Not *his* Lilly. Didn't they know he was protected? Didn't they know that his children were impervious to anything the world could throw at them, no matter how "terminal" or "impossible"? He simply hadn't believed it.

But he did now. God knew he did now.

17

During their resource hour one-day Ben, Ian, and Ella sat down to try and figure out just what in the hell they were doing. Ever since Rutledge had been revealed to be Lilly's murderer, the whole monster idea had been tossed up into the air. After speaking to his parents and the police about his neighbor, Ian was becoming less and less sure that there actually was a real-life monster. Maybe he had just seen Mr. Rutledge walking through his backyard. He hadn't exactly seen any tracks after all—he had just told Ben that he had—and if there really was a monster, then why was it walking around his backyard in the first place? Did it just happen to be tromping through the woods on its way to a yet-to-be-discovered crime scene? Was it going to *feed* on the body? There were no signs of that anywhere on Lilly's corpse, and if that were the case then why would it pick something so hard to access when there were dead deer carcasses every 35 feet up and down every road in Northern Wisconsin? The whole thing was beginning to make less and less sense and the more he thought about it, some creature that had yet to bear any real *effect* on the area seemed to be far less of a problem than a real-life serial killer anyway. After all, Rutledge was the one who was actually *killing* people.

Ben and Ella, on the other hand, both miraculously seemed to agree for once. Both of them were not only sure it was real, but seemed to be even more convinced than they had been five months ago.

"This thing is attracted to death," Ben insisted. Poplar Middle School had entered its next trimester, and the trio's schedules had lined up in a way that allowed them to all have the same resource together, and every day seemed to be a repeat of the last, in which the three of them argued about what to do next. "Of course we'd find a body next to the same place that we found its tracks. That's what monsters are *like*. Plus, how do we know that this thing wasn't working *with* Mr. Rutledge. How-"

At the sound of Rutledge's name, a few heads around the library perked up and then lowered again, trying not to listen.

"How do we know this thing isn't Rutledge's pet?" Ben continued, trying to speak a little more quietly. "We know he likes pets. He kept Lilly's dog, didn't he? Why would he keep her dog and kill her?" A look of revelation washed over Ben's face and he leaned forward, tapping his fingers on the desk they were all seated around. "What if the dog *is* the monster?"

"I don't know man. That thing got brought back to Lilly's parents' house. If it were a monster, I think we would have known by now."

Ben didn't look very convinced, but he didn't argue. "You're with me right, Ella? You know there's something going on—something more than just Rutledge off-ing people, right?"

Ella hesitated for a second. "I think so," she finally said. "I'm just not sure what it is exactly. I have a hard time believing that this is all just Mr. Rutledge."

"That *what* was all Mr. Rutledge? Killing people? People kill people all the time," Ian said, a little louder than he had intended. He quickly glanced around the room to see over a dozen pairs of eyes looking at him, including the librarian, Ms. Shuffer.

There was a moment of silence as they all thought to themselves.

"Claire's back," Ian finally said. "Did you see?"

Claire, Lilly's younger sister, was sitting about three tables away staring at a closed notebook. Obviously trying and failing to ignore their conversation.

"Yeah, I think she had to get out of that house," Ben said. "I don't think her parents are holding up very well. Remember how Pastor Richard looked that day in the church basement? And that was *before* he found out his daughter was dead."

"That reminds me," Ella said, reaching down to dig through the stack of books and notebooks she had next to her. "I think we should look through the books he gave us a little bit more. I've been trying to read them, but they're hard to understand. I think this one might be our best bet though." Ella held up a heavy book that was bound in a soft navy blue leather cover and bore some intricate black design, almost resembling lace. "This thing has a lot to do with creatures of the Bible and other ancient mythologies. It talks about things like Leviathans and Nephilim and Gorgons. I think what we're looking for is going to be in here somewhere."

Ian knew very little about Leviathans, Nephilim, or Gorgons; other than the fact that Ella had absolutely butchered the pronunciation of all three; but he had to admit that the book did interest him; if for no other reason than to learn something about ancient monsters.

"Let me take a look," he said. Ella flipped it around and handed it to him the same way he saw people hand other people guns in action movies, and it was probably because of this that he felt powerful holding it.

Ian flipped through the book casually, letting the dense text and penciled illustrations wash over him. He stopped suddenly.

"Here," he said almost jumping out of the seat. On the left-hand side of one of the pages was the picture of a tall creature with a similar posture to the thing he had seen striding through his yard.

"Really?!" Ben's eyes were wide. "What does it say?"

Ian stared down at the page. There were a few paragraphs of descriptive text, but what caught his eye were a few blocks of verse underneath it.

"*In Tartarus Valley there grows a tree,*

Radial in its infinity.

It bears no fruit but frost.

It sinks its roots in loss."

He let the words wash over him, trying to take in their meaning. He continued to the next block of verse.

"*Opening the blinded eye.*

Called by the one burned in the sky.

Pulling up the serpent horde,

Calling too the Miamani Lord."

The words meant nothing to him but he pressed on, hoping the meaning would be made clear by the end.

"*The fire breaks apart the head*

Feet marching down below instead.

And though the gravestone has been hurled

Still sings The Song that Cleaves the World."

Ian's eyes returned to the top to reread it but before he could Ella was up and out of her seat reaching wildly for the book. Reflexively, Ian yanked it back.

"What the hell are you doing?" he blurted.

Ella looked frantic. "Give it to me!" she said. "Let me see it! I have to-"

And in that moment, Ian felt the book yanked out of his hand by someone behind him.

"What are you three doing?" asked Ms. Shuffer sternly. "Where did you get this book? Did you take this out from behind my desk?"

"No!" Ben and Ian blurted at the same time. Ella slumped back in her seat and folded her arms so tightly that Ian thought she might accidentally break her own ribs.

"That's mine, actually," Ben said. "I brought it from home. We were just-"

"I highly doubt that Mr. Ryewheeler," said Ms. Shuffer. "Now I think the three of you should separate for a while, wouldn't you agree? You've been nothing but a distraction since you walked in here."

The three of them sat silently where they were, trying to figure out an excuse as to why this wasn't a good idea.

"Now!" she said loudly. "Go! There are plenty of open seats."

Reluctantly, the three of them pushed out of their seats, gathered their things and walked off toward different tables. All, that is, except for Ella who remained standing, her things in her arms, looking desperately at the book Ms. Shuffer clutched in her hand.

"Yes, Ms. Windthrope?" Ms. Shuffer asked.

After another moment of uncomfortable silence; Ella spun wordlessly around; her long, dark hair flaring out around her head like an umbrella being opened and closed again; and stomped away.

———

ROSALINE SHUFFER COULD HARDLY BELIEVE her ears when she heard the words of the *Miamani Prophesy* drifting through the library. The three kids had been a virtual beacon of noise as soon as they sat down, and if they had been anyone else she would have shut down their conversation almost immediately. But if she had done that then she would have never seen the book, which had been precisely her plan: if not seizing it directly, then at least hoping to find out what had become of it.

But luck was on her side it would seem, for not only had the three students brought one of the books with them right into her library, but they had brought the only one she was concerned about—the one she had hurriedly rushed off to deposit in the church library one disconcerting night. She wasn't worried what *they* would find in it—other than the peculiar fact of its mere existence in a church basement, the knowledge in the book was only sensitive in the right context—no, what she had been concerned about was *losing* that knowledge. She *had* the right context, but without the book she was flying blind.

It was interesting that they had been reading from the exact page the book had opened up to on that chilly fall night. Was it possible that they knew what was going on in Poplar? Surely they couldn't have made it that far without help from someone, but if that were the case, then who? Who could they possibly be involved with that knew of the Omen Tree and its significance?

A cool chill slid down Rosaline's back as a possibility suggested itself to her. *No*, she thought. Surely they couldn't be involved with Marshall Rutledge. Then again, he had carved the Summoning Star onto the heel of each of his victims. But surely, he didn't understand the implications of what he was doing. The ritual was both precise and drawn out. Was it possible that he had done it? Could he have summoned the Harbinger right here in Poplar? But who could have told him, how? And *why*?

Too many unanswered questions. Too many coincidences, like the fact that it was these same children who had found Lilly's body. How could they be involved in both Lilly's murder *and* the Omen Tree? Surely they hadn't bumbled into both.

Rosaline considered that for a moment, lightly tapping her fingers on her desk. She looked up at Ella who was so angry that her rage could almost be seen radiating off of her like waves of heat. It looked as if everyone within her general vicinity could feel it and had moved away from her appropriately.

Thinking back on it, something felt strange about her new friendship with Ben and Ian. Ella had never really made friends in school, or really even shown up most of the time. Ben and Ian weren't exactly the popular kids in school but still, add Ella into the mix and they were an unlikely grouping. Was it possible that she was involved in some aspect of this and they were involved in another? Had they somehow managed to put two-and-two together? It seemed hard to believe but then again, the whole thing seemed hard to believe.

Rosaline thought about the book she had just stuffed into her bag; the fact that she needed it at all was still somewhat surreal to her. She knew the reality of Poplar, Wisconsin; but never had she dreamed that she would actually live to see a day where that reality was actually relevant. The church elders certainly hadn't thought so either or else they would have hired a pastor that they could bring into the loop. Not that Richard was incompetent or anything, but he was too pragmatic for the things that now concerned them—too concerned with finding God and the Devil in the natural than in the supernatural. It wasn't that they couldn't be found in both, Rosaline believed, but Richard's practical view of things didn't leave a lot of room for what they were currently dealing with. Not to mention the fact that bringing him in *now,* after all these years, would be somewhat harder to do than if they had just told him when they had hired him. The best thing to do now would just be to let

Richard focus on his family and to let the Magen Society take care of it.

The Magen Society was small in Poplar, but the fact that it even existed at all here was more than could be said for most other small towns. The society had locations all across the globe that dealt with things like this, and if she were granted permission by the elders who she had yet to truly discuss this topic with, they'd have to reach out to the others and bring someone in that could deal with this.

The incompetence of the elders brought Rosaline to a level of frustration she could hardly fathom. The town of Poplar sat directly on top of what might be called a "thin spiritual membrane," that allowed certain things into the world that weren't typically allowed in other places. It was true that the small rural community experienced an abnormally high amount of hospitality and generosity that wasn't always apparent in big cities, but in spite of this—or, Rosaline sometimes thought: *because* of this—there was an even greater propensity for darkness.

That was why she needed the book. Every once in a while, that darkness would rear its ugly head in a variety of forms, many of which were detailed in the book and a few of which were not. Luckily, the very thing that Rosaline suspected of haunting the town was something that was covered, and somehow, it appeared as if the trio of students had figured it out as well.

Ever since the images of the stars Rutledge had carved onto his victims' heels hit the air she had been searching for that book, but it wasn't until she had gone back to the church basement to check for the third time that she felt the first inkling that she wasn't going to find it there. She knew that Richard had been spending a fair amount of time sleeping in the church's basement—he had had a hard time falling asleep at home, he had told her, something she could sympathize with—but after looking at his cot for about the hundredth time, she began to wonder if he had taken it for some reason.

That was when she had given Richard a visit and discovered just what had happened to what could easily be considered a 'priceless artifact.' He had given it to some kids. *Kids.*

No, not just *some* kids—*the* kids: the very students who had found his daughter's body.

There were machinations working around her that she couldn't perceive, thought Ms. Shuffer as she walked over to where Ben was sitting at his new table. The bell rang shrilly to signal the end of the period and all around her students began to rise as they packed up their things.

Ben was up and turning to go when Rosaline said, "Mr. Ryewheeler, I believe this is yours," and handed the book back to him. Or maybe not *the* book, per-say, but at least *a* book—at least one with a similar cover that she had quickly fished out from a stack of her own personal books she kept on her desk. She had simply made sure it was neither important nor inappropriate for children—she had been known to read the occasional risqué romance novel while on the clock—and when she handed it to him she made sure that she did it facedown, hoping that he wouldn't turn it over. He didn't

Ben looked up at her with shock and amazement, then quickly tried to play it off as if the book bore no real significance.

"Oh, thanks," he said, shrugging. "It's my dad's, ya know. Wouldn't want him to think I lost it or anything."

"Sure thing," Ms. Shuffer said, smiling as Ben turned around and walked out into the hall.

It was his very father she was concerned about actually. As important as her *other* duties were, the last thing she needed at the moment was for some kid to go crying to his parents that a teacher had stolen a book from him. Now at least she could shrug her shoulders and say, "yeah, I took it. He was being distracting so I took it away, mistakenly thinking it was a library book. As soon as the period was over I gave it back to him."

Being one of her own books, it had none of the barcodes that the library books had in the front covers, so there was no way of proving the books had been switched. Plus, who was going to believe a 13-year-old child had obtained an ancient book of mythological creatures and that the librarian—for some reason—had switched the books.

18

"The Animal Kingdom," Ian read aloud as he sat in his cramped bedroom with Ben and Ella. He flipped through the book, brightly colored photographs flitting by one after another. Each page had a vibrant picture of an animal on the left and a block of text on the right describing key characteristics.

"I could kill you," Ella said quietly under her breath. "I could literally kill both of you."

"Oh, I'm sorry," Ben said loudly, waving his hands, "Was it Ian who launched himself across the table like a drunken maniac? Ya know, I bet you were the kid in preschool who bit other kids when they were playing with the toys you wanted. Am I right? Were you the kid on the playground who would go throw sand in people's eyes when they wouldn't get off the swings? Or were you-"

An audible *whump* went out of Ben as Ella jumped up and kicked him in the stomach, knocking him to the ground. Holding his chest with both arms, Ben wheezed on the ground as he tried to regain the wind that had just been knocked out of him.

"*Jesus,* Ella!" Ben said. "What do you think-"

"I did not just hear the Lord's name get taken in *vain,* did I?" came the sing-song voice of Ian's mother.

"No mom!" Ian yelled, embarrassed. He turned back to Ella. "You can't just go hitting and kicking people who disagree with you, Ella. Ben and I are your friends and-"

"I'm not," Ben wheezed from the floor.

"-and from what I can tell, we're the only ones you've got. So you better cool it."

Ella looked bitterly at the floor then she turned toward the door, but before she could reach the handle, Ian spun her around by the shoulder.

"*Stop,*" he said. "No more running out when things don't go your way. No more shutting down. We've been doing this for *months* now and I know you know more than you're telling us. So you're going to tell us *now.* Ben and I are done swinging in the dark. Tell me: what do you know, and how do you know it?"

There was a long silence. Ian stared directly at Ella, who was still looking at the ground, her eyes flitting back and forth as if in thought. Ben got to his knees and sat back against Ian's bedroom wall, listening expectantly.

"They said I'd find answers in the ground," she finally said.

"What?" Ben said almost immediately. "Who? What answers?"

Ella continued to stare at the floor. Then, almost reluctantly, she strode slowly over to Ian's bed and sat down with a huff, the bedsprings creaking as they bounced.

"I was at the river," she said. "You know the river that runs into Poplar Lake?"

Ian nodded.

"Well, one day last Fall, I was down there. Fishing. Or walking. I don't know. I had to get out of my house. So, I was down there and I saw this thing in the water. At first I thought it was a fish. It looked like a small musky and for whatever reason I reached down to try and grab it. I don't know why, it was just *there*."

"That's a good way to lose some fingers," Ben said.

Ian shot him a look.

"Just saying," Ben said, defensively. "I mean, it's not like we all haven't tried to catch fish with our bare hands. That never *doesn't* end in blood."

As much as the interruption annoyed Ian, he had to admit that Ben was right. There wasn't a kid in Poplar who hadn't tried to catch fish with their bare hands down off the dock at Poplar Lake Beach, though it wasn't the teeth that drew blood as much as it was the spiked fins on the fish that lived in the local lakes and rivers. As soon as someone reached in and tried to grab them, the back fins would flare up and act as a sharp row of carpentry nails.

"Well, it wasn't a fish." Ella said. "It was a snake."

Ben and Ian stared in mute horror.

"And it wasn't like the snakes that typically live around here. It was bigger. And blacker."

"Whoa, whoa, whoa," Ben interrupted. "Are you sure it wasn't just a garter snake or whatever? They're everywhere around here. I've seen 'em swimming, and while it may be a bit unnerving I don't think they're-"

"It wasn't a garter snake," Ella snapped. "It was practically *winter* at this point. I think I'd gone in to unhook a snag or something, but it was *cold*. The thing should have been hibernating, and it was *huge*. I've seen garter snakes before, and they all have yellow stripes on their backs. This thing was jet-black."

Ben held up his hands in apology.

"Maybe we can find a picture of the snake you saw in our new Animal Kingdom book," he ventured. "Anything in there Ian?"

Ian glanced around and hesitantly picked up the book they had mistakenly received from Ms. Shuffer, Ella waiting defeatedly.

"Umm, no, not really." Ian said as he flipped through the pages. "It looked like she has extensive handwritten notes next to all of the rabbit pictures and seems to have circled a picture of an octopus. Other than that the only snakes I can find are rattlesnakes and reticulated pythons, neither of which are black. I don't think this is a comprehensive book though; the animals seem pretty random."

"Cool," Ella said flatly. "So can I finish my story or would you rather just read fun and interesting facts out of your new book?"

Ian nodded and put the book down, then he gestured for Ella to continue.

———

EVERYTHING WAS WRONG. Wrong species. Wrong region. Wrong time of year. The thing in front of her didn't just look like a snake. It was a snake. Long and obsidian-colored and shockingly out of place. But there it was, as real as everything.

Ella drew back slightly...

Then the world exploded in front of her.

The snake thrashed around in the water as if it was being electrocuted. It moved in quick and jerking spasms, making the water ripple and foam around it.

Ella bolted. She ran the terrifying run of nightmares, the air around her thick and heavy while her legs felt so weightless they could have floated away on the wind. And it wasn't just the cold and the water slowing her down. A sort of dread had overtaken her.

Ella remembered hearing from her mom once—before she had left—that God had placed enmity between women and snakes. Being five years old, she hadn't known what "enmity" meant, so her mother explained that they hated each other, because of what had happened in the garden.

"Why was God mad at the woman?" she had asked. "Didn't the man eat the apple too?"

Ella remembered how her mother had become quiet, thinking to herself. "I don't think God was punishing women when he said that," her mother said. "I think what he was saying was that us girls have an easier time recognizing bad guys."

"Really?" Ella had asked, excited. "You mean like a power? Like a *superpower*?" They had just watched Richard Donner's Superman the night before, and her mother had had to explain that Superman had what were called "superpowers," an idea that had fascinated Ella to no end.

At the question, Ella saw her mother's smile flicker. "Yeah, babe. Or at least, I'd like to think so. Doesn't always seem to work out that way though."

As Ella ran up the bank, she threw down her pole and snatched up her shoes. With no time to put them back on, she just clutched them under her arm as she prepared to run as fast as she could back home. But before she could, she made the mistake of looking back.

The snake was slithering out of the water like the shadow of a spear being thrown in slow motion. And not only was it moving directly toward her, but it was growing. Right before Ella's eyes, she saw it rise and contort before her, its skin bulging, its bones snapping and rearranging themselves inside its long and serpentine body.

It felt like a frozen hand had clutched Ella's heart and that was when she found herself running into the woods in her bare feet. The snow burned her feet as they pounded the ground, but that was so far in the background, Ella didn't even think about it until later. Then, right before she reached the dense underbrush that grew shabbily along the riverbank, she threw one last glance back.

The snake was gone, and in its place stood a man: tall and shifting and covered in scales. And as shocking as it was to see this, the thing that Ella noticed most were his eyes. She couldn't exactly place it at the moment, but later on, she would realize what was weird about them: they seemed wet and sad, as if he had just been crying.

Ella opened her mouth to scream, but before she could, he spoke.

―――――

"He what?" Ben asked.

"He spoke," Ella said. "And he even sounded normal. He didn't speak with what I'd imagine a snake's voice would sound like. It was just a smooth and even voice like a teacher or doctor or something. And the more he spoke, the more normal he looked. I didn't exactly see the scales melt away or anything; he simply became more and more like a regular person until he was finally just standing there in front of me, so real that it would have been easy for me to think the whole snake-thing had been some illusion or daydream."

"What did he say?" Ian asked.

Ella looked down at Ian's floor for a long second.

"First, he asked where I was going. I didn't know what to say, so I just stood there, my shoes clutched in my hands, the socks bunched up inside of them. I don't know why I was thinking about my socks—it was weird like maybe that's where I wanted to be: curled up somewhere safe. He kept his eyes on me the whole time, just standing down there at the edge of the water."

"What was he wearing?" Ben asked.

Ian gave him a look.

"What? That's a reasonable question. Was he wearing a tux? Gym shorts? Snow pants and a winter coat?"

"It's hard to say," Ella said. "It's like I could see him but couldn't look directly at him. Like one of those tiny stars up in the night sky where, if you try to look directly at it, it disappears, but if you look just to the left or right of it then it's there again."

Ella remembered what it was like being there in his presence. She remembered feeling that he was more like a visible thought than a physical person and that if she were to try and run he would follow her like one, tied behind her like a bad dream you can't forget.

She tried to run anyway.

———

BRANCHES WHIPPED past Ella's face as she tore through the woods, her feet scorched with cold and deep cuts and scratches. She pushed on, barely noticing them.

Time felt like it was slowing down. Her feet fell slower and slower, as if she was trying to push them through thick mud. The sky spun over her, once light blue with glimpses of white and gold, it now took on an amorphous grey color, tiny flakes of snow drifting so lazily in the air that they looked more like specks of sediment in an ocean than anything else.

Ella stopped and looked around her. The amount of time she had spent out in these woods was likely greater than even what she had spent at home. She knew every winding trail and towering tree, every dip and rise and pond and puddle. So, if her calculations were correct, she could only come to one conclusion about her current location: she was no longer in the woods behind her house.

Considering how long she had been running, she should have hit one of the main deer paths that wound around the river. And even if she had missed one of those—even if she had gone either too-far right or left in her mad dash back home, she should have either come out in a big field with overgrown grass and a huge maple tree, or hit a steep hill where rows and rows of evergreens clung tightly to the side like bushy soldiers awaiting their marching orders. But where she was now, she couldn't say.

All around her loomed huge black trees, bigger even than the white pines that grew scarcely in the big open part of the forest downstream. There was also snow. Not just layers of frost or patches of melting slush, but a thick layer of snow so powdery that, when the wind whipped through the naked trees around her, it was swept up in its wake and turned it into a kind of frozen smoke that made it hard to see or breathe.

It was at this point that Ella realized she was still barefoot, and as soon as the realization struck her, so did the cold. All at once, her feet and fingers ignited with pain, the sharp wind slicing through her chest like a lance and shaking her with violent shivering. All around her the trees swayed and moaned like the souls of the croaking damned.

"I don't think you'll find home here," said a voice behind her.

Ella whipped around. It was the same man she had seen down by the river. She could see that he left no tracks and cast no shadow.

"You might want to put those on if you plan on walking out of here," he said, gesturing at the shoes in Ella's arms.

As quickly as she could, Ella dropped them into the snow, fished out one of the socks, and then struggled to hop on one foot as she pulled it on, followed by the corresponding shoe. Embarrassed, she repeated the same steps with the other foot and then stood shivering in the snow, feeling only slightly better.

"You get used to the cold," the man said. "You get used to it the same way you get used to your father slamming his fist into your belly."

Refusing to look up, Ella stared down at the ground.

"You don't have to take that from him, you know. We can make it stop. *You* can make it stop."

Ella looked up at him, still saying nothing.

"Great power comes to those who seize it," he continued. "And right now, I'm offering you a chance to do just that."

"What do you mean?" asked Ella through her chattering teeth, though she could already feel the coldness ebbing away. Was it true? Was she just getting used to it like the man said?

"I mean-" and suddenly the man had closed the distance between them—had come so close that all he had to do now was whisper. "-I mean that if he were to disappear, you could have *new* parents. A new home. New friends." He smiled. "New *teachers*."

Ella thought hard about what he was saying, but eventually stammered, "I can't."

"Why not?" the man asked, not so much cocking his head to the side as swiveling it.

"We're-" Ella almost choked on the words. "We're family."

The man spat on the frozen ground. "*Family*. He is nothing but an anchor—a rope tied around your neck that will pull tighter and tighter until you finally break. Mothers and fathers are nothing but carriers—disease-ridden vermin that pass the virus to their children and die. They build the house to stand just long enough to shelter them, and then when they pass, the roof falls in on who's left, which, if you haven't noticed, is *you*, and *only* you."

Ella remained silent. The shivering had stopped.

"I see you're not cold anymore," the man said. "It's not gone you know. You've just grown numb. The same way people living on the streets grow numb to those ignoring them on their way to work. The same way those people passing by grow numb to those on the streets. In no time at all, we realize we're *all* homeless. There are no roofs that block the fallout of the wars of this world. No walls to muffle the screams. The only arms that hold you are your own, Ella, and someday you'll be holding yourself so tight that, when you finally fall, you won't even put your hands out to stop your face from hitting the ground."

IT WENT ON LIKE THAT. Different voices came and went. Serpents big and small, dangling from trees like vines or curled up in the nooks and hollows where she tried to find shelter. The sun rose and fell with no discernible pattern, every day filled with the tension that comes in the reprieve of a receding fist winding up for another strike. Every night a jab, or a right hook. A knee to the stomach that sucked the breath right out of her.

The best Ella could tell, she was in some sort of valley. Neither north nor south were discernible to her, but at one point she thought she saw the jagged teeth of mountains. At another lay the grey and lapping tongues of a frigid ocean.

Except for the black snakes that wound circles around her like a writhing pit of worms, she never saw any other animals. Occasionally she would discern a shadow pass over her, but when she looked up, there was nothing but the ashen sky. At night she could hear twigs and branches breaking, and once she even thought she saw a pair of burning canine eyes. But as soon as she jumped to her feet they were gone.

Ella never built a fire. Never made a bed. Never ate a meal.

Whispers and words twisted around her, inside and out, and the more she listened to them, the more she felt like—if she were to follow them—they would lead her out.

But she resisted. She resisted the pulling thoughts that drew gruesome scenes of patricide in her mind. She averted her eyes when the shadow puppets played out scenes of hanging men and school shootings. All around her there rose a din of voices that proclaimed the pain and meaninglessness of the world— that asked questions without answers and probed the softest and deepest depths of everything Ella had ever wondered or feared.

Then one day, while walking aimlessly through the tall and blackened forest, the trees began to grow denser and denser. As she struggled through the branches, Ella became almost hot with exertion. She pushed and wrestled her way through the bramble that was so thick with darkness, that when she finally broke through and fell out onto the other side, the bright and golden sun that shone down on her blinded her eyes and burned her skin. She lay there in the thin wet snow, moaning and rolling around, her every nerve on fire as they simultaneously resisted the sensations around her and tried to gulp down every ounce of warmth and sunshine she had been without for so long.

———

"I COULD HAVE SWORN that the sun had risen and fallen half-a-hundred times since I entered that frozen shit-hole," Ella said. "But when I checked the calendar at school the next day it said only four days had passed."

Ben and Ian had listened to Ella's story with an ever-growing fascination and now that it was over they felt as if they had just sat through some tall-tale one of their elementary teachers had used to pass the time during a power outage or to keep them occupied after a lesson ended earlier than expected.

The tale she had told was outrageous—unbelievable even—but regardless of its validity, both Ben and Ian had a hard time doubting that at least Ella believed it was true.

"So let's say everything you said is true," Ben said. "Let's say we believe you. What is this thing then? Is this thing that's been walking around our neighborhood some sort of snake-man or what?"

"I don't think so," Ella said. "None of the people—or...whatever they were—none of them were very specific. But they made it sound like there was something else going on here—that there was something stalking around the woods that was at *home* with the woods—something both alien to the town but also a part of it."

"Well, what the hell does that mean?" Ben asked.

Ella just shrugged.

"Okay, so we don't know exactly what we're up against," Ian interjected, "but we do know we're up against something that the adults won't believe—that *no one* would believe unless they saw it, right? So we have a few options. One: we try and bring an adult along with us when we go out next time, and if we see anything, then they'd see it too. They'd have to believe us."

"Why would we even want that?" Ella asked. "What's an adult going to do? Even if they believe us, no one's going to believe *them*."

"Yeah, but I feel like adults are a little better equipped to handle this sort of thing," Ian replied.

"What, monsters? I don't think anyone is really equipped to handle them. In fact, that might be what makes them monsters."

"What do you mean?" Ian asked.

Ella looked at the ceiling, thinking to herself.

"Think about it this way," she finally said, "let's say you're the first person to ever enter Florida. No one's ever been there before. It's a hot day, and you decide to go for a swim in a nearby pond, and *WHAM*-" Ella clapped her hands together, causing both Ben and Ian to jump, "-a fucking crocodile bites you in half."

"Actually, I think it's alligators that live in Florida," Ian said.

"No, American Crocodiles live there too," Ben replied, "I saw a special."

"Whatever!" Ella snapped. "You're missing the point.

"What is the point?" asked the two boys in unison.

"The point is: you've never heard of alligators, or crocodiles, or whatever. You just went for a swim and something bit you in half. That's a monster. No questions. That thing is a monster until someone gives it a name and films some fucking documentary that Ben watches. Then it's an alligator. Get it?"

"It was a good documentary," Ben said. "Seriously, you should watch it."

"What channel was it?" Ian whispered, then thinking better of it, turned back to Ella. "I get what you're saying though, but how does that help us?"

"What I'm trying to say is," Ella raised her eyebrows, "we need that book back."

19

Marshall Rutledge sat outside the beige, two-story house with the motor turned off. He had been sitting there for the last three-and-a-half hours and the four nights previous. He had watched Rosaline come home every evening at around 4:00, make dinner, do some housework, maybe read a book, then go to bed. Her routine hadn't once changed and Marshall wasn't inclined to believe that it would. If this were any other victim, at any other time, he would watch her for weeks—months even. He would watch methodically sometimes, and sporadically others—change up the routine, record the variables, try and predict the unexpected.

That was the thing with the unexpected though, you never knew it was coming. The whole thing seemed obvious, sure, but how many people said things like "expect the unexpected"? Well, as soon as you expected them, they weren't unexpected, right? And these weren't just semantics either. When someone with Rutledge's...*activities* tried to consider all of the things that could go wrong, it seriously paid to think outside of the box. He had done this enough times to know that *anything* could happen no matter how well you planned.

One time, nearly two decades ago, he had been down in Northern Alabama making his move on a young veterinarian he had been following for the last six months, then on that day—that *very* day—the house next to the veterinarian's house burned down. And it didn't just burn down, it fucking exploded.

According to the fire marshal, the running theory was that the person who lived next door had tried to kill themselves by leaking gas into their basement, but at some point, a timed living room light had automatically switched on, blown out, and then ignited the entire house with a dull *whump*.

And the papers didn't even know the half of it. Fire had engulfed the house almost instantly, and due to the close proximity of the houses, both of the neighboring houses had caught as well, including the house belonging to Marshall's intended victim.

Without thinking, Marshall had bolted inside, run up the stairs, and hustled both the woman and her two dogs out of the house before they were ever in any real danger. He could still remember the shocked look on her face as she staggered out of her upstairs bathroom wearing a pair of light flannel pajamas (she had just been getting ready for bed), the continuous barking of the two dogs, trying to convince her that her house had just caught fire—that yes, the sound she had heard had been an explosion and that she had to leave *right now*. All four of them had pounded down the stairs, Marshall and the woman, the two dogs racing dangerously passed them before they were even half-way to the bottom.

It wasn't until they were out the door and could finally see the huge, orange, serpents of flame slither and stretch up the side of her house that the woman, Patti Weshland was her name, was able to grasp the severity of the situation.

"You saved my life," she had said, shocked. "Who are you?"

Marshall had been so startled, so unnerved and flattered by her obvious appreciation for him that he gave her his real name.

"Marshall," he had said. "Marshall Rutledge."

He explained how he had just been out for a stroll when he had seen the explosion, and oh, hey, did you catch what caused it by the way? He was absolutely himself in front of her, hiding nothing but his real reason for walking by that night, and her acceptance of this was so valuable that it literally saved her life.

Even to this day, Rutledge had mixed feelings about the whole thing. On one hand, he had developed a routine, a *practice*. And he had deviated from it. The *fun* had been in the slow unfolding of his plan—in the power he felt as he brought his dark deeds to glorious fruition. But that was just it, wasn't it? He was in control. And being in control, he could decide whether someone lived or died. Sometimes, his decision that night felt like weakness, but after years of thinking about it, it felt more and more like *power*. He had saved her. He had decided that she was going to live, and she had. It was up to him and him alone and what was more? She knew it. She thanked him. In many ways, he was one of the most important figures in her life now, no matter how brief their interaction. For all intents and purposes, he had still accomplished exactly what he had intended to except for the ritual aspect. She was his, and she knew it.

As far as completing the *Miamani Ritual* was concerned, he had ended up taking someone else the very next day. It was anti-climactic, the ritual aspect being removed from the personal one, but it was satisfactory if nothing else. After all, he had still exercised his power over someone in an extreme way after meticulous planning and stalking. Then, the very next day, he had completed another step in his slow march toward ultimate importance.

· · ·

ROSALINE WOULD BE DIFFERENT. This was one of the rare cases where the victim knew him—*really* knew him. She may have even suspected him of being something...*more* when they had been kids. He could still remember her from when they were in school—remember how she had looked at him with interest in her soft green eyes as he asked what she was reading. Interest and enthusiasm. Not disgust. Not apathy. Not like the other girls. Rosaline had regarded him as a real person, even when his own family refused to.

Marshall didn't know why that was the case. Maybe it was because he actually listened to her, the girl just a little too plump to be of any interest to the usual pack of wild boys. Back in those days, if you were fat or ugly or stank because your water had been shut off, you only had three choices. One was to lean into it as others had done. You could join in on the joke as long as you acknowledged the joke was about you. It was horrible and self-deprecating, and most of the kids who took this route ended up both confident and successful, all while carrying around an absolutely intoxicating self-hatred that was almost impossible to purge later on.

The second option was to pull back from the crowd as Marshall and Rosaline had done. They kept their grades up and their heads down throughout the entirety of grade school, and once they were out they looked ahead toward nothing but the future. Or at least, that's what they had tried to do.

And then there was the third option: fight. This option wasn't an option as far as Marshall was concerned. A kid who fought was a kid who got crushed. And not just by the other kids. In Poplar, the kids were nothing but the alarm bell—the smoke detector to let the adults know that, *hey, we've got a trou-ble-maker over here. Tell the teachers, tell the parents, tell the cops. Keep an eye on them and dog their every step, telling them exactly what they are until they finally can't become anything but that.*

Option three was a death sentence. At any time, Marshall could drive down Main Street and watch the "option threes" slouch along the sidewalks as they chain-smoked cigarettes and cussed out cars that almost hit them jaywalking.

Those people were nothing to Marshall. He didn't care to be a part of their story because *they* couldn't even be bothered to be a part of it. They'd almost all die before the age of sixty, if not from drug use or automobile accidents, then simply from losing the will to live. Because if there was one thing that he had learned, it was that fighters got tired.

Marshall wasn't sure if he was a psychopath or not. He had done some research but didn't think he really fit the bill. It seemed that a psychopath didn't have any regard for others, which wasn't true about him, was it? Of course, he had regard for others. That's why he wanted them to be a part of his story. It's not that he regarded them as objects or obstacles or trophies; they were *people* and they deserved to be treated like *people*. It was just unfortunate that not everyone agreed with him on how people should be treated—on what constituted importance or meaning. That's what he was doing, he was giving them meaning. *Purpose.*

Purpose.

How could they not see that that was what he was trying to do? He was drawing lines between each wayward person he came in contact with, just like the ancient civilizations that drew lines between the stars to form constellations—to form meaning. He was drawing people together. Making them part of his story. Creating something from the nothing of their lives.

And now it was time for Rosaline; Marshall's first glimpse of what it meant for two people's lives to converge had been when they had spoken in the library one day so long ago and in that moment he had realized that she had a story inside her as well.

Why not combine them? Why not intertwine the whole world's stories? With Marshall as the focal point.

The North Star. Guiding everyone home.

———

WHEN ROSALINE HEARD the knock on her door, she was all at once surprised, excited, and suspicious. Who could be knocking at this hour? It wasn't like she had a lot of friends that just dropped by unannounced.

Her first thought was that Richard had brought the books back. But wait, she had the one she needed didn't she? She hadn't told him yet, but maybe he had the others?

Then, as she walked to the door, she figured that it was probably just Tony asking for help fixing his toilet or something. The boy could be so clueless sometimes.

Rosaline unlocked the door, but left the chain on, because well, you never really did know, did you? Better safe than sorry.

It didn't matter though. Before she could even look through the gap out onto the front step, the door exploded in on her. The bulk of it hit her in the mid-section, sending her sprawling to the ground, the broken chain whipping her in the face on the way down.

She tried to speak—tried to scream—but nothing came out, just a hoarse moan from the back of her throat as a ghost from the past entered her house. Marshall didn't say a word as he stepped inside. His actions were calm but the flush in his face betrayed his excitement.

The deadbolt made a smooth clack as it was slid into place. Marshall Rutledge turned around.

In an instant, Rosaline was desperately trying to scramble to her feet, but then he was there behind her yanking her up by her hair and slapping a huge hand over her mouth. She tried to scream but it just ricocheted off the back of her teeth and into her brain like some sonic bullet.

"Don't scream," he said, and as he did he emphasized the statement by gently pressing the blade of some sort of long hunting knife against her throat. He slowly removed his hand. "Your phone lines are cut, and Tony's gone for the evening. I watched him leave a few hours ago. It's just you and me."

"M-M-Marshall, wh-"

"I don't usually do this," he said, cutting her off, and as he spoke, Rosaline thought she detected a faint quiver in his voice. She still couldn't believe this was happening. She looked desperately around for a weapon. A phone. Anything.

"Do what? Murder people? Because it sounds like you do it all the time," she heard herself say, the words feeling as if they had come from someone else. She still couldn't believe it. This was happening. Now. She was going to die and there was no one to stop it from happening. A part of her wished Tony would come through the door and save her, but another part of her prayed that he wouldn't. Not for anything.

"I don't usually talk to people before I kill them," he said, and the matter of factness made it sound so bizarre that it could have been some other language entirely. "Usually they don't even know they're gone."

"So why are we speaking now?" Rosaline asked. She needed time—needed to stall. For what, she didn't know. But she felt like she needed to keep him talking, if for no other reason than to prolong her life just a few moments longer. "Is it because you know you shouldn't? Because you know you want to stop?"

"Ha." Marshall let out a short and humorless laugh. "No, no, not really. This is going to happen. But I think it might be worthwhile for me to try and convince you of what I'm doing. I don't know, it never really bothered me before this but, well, I'm probably going to die soon, you see?"

Rosaline didn't see, but she hoped it was true. In fact, she hoped it would happen sometime in the next 30 seconds.

"I know how it is. I know how it ends for guys like me, in towns like this. It almost seems preordained, even though I loathe that notion. No, this town wanted to be rid of me from the very beginning. I pulled back, just like you did, tried not to engage. But I was just too—I don't know—different. They knew it from the very beginning. Everyone did. They knew that there was something special about me and if they couldn't have that special something for themselves, then they needed to crush it out altogether."

Rosaline couldn't tell if it was fear clouding her mind, but as Marshall spoke he seemed to be in a world all his own, almost as if he were just speaking to himself.

"But you, Rosie, you understood. You knew what it was to be involved in the tale. Even though you probably didn't know it, you understood me better than anyone else, simply because you read the same books I did—because, in experiencing those characters, you knew the same things I knew."

Rosaline stifled a *'you know that's insane, right,'* and instead said, "If that were true Marshall, then how come we ended up on such...different paths?"

"Well, you simply didn't have the right framework, the right perspective. But I'll give you that soon, don't worry."

"Marshall, you need to stop this. There's more at stake here than just the people you're killing."

Marshall gave her a look that said, *oh?*

For a moment, Rosaline considered telling him everything, if for no other reason than to at least tell someone before she died. The knowledge she had wasn't something she could take to the grave, not when the elders were as incompetent as they were. Hopefully, she had taken care of that, though. Just two hours earlier, Rosaline had gone over the elders' heads and penned a desperate letter to the higher-ups of the Magen Society. The letter was sitting in her mailbox at that very moment, the plastic red flag stuck straight up in the air as a silent plea for help. With any luck, they'd send out a few officials with actual field experience, rather than what she was dealing with here in Poplar.

Plus, there was a part of her that thought, of all people, Marshall might be the one to believe her. He was insane after all, wasn't he? And didn't it take an insane person to believe what she knew?

"There's something—well, the thing is," Rosaline took a moment to try and gather her thoughts. Fear was still coursing through her though, and she didn't really know where to begin. It felt like everything she knew had gained a mind of its own and was now running around loose in her head like so many scurrying mice. "Did you ever read *Crime and Punishment*?" she finally asked.

Marshall nodded.

"Well, what did you think that was about?"

"It was about a lot of things," Marshall replied. "But the central theme was simply about what the title suggests: crime and punishment."

"Yes," Rosaline nodded, her mind slowly slipping into her librarian mindset. "It was about how regardless of whether you can get away with a crime or not, punishment will still find you. It's about how the consequences of crime are not only inevitable but, in a way, something that even the perpetrator will gravitate toward, however subconscious that attraction might be."

"Are you saying I want to be caught?" Marshall asked. He had begun twirling the knife casually in his hand, the point of the blade swiveling its sightless gaze from the floor to the ceiling and then back toward the floor again.

"What I'm saying is-"

"Because I do," he interrupted, the blade halting in his hand, pointing directly at Rosaline's face. "I want to get caught. I want to face the punishment. I know I'm not long for this world, and to tell the truth, getting caught is the whole idea."

"It's not just about you, though," Rosaline implored, her voice beginning to crack again, the fear that had taken a momentary rest now came back in full force at the sight of the knife. "To commit a crime—and not just crime against the law but against humanity—against *reality*—it ripples out and affects everyone. You could even say that it forms *cracks* in our world—cracks that let things in that neither you nor I can even imagine. Things that will grow so huge that they will dwarf even what *you* have done. The pain you cause will become its own entity, and once it gets big enough it will get a name, and once it gets a name you'll simply become a footnote to it."

At this, Marshall's face fell and flooded with anger.

"You're wrong," he snarled in a low voice. "They won't forget me. No one will be able to forget what I've done. You say what I'm doing is forming cracks in reality, but you're *wrong*. I'm making cracks in *your* reality, and not only that, I'm about to smash it and show you what's on the other side. Getting caught will reveal me to the world. The real me. I don't even *care* if they forget my name, because they will know my *face*. I will have ascended beyond death and the whole world will look through the broken pane of their existence and they will see me, the god of everything, and the stars will bow at my feet."

After a moment of strained silence in which despair truly engulfed the entirety of Rosaline's heart, she finally said, "I didn't want to believe it. I didn't want to believe you were this...*insane*." She spat the last word.

"In my experience," Marshall said calmly, "'insane' is the word people use to describe things they don't understand. Like school shooters are *insane*. Terrorism is *insane*. Hate crimes are *insane*. But let me tell you, Rosie, my love, my shining star, I understand why they do it. I understand why they rebel against reality itself. It's because it isn't their reality—it isn't their story, and they're trying to make it theirs. They're trying to be heard in a world that refuses to listen to them. You see, everyone has this feeling that there's a place just for them and they're always subconsciously trying to make it. Their own ideal world. Their home. We're all trying to create Heaven or Hell, and we're always willing to cleave off a part of the world to do so."

The word "cleave" all but slapped Rosaline in the face. Did he know? Was it just a coincidence that he used that specific word? *The Song that Cleaves the World* was an old ritual. Dangerous and forgotten, not even she knew the specifics. Was it possible that he had unearthed the old spell? If so, then they were truly doomed. It took someone of extreme skill and training to pull off a spell like that. And if done incorrectly? Rosaline shuttered at the thought.

But she had no more time to think about that. No more time for anything. Marshall was moving in closer now and she tried backing away like a wounded animal, but there was the wall. She hadn't known it, but she had been slowly backing up, inch-by-inch the whole time, and now she had finally run out of space, and run out of time.

"You'll see, and when you do, what you'll see-" Marshall pressed forward, his knife bared like a single serpent's fang, "-is me."

20

"Where do you think she is?" Ben asked disconcertingly.

Ben, Ian, and Ella had all arrived twenty minutes before school started the next day to try and catch Ms. Shuffer as she went about her morning routine. The plan was pretty simple: tell her kindly that she had given them the wrong book by mistake, and if that failed Ben and Ian would distract her with naive questions about Harlequin Romance novels as Ella pilfered her desk. The problem was that she wasn't there yet, and she was *always* there by now. There had been times that Ian had asked his mom to drive him in early so he could feverishly bullshit his way through a book report he had forgotten the materials for the previous day, and the best place to do that was always in the library as Ms. Shuffer went about re-shelving books. And through Ian's long career of forgetting to do his homework, never once had Ms. Shuffer failed to be there.

"Maybe she's sick," Ella said, as they waited outside the two big wooden doors that, if they had been unlocked, would allow them access into the library.

Ben and Ian slowly and meaningfully turned their gazes on Ella.

"What?" she said, confused.

"Do you know how I know you're tardy half of the school year?" Ben asked.

Ella pursed her lips and her gaze hardened.

"I know you're tardy half of the school year because you have somehow managed to miss the fact that even if Ms. Shuffer had just had her legs ripped off by a couple of velociraptors she would still find a way to cauterize the wounds with a searing-hot clothes iron and drag herself through these doors."

Ella let out a huff but resumed her silence, and inwardly, Ian congratulated her for that tiny morsel of self-control.

Baby steps.

The three of them waited there fidgeting right up until the 8:00 bell. Regardless of their certainty of Ms. Shuffer's dedication to being a librarian, they all hesitantly agreed that, well, maybe she *was* sick. So they deferred their hopes until later.

By the time they hit their resource period however, they found that the doors *were* unlocked, but the seat that typically held Ms. Shuffer was now occupied by Mrs. Reinhart, the most ill-tempered substitute teacher cursed to walk God's green earth; and as they walked in Ian noticed that the woman was glaring at them acidly through a pair of slime-green eyes that were nearly hidden beneath a mop of frizzy, black hair.

Ben went for it anyway.

"Good morning Mrs. Reinhart, I was-"

"Sit," said the substitute, the word coming out as if she had just commanded a cobra to tie itself into a pretzel.

"But my-"

"Sit *down*."

Defeated and forlorn, Ben slowly trod over to the desk that Ella and Ian had chosen.

"Nice one," Ella said, almost triumphantly.

"I don't see you doing any better," Ben said.

Ian lifted his backpack up onto the table searching for something—anything—that might help them in their predicament. That, or possibly just a place to hide while his two friends slowly ripped each other apart.

Ella opened her mouth to say something, but just as she did the bell rang overhead, signifying the beginning of the period.

"No talking. No sleeping. Do your homework, or go to the principal's office," Mrs. Reinhart said.

All of a sudden, there was a soft scuffing noise as Ella slid her chair out and stood up.

"Gee gosh, Ella, that was pretty smooth," Ben said. "Can you teach *me* how to be that inconspicuous?"

After Ben and Ian swung by the principal's office at the end of the day to pick Ella up, the three of them walked out the school doors having no more ancient texts than they had walked in with. Ella had tried to walk up and sweet-talk Mrs. Reinhart into giving her the book, which they didn't actually have visual confirmation of yet. Having failed that (and having failed it rather quickly) Ella had tried to improvise by creating a distraction. Unfortunately, the distraction she tried to create involved tipping over a stack of books onto the floor and—having little experience in creating diversions—Ella's act of carelessness looked exactly like what it was: an overt act of vandalism.

Mrs. Reinhart had glared disbelievingly at her before hastily grabbing for the phone to call the principal's office. Refusing to accept her failure, Ella had then lunged over the desk at the nearest pile of books and promptly received what—up until now —had only been a rumor that circulated the hallways: Mrs. Reinhart's Fiery Kiss.

A written report of the incident would later reveal that, fearing for her own wellbeing and safety, Mrs. Reinhart felt she had no other choice but to defend herself by any means necessary. Ella didn't see the shocked and vindictive substitute teacher reach into her giant handbag at her feet, nor did she see her withdraw the tiny white spray bottle. At first squirt, Ella thought she had been sneezed on and stopped dead, mortified. At the second squirt, she realized she was being sprayed in the face like an unruly cat and tried to slap the bottle out of Mrs. Reinhart's hand. Then, as Ella was sprayed for the third time, she suddenly felt like someone had just doused her face in gasoline and flicked a lit match into it.

"I haven't seen anyone roll around crying like that since Ian's parents wouldn't sign his permission slip for the class trip to Six Flags," Ben said.

"Yeah, it was hard to tell what was happening at first, actually," Ian added. "I thought maybe you were being electrocuted."

"Yeah, well, it hurt like hell," Ella said, her face still red and swollen.

"What did they do in the principal's office?" Ben asked.

"Oh, not much," Ella said. "At first they tried to give me the stern, discipline talk. But they realized pretty quickly that I was in no state to listen to anyone or anything."

"Oh, that's new," Ben snorted.

The early evening had begun to descend on the three of them as they walked along the slushy sidewalks and made their way toward Ms. Shuffer's house. They were bound and determined to get that book today, and all three of them refused to go home until it was in their collective set of hands.

The trio made their way lightly chattering to each other about the exciting events of the day and what they were going to do when they made it to Ms. Shuffer's. Providing she was home, they were going to follow through on the same plan they had

had earlier: simply tell the old librarian that she had somehow switched the books up yesterday, and politely ask for it back. If she wasn't there, well...then they'd just have to get creative.

Within record time, Ian was knocking firmly on Ms. Shuffer's front door. The sun was hanging low in the West, trying to stretch its long orange fingers through the hazy atmosphere to dully illuminate the dying winter world around them. Every four feet or so there had lain a puddle one couldn't avoid unless they stepped into either the woods or traffic, so by this time all three pairs of their feet were soaked through and throbbing with cold.

"Ms. Shuffer!" Ian yelled, hoping she'd come out. They hadn't been there very long, but her car was parked along the road and she certainly should have been out by now.

"Try looking in one of the windows," Ben whispered to Ella, who then stealthily tip-toed down the front steps, over the snow blanketed garden patch that ran alongside the house, and up to one of the semi-curtained windows.

"Well, can you see anything?" Ben asked.

Ian continued pounding on the door.

"Not really," Ella replied as she tried squinting into the darkened house between the curtain and window frame. "It's pretty dark in there, but I think I - *AHH!*" she suddenly cried, stumbling backward. "Face! There's a face!"

Ben and Ian almost tripped over each other as they scrambled toward where Ella had been peering in. But before they could get there, they heard the smack of the front door being unbolted and thrown wide.

"What the fuck are you guys doing here?" said a drawn and pale face that hovered gaunt and ghost-like in the darkness of the doorway.

"Tony?" Ben asked incredulously. "What are you doing in Ms. Shuffer's place?"

"*Get in!*" Tony hissed. "*Now!*"

The three, cold kids piled quickly inside, each of them throwing at least one furtive glance over their shoulders.

"*In! In!*" Tony said as Ben entered, followed by Ian, and then Ella. Tony, smelling like sweat and some other pungent odor, gave one final wary glance at the street outside. Then, in one fluid motion, he slammed the door shut, threw the bolt, and then turned the lock on the knob.

"Geez man, what are you so worried about?" Ben asked, trying to keep the fear out of his voice. All three of them were properly worried now, Tony's disheveled look and atmosphere already beginning to infect them.

"Did you guys see a grey car out there on your way here?" Tony asked.

When no one answered immediately, Tony hissed a frantic, "*Well? Did you?*"

"Not that I can think of," Ben said in a daze. "Why?"

Tony hurried over to the window, crouched down, and then peeped a single eye out toward the street, much in the way he must have done when Ella had seen him.

Observing that Tony wasn't going to immediately give them an answer; Ian turned to look around the small, dark room.

And felt his stomach lurch.

Not four feet away from them was a huge patch of something dark that had recently soaked into the carpet. Ian tried to say something, but the words flapped and failed in his throat.

Sensing the tension, Ben turned to look at what his friend had so clearly become enamored with, and was stricken ill himself. The two children stood there staring at that dark mark feeling like just that: children. Kids locked inside a dark closet that they can't get out of, their panic rising, their anxiety beginning to buzz in them like a swarm of hornets. As they stared into that slick and noxious hole that had been torn in their reality, they felt as if all of the evil in the world had been condensed to a single point that lay on just the other side of it staring back with the hungry eyes of every imagined monster and killer that had ever plagued the nightmares of children since the dawn of time.

"Yeah," Tony said dryly. Both he and Ella had turned to face the patch of blood as well and the four of them stood grimly together in the dark.

"What happened," Ben finally asked.

It took a second for Tony to answer. "It began a couple days ago," he finally said. "I just happened to look out the window when I noticed a strange car I hadn't seen in this neighborhood before parked on the other side of the street. I'm always on the lookout for that sort of thing, you know."

"Why?" Ella asked.

There was an awkward moment as Tony shifted from his left foot to his right.

"Well, you know cops around here," he said impatiently. "They're *bored* and always looking to mess with guys like me. Straight-up harassment is what it is."

For a second, Ian was afraid that Tony was going to launch into some digression that he had neither the time nor patience for, and if he wouldn't have been so scared he would have rolled his eyes so hard they'd have been likely to fall out onto the floor and roll away. But, mercifully, Tony continued his story.

"So I see this car, and it give me pause. *Now why's that giv'n me pause?* I ask myself. So I sat there looking at it from my window upstairs when it hits me: I've seen that care before. It wasn't in the same spot, but I'll be damned if it wasn't there yesterday and the day before. And didn't I pass right alongside it a couple days ago when I was coming back from the grocery store and look inside the window and see someone just *sitting* there?"

A moment passed as the three children wondered if the question was rhetorical or not, but then Tony went on.

"*I'll be* damned *if that's not a cop*, I think to myself. So yesterday, I make like I'm leaving, right? I get all bundled up, spend some time on the phone making sure none of my —uh— *friends* are coming over unannounced, then I leave out the back, walk around the house, and stroll on down the sidewalk, right?"

And this time, it appeared as if Tony did expect an answer, because after a few seconds he repeated himself: "*right?*"

"Right," all three of them replied, not quite in unison.

"Wrong!" Tony snapped. "I turn the corner a few blocks down, walk through the woods, and then loop right back here, where I sneak through the backyard—it's dark now, mind you— and I tip-toe up the steps, slip through the back door, and *voila:* I'm home."

"Why?" Ella asked, confused.

"What?" Tony replied.

"I mean, who cares if you're home or not?"

"So I can catch *him!*" Tony said impatiently.

"Catch him where?" Ben cut in. "Catch him *here*? In *your* house? Full of *your* drugs?"

"*Easy,*" Tony said, and he made a motion like someone running their fingers along a thin thread.

"What?" Ben asked.

Tony tried to mouth something.

"What?" Ben asked again, louder this time.

Wi-red, Tony mouthed in two big syllables.

"Jesus Christ," Ella muttered under her breath.

"Yeah, can we just get on with the story," Ian said, trying to push them along. "So what happened then?"

"So, I'm up there watching this car through a crack in the curtain, right?" Tony said, instantly back in the story. "I figure: *yeah, you just wait to see what you have coming, pig. Teach you to go breaking into people's houses without a warrant.*"

Ian wanted to ask why Tony was so sure that the police officer wouldn't just knock on his door or continue watching the place, but in the interest of time, he suppressed it.

"So I'm up here waiting for hours, right? And just when I was ready to give up, *boom*, the guy gets out of his car."

The small audience of three was now riveted with attention.

"And it weren't no cop, I could tell that right away. Then I think I seen him somewhere. *Where you see this guy*, I ask myself. Then, as he gets closer, it hits me. WHAM!" Tony smacked his hands together and all three of them jumped. "It's the guy!"

"The guy, what guy?" Ella asked.

"The *guy*," Tony said meaningfully. "The guy from the news who they think been killing all those people. *That* guy."

All four of them stood frozen in silence.

"So now my heart's just hammering, right? Like, *holy shit!* This is the *guy!* That fucking killer, and he's walking toward *my house!*"

"So what'd you do?" Ben asked.

"What'd I do?" Tony said, and the way he said it made him sound as if he himself didn't really know the answer. And then after a few moments of thinking, he finally said, "I just watched him walk up to the front door, I guess. Dude knocked a few times, then Ms. Shuffer must have come to the door, 'cause suddenly I see him—*wham*—kick the door in."

Ian felt Ben turn to look at him, and the two boys' eyes met with matched horror: *this guy was our neighbor.*

"I can hear them making some sort of commotion downstairs, some mild shouting and loud talking and whatnot. Meanwhile, I'm just up here curled up in a corner scared shitless, just praying the dude doesn't come in here too. I think about running, but when I try to get up my legs feel all wobbly and I just sink back down. Plus, I'm afraid he'll hear me and know I'm up here. Remember, best he knows is I'm out for the evening, so I eventually figure the best thing I can do is just stay put."

"Then what? Where's Ms. Shuffer?" Ben asked, almost stuttering.

But Tony just shook his head. After an hour or so—or maybe it was like, ten minutes, hell, I can't remember—I hear the back-door to Ms. Shuffer's place open. So, then I creep quietly over to the opposite window and look out. There's no light on back there really, so it was hard to see. But I coulda sworn I saw that guy dragging something out into the woods."

No one said anything as those final words hung in the air like a group of hanged men.

"Then what?" Ian asked hesitantly.

"The fuck you mean *then what?*" Tony said derisively. "Then I stayed-the-fuck-*put*, the fuck else I'm supposed to do?"

"I don't know, call the cops?" Ian said.

"Oh, yeah, right?" Tony said, rolling his eyes. "Like they'd believe *me*. They'd probably just try and pin the whole thing on me."

"So...what? You just planning on never leaving again?" Ben asked.

"*No*, man—*fuck*, I-" Tony ran a hand through his greasy hair. "I don't know, man. I got no clue what to do. I was trying to think of something, but...Well, then *you* showed up, and well..."

"*Then we showed up?*" Ben asked. "This was like...a *day* ago. What have you been *doing?*"

And as soon as Ben had asked the question, all three of them were able to identify the mysterious odor that hovered around Tony.

Tony just shrugged and lifted his hands as if to say: *well, whatcha gonna do?*

"Well shit, this complicates things," Ella said. And for a

moment Ian didn't know what she was talking about. To tell the truth, he had wholly forgotten the reason they had even come in the first place, so immediately pressing was Tony's story. But then, all at once, he remembered: the book.

"Look, Ella, maybe the book needs to take a back seat for now," Ian said hesitantly.

"For *now?*" Ella snapped. "This is the *only* time we're going to have a chance to get it. This place is about to become ground-fucking-zero in terms of cops and journalists and God-knows who else."

"Guys," Tony said.

"Look, I'm not going to go rifling through some dead woman's shit," Ben said to Ella. "No way. That's just wrong."

"Guys," Tony said again, this time a little louder.

"Yeah? Well how 'bout you just scamper on home like a *bitch*," said Ella.

A roaring fire ignited in Ben's eyes, but before he could let loose Tony cut in for a third time, "Guys! There's a fucking *body* out behind my house. Don't you at least want to go make sure that she's dead? I mean, who knows? Maybe she's just back there hurt or something."

"Yeah, fat chance," Ben said, his blood boiling almost visibly beneath his skin.

A pregnant silence passed. The four of them stood there, not wanting to leave, but knowing they had to.

Ben was the first to start walking to the back door, followed by Ian, then Tony. And when Ian looked back to see if Ella was coming he was struck by what he saw. It was as if everything toxic and terrible about Ella had receded to reveal the child she could have been under other circumstances. There she stood, just as scared as the rest of them, not wanting to leave the comfort of this house for the unknowns of the dark forest outside, no matter how foreign this cramped and horror-stricken living room was.

"Aren't you coming?" Ian asked.

Ella didn't respond immediately. She seemed frozen as if on the edge of some huge precipice. But then, finally, she took a hesitant step forward. Then another. And then another. As she walked toward Ian, he saw that crazed and wild look of hers slide back over her face like some protective shell, and by the time they were both out and jogging across the unlit backyard to catch up to their friends Ella had fully morphed back into the girl Ian was used to—the girl that he had fought and shared dinner and hushed conversation with over the last few months. And for many years afterward, Ian would think back to this first glimpse of the real person he would eventually fall in love with, and his heart would ache painfully with the thought of it.

21

———

The forest stretched up around them like uncountable fingers on some ancient, wooden hand, buried beneath stones gradually ground into dirt, and the entire time they walked back, Ian couldn't help but feel that those fingers were about to close shut on them. The sun was completely down by this point, and they had no flashlights. Luckily, the thick branches overhead were responsible for a substantial amount of shade in the early spring that kept the snow from melting as fast as it did in more exposed areas, and the landscape around them reflected the moon in a deep turquoise color, as if the very stars themselves were drawing light from the Earth and not the other way around.

"Do you know where we're going?" Ben whispered to Tony, who had taken the lead.

"I'm just following the footprints man." A moment of silence. "And the drag marks."

They didn't actually have very far to walk, but the night around them seemed to distort time in the same way it seemed to distort light and space, because Ian could have sworn they had been walking for days.

And then suddenly, they stopped.

Tony stopped walking first, the others coming to a halt behind him.

"What is it?" Ian asked, stepping around to get a better look. "Did you find-" and the words came crashing to a halt.

There, as if she belonged amongst the fallen logs and mounds of snow and all the other bits of landscape, lay Ms. Shuffer. Eyes closed in her snow-dusted evening wear, she had her legs curled up so as to reveal the tiny, knife-etched star on her heal. Ian thought that she could have even looked like she was sleeping if it hadn't been for the huge, gaping grin of a knife wound hacked across the length of her throat. Looking at the wound now and thinking back to how much blood had been on the carpet in the living room, it was obvious to Ian that she had died quickly once the actual violence had begun. It was a small comfort, but in the grimness of the situation, it was better than nothing at all.

"So what do we do now?" Tony finally asked. He had started to shiver, and Ian realized that he had come out in nothing but a pair of jeans, tennis shoes, and a long-sleeve flannel shirt.

"Well, you gotta do it man," Ben said. "You gotta call the cops and tell them what happened."

Tony gave him a tired look, but for the first time that night, it looked like he was actually about to take responsibility for something in his life.

"Okay," he finally said. "I gotta take care of a few things first. But ok."

"Should we say something?" Ian asked. "I mean, I feel like we should right?"

No one ventured anything at first, but then, seeing that no one else would, Ben started.

"You deserved better than this Ms. Shuffer," he said. "You were nothing but a shelter for us. You were a place we could come when the rest of the school didn't want us. You gave us a place to sit and read and talk if we needed to. Hell, you even gave Tony a *home*. You didn't just care about us like it was your job, you cared about us like it was your purpose."

"I remember, one time I got sent to the principal's office for tying my shoes together in a knot."

Ian gave the smallest sniff of laughter, remembering the story.

"Alison Beemer dared me to, so I did. Then, once I realized that I couldn't get them untied myself, I had to hobble to the front of Mr. Lekke's class and ask him for help. Well, you know Mr. Lekke. He thought I needed to learn a lesson, so he made me leave the classroom and walk all the way to the principal's office with my shoelaces tied together. I think I probably made it about three hundred feet before my legs were burning so bad that I just sat down on the floor and cried—*this was in the first-grade mind you*."

"So I was sitting there balling my eyes out when you came up and asked what was wrong. I tried to tell you, but I was just so ashamed that I couldn't get the words out. So, instead of making me continue my arduous journey, you just picked me up and brought me to your room where we sat there and talked for the rest of the period. You helped untie my shoes, and while you did, you asked me why I felt like I needed to listen to Alison when she dared me to do stuff. It was a bit of a long conversation, but well," and at this Ben laughed out loud, "I think I learned about romance that day. You taught me that I didn't need to do stupid stuff to impress people. You said—and I remember this quite well—you said that I was going to do enough stupid things in front of girls while growing up and that maybe they'd be more impressed by wisdom than by my lack of it."

"Well, Ms. Shuffer, Alison and I actually talked at the spring dance last year. We went into the gymnasium and chatted about her parent's divorce and what she wants to go to college for and how she'd like to visit Italy someday. Then we made out for an hour, until *you* came and separated us. So, I hope you're happy."

Everyone was looking down at their feet with smiles on their faces, imagining a horror-stricken Ms. Shuffer running over to separate the two kids.

"You didn't just see what we were," Ben continued, "you saw who we could be. You saw our futures and nurtured our potential. And I don't think this town—this *world* —will ever be the same without you."

The other three gave nods and murmurs of agreement. Tony, who had begun crying quietly, gave a soft snuffle. Ian could feel Ben's words sink into him slowly, and with them, the hideous weight of what was actually going on around them began to press downward on the group. All four of them stood in silence, contemplating the life that lay extinguished at their feet.

Ella was the first to turn back toward the house.

"I don't think there's anything else to see here," she said quietly.

Then she stopped.

Ian, who had begun to follow, stopped too.

"What is it?" he asked. Ben and Tony were looking around in confusion now, probably in fear that something was about to come out of the woods around them.

Ella remained silent, staring straight ahead.

At first, Ian couldn't tell what the problem was. Then he realized that something was off—something about where they were. No, that wasn't it. About the way they had come? Something was different about it.

Ian looked down at the tracks they had left on their way into the woods, verifying that they were still there and that they could follow them back if they were to get lost. And it was then that he realized what was wrong.

He followed the tracks with his eyes, there were five sets of them: Ben's, Ian's, Ella's Tony's, and Mr. Rutledge's both in and out. But when Ian tried tracing them back, the path they had taken looked as if it went directly through a tree.

The tree was tall, but not as tall as the others, and it looked as if it had been shorn off at the top. It could have just been short, but even so, it still stood a good three meters high.

Then it moved.

It was subtle at first, and one could have easily been forgiven for thinking that it had simply swayed in the wind. But then it kept moving. The tree that had not been there before split at the trunk and a huge piece of it resembling something close to a leg took a huge lumbering step forward.

"What the *fuck*?" Tony cried out as all four of them scrambled backward.

Arms had separated themselves from the main trunk of the tree now, and the huge shape strode forward almost human-like. Ella took four big steps backward and almost fell down trying to get away, but the thing seemed to not only be ignoring her, but was in fact ignoring everyone.

That is, except for Ms. Shuffer.

Ian stared in shock as the tall monster walked slowly toward Ms. Shuffer's body, and as it bent down, a ray of moonlight flashed luminescent through something that lay thin and crownlike atop the creature's head.

Fangs, Ian heard in the back of his mind. He wasn't sure where it came from—maybe some deeply lodged instinct from ancient ancestors—but as soon as he thought it he knew in his gut that it was true. It was wearing a crown of fangs.

"You stay away from her!" Tony cried as he fished a long and solid-looking stick out of the snow and hurled it at the monstrosity.

The stick clattered against the monster's bark-like flesh and fell benignly to the ground.

A sound like wood moaning in a winter storm rose as the creature turned its head toward the four companions, and in that movement, Ian saw it. It wasn't just a monster. It was *the* monster. The height, the color, the way the thing walked. This was it. This was the thing that had kicked off the whole thing for him—the creature that had strode through his backyard. Ian didn't think he could be any more shocked, that was until it spoke.

"She is dead," it said simply, its voice was surprisingly soft and sorrowful. "There is nothing for you to accomplish here."

"And what do *you* hope to accomplish here?" said a voice from behind Ian, and it sounded so calm and sure of itself, that he was surprised to turn around and see that the voice had come from Ella. "What are you? And what are you doing here?"

The creature looked appraisingly at her, then said, "I am the Harbinger, the Omen Bearer, the Dead Tree. I follow death and where I go death follows. I am the shadow of the Tree of Life. I am the tree upon which Christ hangs, and Odin hangs, and every victim of every lynch mob hangs. The world has a heart of stone, and every time that heart is cracked, I rise up from Hades and stretch my limbs into the night sky above."

"Are you going to kill us?" Tony asked, trembling now.

"I do not kill," the creature croaked. "I merely water my roots with blood and draw my life from that which has been expunged. I go where the reaper leads me, and it would seem that he has chosen to make this town his home."

"So what then?" Ben ventured. "You just go around crouching over dead bodies? You say that you follow death, but death follows you. What does that mean? What happens if we just burn you down?"

At this, the creature turned to face the four of them full on. It had no visible eyes, but the bark on its "face" appeared to move and separate as it talked.

"You are children," it said. "You show courage speaking to me as you do, but only because you fail to comprehend the magnitude of the situation. You all stand upon the edge of a chasm. One step further and you will fall into the black water that lays below. The depthless chaos is a lake of fire that cannot be quenched. I am the tree of Revelation and Ragnarok and of the torn flesh of Prometheus bound in agony atop the mountain. I do not accept the words of children, but children should heed mine: the world is tearing apart all around you and from the black ocean of death will rise a storm the likes of which you have never seen."

The Harbinger, ancient and wooden, craned its neck looking as tall as everything.

"And you, child," it looked straight at Ella who took a step back. "You, who have walked in my forest and resisted the words of serpents. You think you have the strength to bear the weight —to fight the good fight—but you do not. Your desperation is the world's swan song. You will fail, and your friends will fail, and in your failure, the jaws of Hell will open wide and its teeth will be my branches."

And with these words, the creature plunged one of its long, branchlike arms into the earth beneath and around Ms. Shuffer's body. Roots flew out and thrust themselves down like a video of a tree being uprooted played in reverse.

"The storm will rise," the creature said gravely, "and when it does..."

Silence struck the night like a final death knell, and from it rose the creature's final words:

"...it will swallow you."

The Harbinger ripped its arm from the ground in a gout of frozen dirt and snow, leaving a countless number of holes like buckshot drilled into the earth below, and out of them came a gushing wave of writhing, black serpents. Ian screamed as the lithe, obsidian bodies poured over his feet in a noxious wave of reptilian stench and his terror rose again and again from his mouth in chorus with the others as they all stumbled backward and began racing back toward the house, away from the body, away from the monster, and away from the eternal blackness of night.

22

Hot water poured over Ian's face as he tried to wash the stink of snake off of him. He had washed his hands at Tony's after they had come crashing back through the door, but it wasn't good enough. Ian thought that the smell would stay with him forever. The stench was like a mixture of feces, dead leaves, rotten meat, and sour sweat. Ian squirted a huge dollop of honey lavender body wash into his hand for the fourth time and began scrubbing his chest with it.

And it will swallow you.

The shower steamed and hissed as it ran but it still wasn't loud enough to drown those words from his head. What had the thing meant by that?

Ben, Ian, and Ella had all left Tony's immediately, making him swear that he would call the police but not to mention them. The last thing they needed was to be tied up in not one, but two murders.

The trio remained silent the whole way home, and when it came time for them to split, Ben just kept walking without a single word of farewell. When Ian and Ella stepped through the door, stomping the snow from their boots, they were addressed by a pair of worried faces belonging to Ian's parents. They simply explained that they had stayed late after school with Ben and lost track of time. Ian's mom accepted this answer, but not without a stern talk about calling home when they were staying after. Ian nodded and Ella nodded and Ian's dad looked with solemn approval as the two kids walked down the hallway in what must have seemed like an air of regret.

When Ian got out of the shower, Ella passed by him with her own stack of clothes and towels in her arms. They passed by each other without a word, and Ian wondered how she was taking all of this. She hadn't actually known Ms. Shuffer that well, but then again, she had just been confronted by a massive, tree-shaped monster that ripped a bunch of holes in the ground for snakes to pour out of.

That night, Ian's dad had rented *Young Guns* and they all gathered around to watch the dubiously historic account of the mythic figure of Billy the Kid set to stadium rock 'n roll. There was a point pretty early on where the unspoken question floated into everyone's minds about whether or not the movie was appropriate for children of Ian and Ella's age, but ever since Ella had unofficially joined their family, every instance of violence on television seemed cartoonish in light of what she had endured and what both her and Ian had seen over at Mr. Rutledge's house.

An unexpected connection had arisen between Ella and Ian's dad, and it did so in the form of movies. There was no "movie night" in the Whelan household because, for Mr. Whelan, every night was movie night. Whether he was watching one upstairs in the living room with the family or downstairs at night by himself, hardly a day went by where he didn't sit down for at least one-and-a-half hours and watch some cars chase each other, or people fall in love, or buildings explode, or Adam Sandler do some outrageous and unbelievable character. Ian's dad didn't just love movies, he lived for them.

Ian had always gotten along well with his father, but he tended to skew more toward his mother's love of reading. Sure, there was enough overlap of theme and characters between the two mediums that he had a sort of built-in vocabulary with which he could speak with his father, plus there were all the movies he watched with Ben, but when Ella entered the picture, the two of them connected almost instantly. In fact, Ian wasn't so sure that Ella didn't spend more time with his father than he did. It seemed like almost three times a week he would walk into the living room and the two of them would be sitting silently on the couch together with a bowl of popcorn between them as cowboys mimed being shot by each other on-screen. Ian wasn't jealous, to be sure—in fact, he thought it was a bit of a relief that Ella was getting along so well with his dad—he just felt weird about having this sudden new addition to their family that he hadn't even been consulted about.

If Ian's parents noticed that something was off about the two children they didn't say anything. Ella's eyes were on the screen but they weren't watching. Not that Ian could blame her; they had just found one of their teacher's murdered out back behind their house, the killer was still at large, and on top of all that there was some sort of *monster* out there. A *real* monster. Ian realized that no matter how much he wanted to believe it before, he hadn't, not totally. It wasn't until he saw it move—heard it speak—that he knew it. It wasn't until then that he had felt the truth of what he had declared for so long: that there was indeed a monster roaming the woods of Poplar.

He hadn't actually been able to think about the events of the night at all, not really. It was like some dark eye that had followed him out of the forest, and to think about it was to look at it, so instead, he resorted to skirting around it with thoughts of Ella or Ben or Tony and just what the hell they were going to do next.

Unsurprisingly, Ian found that he couldn't really sleep that night. He rolled around in the covers for about twenty minutes before he finally gave up, got out of bed, and went to the window. He thought back to that night a few months ago when he had first seen the creature striding like a flitting shadow across the lawn. He saw the thing in his mind's eye and when he projected it out onto the moonlit landscape outside he could see it clearly.

He had seen it, no doubt about it. It must have been attracted to Lilly's body that night and had gone over to it to do whatever weird ritual it was want to do. What was all that anyway? Snakes? He wasn't entirely wild about them, but what did a few more mean? Less toads? Competition for owls and stray cats?

But then he thought about Ella—thought about the story she had told about the snake in the river and the snakes in the woods as they followed her for days, speaking to her. No, that wasn't it—trying to *coerce* her into something.

Into what?

A quiet but urgent knock sounded at Ian's door. He waited for a few heartbeats, afraid to move, then the knock came again. Ian stepped away from the window, padded lightly across the carpet in his bare feet, and opened the door.

It was Ella. She looked like she couldn't sleep either and was fully dressed in jeans and a winter coat.

"What's up?" Ian asked, feeling conscious about the fact that he was only wearing a t-shirt and a pair of boxers. He tried hiding himself behind the door as best he could.

"Can I ask you a favor?"

Ian was taken aback. Since when had Ella

ever *asked* for *anything*? Normally she just *took* and asked for forgiveness later, that was, as long as someone *made* her ask for forgiveness.

"Sure," Ian said, matching Ella's wakefulness, the only two in the house that couldn't yet face the night with their guards down.

"I want to go back to my house," Ella said, then hastily added, "just for tonight. I need to see something. Will you go with me?"

"Yeah," Ian said stupidly, "We can stop by Ben's and-"

"No," Ella interrupted. "I don't think I can withstand any more arguments. Not tonight."

Ian was reluctant. He had probably spent more time with Ben than his own parents over the last few years, and to tell the truth, he still didn't trust Ella a whole lot. But there was something in her voice—in her eyes that reminded him of that moment back in Ms. Shuffer's house when he saw her take that hesitant step forward toward the unknown. What was it? He couldn't quite put his finger on it, but in the end, he went with his gut.

"Okay," he said. "Just, ya know—let me put some pants on."

Ella blushed.

"Yeah, I'll be out front." And with that, she pulled the door closed.

THE NIGHT WAS COLD. Colder than it had been just a few hours earlier, even in light of their unexpected company. The stars were crisp and brittle overhead. Ian looked up at them, his breath crystallizing as he exhaled.

"Why do you think Mr. Rutledge carves stars into people's heels when he kills them?" Ian asked quietly. The night around them had frozen what water had been left standing by the day's thaw, and their boots made loud scuffing noises as they walked. They tried to move more quietly, but the wind was down and even the smallest noises felt as if they could be heard for miles.

Ella was silent, but she had an air of thought around her, the two children connected by something neither physical nor verbal

"Not sure," she finally said. "They look like pentagrams— like the things you see in old horror movies that demons come out of."

"What do you think they're for? I mean, they seem to be connected to the monster somehow. But how?"

"I don't know," Ella said. "I think it might be something like a calling card. I think the stars mean something to him that they don't mean to anyone else. When he draws them, I think he's drawing a part of himself—a part that he wants us to see."

They chewed on that as they walked down the moonlit street.

WHEN THEY ARRIVED at Ella's house, the structure seemed to loom out at them, dead and foreboding, and Ian was more than a little relieved when Ella suggested they take a short detour to the work shed out back before they went in.

"What do we need in here?" he asked as Ella examined a rusted padlock on the latch of the shed's door.

"Shovels," Ella said.

"Shovels."

"Yup."

"Ok." Ian looked down at his feet; once again, snow had melted through his boots and soaked his socks.

"Guess I'll find out what those are for soon enough."

"Yup."

· · ·

BREAKING the padlock was less of a problem than Ian would have anticipated. There was something about locks that had seemed indestructible to him until now, but after finding a big rock nestled up against the wall of the shed, Ella had the weak piece of metal in pieces after only a few well-aimed swings.

The door creaked open to reveal piles of dusty junk. Flower pots and plastic buckets cluttered the floor, each one filled with its own assortment of rusted hand tools and odd lengths of rope. An old lawnmower with its engine removed lay dead and gutted amongst a heap of smashed drywall and torn shingles. Over in a corner, there leaned a forest of rakes and hoes and shovels of different kinds. Ella waded through the junk, grabbed two shovels—one with a wooden handle and one made out of some sort of aluminum—and then led Ian back out into the yard where they cut across the unmarked snow to the back door.

"Are we going to smash this door down too?" Ian whispered.

"Probably." Once standing directly in front of the door, Ella reached overhead to the warped trim and fished out a small key. "Or we could just open it like regular people." She jammed the key in the lock, jiggled it, then slammed her shoulder into the door a few times before it finally opened with a big crack, the inky black of the abandoned house yawning out at them.

"Like normal people," Ian said. "Right."

"Follow me," Ella said. "Be careful, the stairs are right in front of us,"

"That's a good design."

"Just don't fall. There are some flashlights downstairs— hopefully the batteries still work—but for now you're just going to have to follow me through the dark."

The basement was no darker than the rest of the house, but as he slowly descended the steps, holding Ella's hand for guidance, it *felt* like it was getting darker. He wasn't sure if it was because he was moving away from the ambient light that filtered in from the moon outside, or if it was simply the knowledge that he was entering the basement of a strange house. The stairs were bare and wooden and creaked with every step, a long series of constant alarms.

Ian wanted to say something—to ask where they were going or why they were here—but every time he tried to speak, the words wouldn't come, so enamored was he with the sensation of Ella's hand in his, leading him to face the dark world below.

His feet suddenly hit dirt and as he stumbled and almost lost hold of his shovel, Ian felt the odd sensation one feels when they go to take another step down and realize that there is nothing lower—that they're at the bottom. He stumbled, but Ella caught him, leading him on into the black. The basement was cold, but not as cold as Ian would have imagined. The earth beneath his feet was mostly dry and he could smell the familiar scent of dust and dirt mingling in the air as he kicked it up.

A light flared without warning and as his eyes adjusted, Ian could see Ella fiddling with a lit flashlight, the circular beam dancing unsteadily on the walls, throwing shadows around the room like black leaches being shaken in a jar of water.

"Can you take this?" Ella said, handing him her shovel so that Ian was now holding two. Despite how cool he might have felt "dual wielding" shovels, he couldn't help but feel vulnerable to anywhere the light didn't shine, particularly from behind.

Ella used the flashlight to illuminate a small, wooden shelf packed so tight with junk that the individual items had long since ceased to be anything but what they were in their accumulation: a big pile of sharp and dusty shit. The inconsistent light made it look like some sort of flea market one might come across if they were shopping for lawn ornaments in the underworld. Jagged pieces of metal jutted out dangerously and without any sense of order. Paper was crumpled and folded and jammed into nooks and crannies so as to give Ian the impression that a single lit match would cause the shelf of junk to literally explode.

Ella sorted through it, tossing things aside without caution, clearly forgetting Ian's warnings of tetanus from a few months back. She dug through and dumped out boxes until she finally found what she was looking for: a small Coleman lantern. She shook it lightly to make sure that it still had oil in it, and then, after setting it down, she fished through her pockets until she pulled out a small book of matches.

"Where'd you get those?" Ian asked.

"From the kitchen."

Ian recognized that she had said *the* kitchen, not *your* kitchen. She was undoubtedly talking about Ian's kitchen—they had yet to step foot in hers—and for some reason it made him feel uneasy, as if he had just received a confirmation letter from adoptive services about the Whelan family's brand new 13-year-old daughter. Ian pictured brand new family pictures with an extra child in them. Another spot at the table. Another person opening presents on Christmas.

But it had already begun, hadn't it? She was already living in their house and eating dinner with them every night. She had already come out on Christmas morning to find a slew of presents with her name on them sitting underneath the tree. He wasn't sure how he felt about it, other than simply feeling *weird*.

Ella lit one of the matches, cupped it in her palm as if it was some sort of fragile firefly, and then lit the wick inside the lantern. It took a few seconds, but eventually the wick was burning as well, and as it got brighter it illuminated the basement in a haunted orange like the death of evening where the shadows have swallowed the world up to the neck. All around them the darkness shifted and shrank into corners, and as Ian looked down, horror dawned on him as he realized that he was surrounded by holes.

Some of the holes were small, about the width of a bratwurst, but one of them near the middle of the floor was huge. Ian thought that, if he had wanted to, he could have fit his whole leg down it. The rest seemed to congregate around a section near the far wall and as Ella focused in on them she began to walk.

"Don't get too close to that," she said as Ian peered down the big one. He couldn't tell, but it felt as if it could have gone straight through the bottom of the world.

"What made these?" he asked, already sensing the answer. His stomach involuntarily churned inside of him.

Ella simply shook her head, and then in a hoarse voice: "Bring the shovels."

"What? Ella, why-"

Ella whirled around. "Ian, I need you to do this with me." Her tone sounded flat and dead, and Ian could see both determination and desperation roiling in her features.

After some careful consideration, Ian solemnly handed her one of the shovels.

The ground was cold and hard, but due to a miraculous lack of moisture in the basement, the dirt came away far easier than it would have outside. It still required a fair deal of their strength, however. Their two spades independently bit the dirt like a pair of dull teeth, and it wasn't long before they were huffing and sweating.

Ian had just taken off his coat when Ella found what she had been looking for.

23

———

"I thought I would feel something," Ella said. "I thought I would scream. Cry. Explode. Something."

Ian held her hand as the two of them sat outside on the hood of a rusted car Ella's dad had never gotten around to disposing of. The moon burned bright and fat in the sky like a second sun, the night around them cold and silent.

"But I felt nothing," Ella said, "nothing at all. The whole time we were digging I knew. I think I've known for a while now, ever since those nights in the woods. They virtually told me, but I didn't want to listen."

Ian nodded. He had no words. Everything warm and comforting had been sucked out of him when he saw the shrunken, hollow face of Ella's mother, unearthed from her shallow grave. He couldn't tell exactly what it was at first, not with the chunks of dirt still clinging to her. But Ella kept working—kept chipping diligently away until a crude outline of a body lay wasted and rigid before them.

"It's like my mind knew what was coming—like it knew some horrible truth was about to invade my life, so it made a built-in lever to just...shut everything off before it could get to me."

"Do you feel anything now?" Ian asked.

Ella screwed her face up, thinking. "I don't know. It's like I keep throwing doors open in my mind, expecting grief to be on the other side, but...it's never there. Just emptiness."

The thought seemed alien to Ian as he tried to imagine what it would be like to lose his mother. And then, after a few moments of thought, he decided that he might feel the same way. Then another thought invaded his head, something he longed to know but dreaded asking.

"Ella," Ian said slowly, "who killed her?"

"My father," she said stiffly. "It must have been. He told me that she had run off. That she couldn't bear living with me any longer so she left. He was angry. He was *so* angry. I don't really know what could have happened, but I doubt he tried to do it. I don't think he really tries to do anything, really. He just *reacts* to the world with shitty choices, and after this one, I don't think he was sad she was gone, I think he was just pissed that he had to take care of me."

"Why didn't he just give you away or something?"

"He's not like that. He's not one to give something up, even if it's a burden to him. Not if he thinks it's *his*. Just look at this car we're sitting on."

Ian shifted and looked down at the hood he was perched on. Most of the paint had been chipped and worn away and all of the windows were gone but for the jagged bits that jutted out like so many teeth around the edges. The whole front of the car groaned under his weight.

"I don't know what he was thinking burying her down there," Ella said. "Then again, he wasn't much for the outdoors. He worked the night shift, hated the sun, all that jazz. I guess he would have had to bury her in broad daylight if he tried to do it outside."

"Can I ask you a question?" Ian asked hesitantly.

"What is it?"

"Why do you call your mom 'mom' but you call your dad your 'father'?"

"It's something she taught me," Ella said after a second. "Some piece of misplaced love or respect or something. The only reason I still do it is because of her. It's like a piece of her is still here with me. One of her only lessons."

"Where do you think he is now?" Ian asked after a pause.

"Not sure," she said, then, "I have a brother too, you know."

Ian sat up a bit straighter and looked at her. "Really? Who? Where? Does he go to school with us?"

Ella laughed. "No, I'm not sure where he is. He left when I was little to go live with my aunt, I think. On my father's side. This was a few years before my mom left." She caught herself and swallowed. "Before she died, I guess. The memory's all fuzzy in my mind, but they practically took him away. The whole thing was strange, and looking back, I think that was the beginning of the end for my parent's relationship."

"Do you think you'll try to find him someday?"

"Maybe," she said. "Someday." She exhaled a sigh of frustration. "I'm not sure what I'd say to him. How would I tell him about this? How could I go about explaining what's happening up here without getting the cops involved?"

"Why don't you want the cops involved?" Ian asked.

She didn't respond right away; instead she hopped off the car, took a few investigative steps, then carefully lay down in the snow facing up at the stars. Ian thought she could have looked like an angel if she hadn't looked so forlorn.

The hood of the car creaked as he slid off to join her.

"I hope he's in Hell," she finally said. The words were so

quiet that at first, Ian thought he misheard her. "My father, I mean. I hope he's stumbling in the woods like I was. I hope he's got snakes wrapped around each of his ankles like a pair of demonic toddlers. I hope he's suffering."

Speechless, Ian just laid there without moving. The snow was comfortable and molded around his body, holding him there like a cold but comfortable hand.

"What do you want, Ella?"

"What?" she replied, seeming almost startled.

Ian hadn't even thought about the words before he said them and was even somewhat surprised by them himself.

"What do you want to do with your life?" he asked. "We're young, I know, but what do you want to do when you're older? I want to be a police officer. Maybe in a big city or maybe not. I'm not sure yet, but I know that that's what I want to do. So how about you?"

"I don't know," she said.

A small gust of wind rattled through the trees, reminding Ian of the giant living tree they had seen, but when he thought of it, he wasn't afraid for some reason. He felt safe around Ella, as if for once her fearlessness was more than just a mask she wore but was actually something solid and secure. Whether it be talking snakes or walking trees or murderous fathers, there was nothing that could touch them here in this moment.

"I feel safe," Ella said, echoing Ian's thoughts. "I feel this way sometimes, ya know? Like I can disconnect myself from my body, float up and above the tree-line and scope out the future for danger."

"See anything?" Ian asked.

Ella exhaled, her breath like a huge, white mushroom cloud in the cool air.

"Nothing tonight at least," she said, then turned her head over to look at him. "Sometimes I feel like I can go up really high

—like I can just float up like a balloon, looking down at all of existence. And ya know what?"

"What?" Ian said after a beat.

"It's strange. The whole thing's strange. It feels like a big car that no one's driving. And when I float up, sometimes I feel like I can put my hand against the glass."

"The glass?"

"Yes, the glass. Like, one of those two-way mirrors you see in cop movies. It feels like that. Like there's a border, and on the other side is a whole different world, or *worlds* even. Who knows?"

Ian didn't know what to say.

"That's what I want."

"What about that do you want?" Ian asked, confused.

"I want to see the other side."

24

When Tony had called 9-1-1 he had expected the local sheriff to show up with one of his deputies. It turned out that his assumption was partially correct, in that the sheriff *did* show up and he *did* have one of his deputies along. What he hadn't expected was what looked like a *battalion* of FBI personnel to show up with them.

The crime scene crew immediately swept him out of the house and taped off a perimeter.

Everything was a crime scene. His house was a crime scene. The woods were a crime scene. He wouldn't have been surprised if the whole damn town was a crime scene. Sheriff Anderson transported him down to the police station where they shoved him in a stuffy interrogation room, handed him a shitty cup of coffee, and then asked about 1,000 questions over and over again until he felt like he might not even know who he was anymore.

"What is this guy, Osama Bin Laden or something?" Tony asked as they were wrapping up. "You really need this many people working on this?"

"Look," said the FBI agent across from him. The man had thinning hair, was thick around the middle, and looked eternally out of breath. "We think this guy's killed people in at least four states, that makes this federal. Plus, we have no idea how far back this goes. I can't give you any specifics right now, but it looks like this guy's done a lot of bad things for a really long time, and that has people scared. People want this solved. They don't want to think that a man can go around killing people for decades, and then, even after he's been identified, just continue on as if nothing's changed. So yeah, we've got a lot of guys working on this."

"Huh," said Tony. "Do you think I'll be able to go to sleep in my own bed tonight, or...."

"No, you got somewhere to stay?"

Tony exhaled. "Yeah, I got some friends I can crash with." He wasn't actually thinking about sleeping as much as he was concerned about his upstairs living quarters that were both full of marijuana and federal agents. Then again, Sheriff Anderson had made some remarks in the past about how he was basically "allowing" Tony to deal in Poplar, mostly because he was, in Anderson's words: "stupid, incompetent, unambitious, easy to keep track of, and relatively harmless. At the time, Tony had just read the words as the sheriff trying to cover his own ass because he couldn't pin anything on him, but now he hoped the sheriff had actually been telling the truth. After all, they hadn't really brought it up yet. And wasn't dealing a little weed small potatoes when it came to state-line-crossing serial murderers?

When Tony left the station, he began to wander slowly toward Jeff Adams' house, a shitty friend and loyal client. Jeff was mean-spirited and smelled like sunbaked garbage half of the time, but hey, it was a couch to sleep on.

Tony was surprised when he realized how light it was outside and that he had been awake almost the entire night.

Man, had they really kept him that long? The air was cold, but Poplar glowed around him with the bright, baby-blue of first light in spring. Tony wrapped his arms around his chest, wearing only a light jacket, and by the time he cut south through the small park toward Jeff's his teeth had begun to chatter. A black pick-up truck passed him on his left and air rushed through him in a brief gust, the red taillights flickering briefly before the truck turned at the next intersection.

"*Damn* it's cold," he said to no one. Tiny storefronts sat unlit and snoozing around him. The sidewalks lying long and empty, the town so quiet he thought he could still hear his voice echoing down the streets.

Two more blocks and Tony turned onto Jeff's road, a winding and unplowed thing that was as pothole ridden as it was sparsely populated. To the best of Tony's memory, the house was less than a mile away. Then again, he had only ever ridden there in people's passenger seats; he'd never actually *walked* there before.

Tony heard another vehicle coming up behind him, its wheels crunching through the frozen slush still left blanketing the road. He stepped off to the right just to make sure the truck had just enough room to pass when he realized that it was the same truck that had passed him before.

He realized it too late.

———

RICHARD CARLYLE HAD BEEN JUST about ready to pack it in when he heard the dispatch come over his police scanner. He had picked up two of the handy machines—plus a small chrome revolver he had bought on a whim—from a somewhat less-than-reputable pawn-shop owner in Superior, Wisconsin just a few days after Marshall Rutledge had been identified as Lilly's killer.

He kept one by his bed, much to Helen's dismay, and one fixed to the dashboard of his truck. Every day since then he had spent huge amounts of time listening to the boring blather of small-town police radio chatter, all the while imagining what he might do to Rutledge if he got to him first.

Like all things, it started rather small. He rationalized it to himself by saying that he only wanted it so he would be among the first to receive news on Rutledge when he was eventually caught. It had been easy, as if some part of him had a secret use for the scanner and was keeping it from the rest of him.

At first, Helen was merely annoyed with his decision to keep the scanner on next to the bed, but halfway through the second night after what seemed like the hundredth stream of police chatter came over the air, she asked Richard if he really needed that on while they were sleeping. She had tried to have a few conversations with her husband once he had returned, but Richard kept their interactions to a bare minimum. After pleading with him to shut it off, a conversation that snowballed into a nasty argument, Helen eventually kicked him out to go sleep downstairs in Lilly's bedroom.

Richard could have slept on the couch—probably *should* have slept on the couch—but being in Lilly's room after all those months was like a red-hot knife wound in a world that had become drab and grey. On the night he had left his home to go sleep at the church, he couldn't even bring himself to walk down the stairs, but now he found himself sleeping where she had slept every night. Surrounded by all of her personal belongings, a crypt of accumulated memories, Richard found himself submerged—almost masochistically—in a sea of painful memories.

Helen no longer seemed to be putting up with him. He could be days away from being fired from his job, but he'd never know.

He barely talked to anyone at the church. The only one that seemed to still care about him was Claire.

That almost stopped it right there—almost made him stop the whole thing and ignore that whispering part of himself and go back to his family. But wasn't that why he was doing this? Wasn't he doing this to protect her? To protect all of them? Yes, he had to. It was his duty as a father and pastor to protect his flock. Granted, he hadn't preached a sermon in months now, and would probably soon be replaced by some swoopy-haired, acoustic guitar-playing youth pastor that stammered out directionless prayers and preached almost exclusively on the "goodness of God's name," but that didn't matter. There was more to being a leader than giving speeches and he was about to prove that.

So it was with absolutely no self-awareness of his gradual transformation over the past few months that Richard Carlyle stalked Tony Langley from his house to the police station and then down some God-forsaken stretch of road that was so desolate it practically begged to be the scene for what was about to happen. Richard had waited in the parking lot all night waiting for Tony to come out, slowly nodding off and jolting awake again, praying that he hadn't missed him; and it was just about 5:30 in the morning when he was awakened by the slamming of a car door. His eyes shot open and he frantically searched around the parking lot for any sign of his prey before he saw the doors to the station serendipitously swing wide and cast forth a slumped and exhausted looking Tony.

After pulling out of the lot, Richard watched carefully from afar as the young man ambled down the empty streets. Keeping a few blocks away, Richard pulled incrementally forward. He could feel the pull of sleep somewhere deep down in the lowest parts of him, but adrenaline was coursing through his blood now and he was so focused on his task that he felt as if he could run an entire marathon.

At one point, Richard saw in his review mirror that a police cruiser was making its way down the road behind him—probably fresh from the station—and Richard sped up to a normal pace to make sure that the cop couldn't get his license plate number. It was a slim chance, but then again, he did look pretty suspicious crawling down the road like he was. Thank God Polar was so small, or this would have been impossible. He needn't have bothered however, as the patrol car turned a few blocks later at about the time Richard was passing Tony and then pulling up to a stoplight. Richard turned and looped back around and was delighted when he saw Tony turn down the road he did.

Five minutes later, and he was swerving to cut Tony off, jumping from the truck with the small pistol in his hand, turning, screaming "get on the ground! Get on the ground now!" And Tony being Tony tried to run, tripped, fell, and then curled up into a ball. Richard ran over to him and shoved the cold muzzle against his cheek.

"Tell me about him!" Richard hissed.

"What? About who?"

"Rutledge. You must have seen him. Seen what he was wearing. What he was driving. Did he look clean to you, or did he look dirty? Did you see him kill Rosaline?"

Tony didn't say anything. He flinched and visibly tried to grapple with the questions that were flying rapid-fire out of Richard's mouth.

Richard hit him. He hadn't tried to hit him hard, but his adrenaline was up. That, and he had the added weight of a .38 revolver in his hand. The handle left a bright, wet gash on Tony's cheek.

"Okay, okay!" Tony was whimpering now. "He was driving a grey car. And—geez—I don't know I guess he looked dirty, but-"

"What kind of car?"

"I don't fucking know, man. A car. A fucking car. With a windshield and shit."

"Oh, a windshield. That's really helpful. Tell me, did it roll around on four big circles too?"

"Fuck you man."

Richard pulled the hammer back on the pistol and leveled it at Tony's right eye.

"W-w-w-w-wait! There was something else! He said something else, too."

Richard didn't say anything. He just waited.

"He—a—*shit* man, I totally forgot!"

"What?" Richard asked. "What did he say?"

"He said something about Ian. About the kid. Ah shit, I think he's going after Ian!"

"What? Why would he do that?"

Tony looked around frantically, as if the answer might be hanging off one of the branches of the trees across the road. Richard moved in closer, almost touching Tony's eye now. Somewhere in the back of his mind, he thought that he must have smelled like Rutledge did. Maybe even looked like him, considering what kind of stress the two of them had been under.

"I don't know, man. He must have spoken to him or something. Like before we all knew who he was. Dude was talking about stars and shit. Man, his mind is *fucked.*" Then Richard saw the comment form on Tony's lips before it fell back down his throat.

Like mine, right? You think both our minds are fucked.

Then Richard felt something wash over him. Something new and hot and feverish, like a wave of something both calming and electric. It spoke to him. Richard suddenly felt the gun's grip in his hand. Felt the trigger begin to itch, the mouth of the barrel suddenly wide and hungry. He wanted to pull the trigger. He wanted to end this miserable insect's life.

He fought back against it, like a rising urge to vomit. He swallowed and tried to push it back down. The urge to pull the trigger wavered and he focused on his trigger-finger. He didn't think about anything else—didn't try to reason or debate. Nothing. Just the solitary digit and what it was *not* going to do.

The feeling passed. Richard's skin felt suddenly cold. The gun heavy in his hand.

"Look, Tony," he said, "I'm sorry. But I gotta find the guy who did this. It's gotta be me, understand?"

Tony nodded.

"Just—just don't tell anyone about this. Not the cops, not your buddies, not even Ian, got it?"

Tony nodded again, his eyes closed.

"Good," Richard said. "This will all be over soon."

That's when Richard made a mistake. It was almost as if some part of his body was conspiring against another part—as if it knew there was some foreign body attached, pouring poison in. It was hard to say how long the presence had been there, infecting the man's mind, but if he had to guess he probably could have traced it all the way back to the night he decided he had to leave the house. The pain. The hatred. The need for isolation. They had all been a perfect cocktail to feed the thing attached to him. They would leave his body and then flow right back in, magnified ten times what they had been. A toxic feedback loop of bitterness.

Richard almost screamed when Tony reached up and grabbed his forearm. Pain and revulsion shot through him as his very flesh contorted beneath his shirt. Lashing out in anger and surprise, he backhanded Tony as hard as he could with the gun in his hand. The boy's skull cracked and he went down into the snow, unmoving.

He was still there as the pair of headlights swept across him as Richard turned around on the small road and began to head back the way he had come.

25

The next day at breakfast, Ian begged his mom if he could stay home from school. He didn't particularly relish the idea of having to go sit in a classroom where he would then have to wait for the dreaded announcement that called everyone to the auditorium for a special assembly. They'd then have to sit through a feeble and meandering tale about what had happened to their librarian in the vaguest and most well-meaning way possible. After that, there would be the boundless speculation among the students. The look of unease on the teachers' faces and in the way they held themselves. The thick and heavy impatience that would connect Ian with Ella and Ben.

It was horrible. The things that the three of them had experienced were quickly creating a life that felt wholly alien to the one they had had just a few months ago. What was pre-algebra to serial killers lurking the streets? What was historical French politics to monsters that stalked the woods?

"No way, mister. No temperature, no absence. You know the rules." Ian's mom dropped a paper plate of toaster oven waffles on the table as Ella pulled out a chair across from him; her hair in a messy, dark tangle; eyes heavy with sleep.

"But mom, I-"

"But nothing. You don't look sick to me and the last thing you need is to be home alone. Not with all these...*scary people* running around."

Ian relented and poured a rebellious amount of maple syrup onto his waffles, a decision he would soon regret as the flimsy paper plate began to show its lack of structural integrity.

"Here ya go sweetie," Ian's mom said as she put one of the three heavily-used ceramic plates down in front of Ella.

"Why does she get the good plate?" Ian asked through a mouthful of sugar and carbohydrates.

"Because dear, we want her to feel welcome here. *You're* here whether you like it or not."

Ian crossed his arms indignantly but soon returned his focus to his breakfast.

"And because you typically gobble down your food faster than the syrup can eat through the paper," his mom added.

That day at school went almost exactly as Ian had predicted, right down to the rampant rumors that began to spread almost immediately following the assembly addressing Ms. Shuffer's death. Ian thought that the best one was that Mr. Rutledge didn't actually exist and that the killer was actually Mr. Tadler, who not only hated the children he taught, but now: life in every form. During their lunch period, known bullshitter, Joshua Davis, narrated a tale in which Mr. Tadler, "sucked dry by a life of banality and resentment, had turned on student and faculty alike in an unquenchable bloodlust that would soon hit a fever pitch as he led a few more rogue teachers in bloody rebellion against life, liberty, and the inherent decency of civilized society."

While the idea was somewhat amusing, Ben and Ian agreed

that it would have been more amusing a few months ago. Now it just seemed...exhaustingly wrong. Facing no opposition, Josh utilized the entire lunch period by weaving fact into fiction, fiction into myth, and then pushing myth off of the cliff of reliability and down into the dark mirk of bullshit that lay below. By the time the bell rang, he was whole-heartedly proposing the idea that Mr. Tadler was *actually* an inter-dimensional crab monster who would love nothing more than to snip every male student's dick off.

"So what's our next move?" Ben asked as they claimed a table in the library during their resource period.

Ian glanced hesitantly toward the front desk and thought that it looked like Mrs. Reinhart was likely to become a permanent fixture now that Ms. Shuffer was gone. The tough, old woman sat ramrod straight in the former librarian's chair, her gaze fixed on something in her hands, eyes flicking up and around the room in discreet little jerks of movement.

"I don't know," Ian said, but let's try to look like we're reading or something. I don't want any of Mrs. Reinhart's homemade hot sauce recipe in my eyes.

"Ha," Ella said flatly, though she did immediately pulled out a book and began pretending to read it. Ben and Ian did the same.

"So? What next?" Ben said, eyes looking through the book in his hands; a big blue biology textbook that featured orcas breaching the ocean surface.

"We need to destroy the tree," Ella said firmly.

"How do you propose we do that?" Ian asked.

"How does one *typically* destroy things made of wood?" Ella asked.

"I don't know," Ian said. "Birch worm?"

"What the fuck is birch worm?"

"It's really awful, actually," Ben interjected. "It was a big thing a while ago. A kind of invasive species that came through and wiped out all the birch trees. I imagine you're thinking about fire though."

"Yes." Ella gave a gesture of thankfulness. "Yes, fire. Obviously."

"I know. I know. That sounds so—well, dangerous." Ian felt dumb saying it.

Ella shot him a withering look. "What, are you suddenly afraid for my safety?"

Ian was actually. He felt like they had shared something the other night, and he had no idea what to do with that fact. The only thing he had was the hundreds of movies he had seen and books he had read that came rushing in to give him advice. It wasn't unanimous, but the general consensus seemed to state that he had to sacrifice his own safety for hers. That no matter what happened, Ella was now his responsibility.

"I just think we should be careful about this," Ian said.

"I think Ella's right," Ben said. The idea of burning down a tree that was also a monster was clearly igniting a fire of a different kind behind Ben's eyes. "It's the best way."

Ian doubted that, but then again...it did sound really cool.

WALKING home after school with Ben and Ian, Ella imagined what it would be like when the tree went up. Would big ropes of flaming snakes gush out of it in burning red ribbons? Would it scream? Would it tear itself apart? She didn't know, and to tell the truth, she didn't even know what she wanted to happen. To tell the truth, she couldn't really grasp the big, walking tree's place in this whole thing. It seemed obvious that it was some sort of gatekeeper to the *real* monsters. But none of them had really shown their faces since those days of wandering in the wilderness.

"Should we try to make cocktails?" Ian asked.

"What?" Ben shook his head. "What are you talking about?"

"Ya know, cocktails. Like they used in that zombie movie."

"Do you mean *Molotov* cocktails? Because those are different than cocktails."

"Not really," Ian said defensively. "One just has a burning rag at the end."

"I don't know about that," Ben said. "I think Molotov cocktails use pure gasoline."

"We're not going to make Molotov cocktails," Ella interrupted. "If we did that, I'm pretty sure we'd all die horribly."

"Well, what do you suggest?" Ben asked.

Ella looked straight ahead. The day was warm and there were big patches of brown grass and exposed dirt where there had recently been snow. Despite the warmth, Ella noticed that Ian had continued to wear his ridiculous looking hat with the big flaps that flopped over his ears. Gosh, he must have been roasting in that thing. Ella wasn't wearing much over her school clothes beside a light spring jacket and she was still a little warm from all of the walking. They were less than half-a-mile from home now.

Home, she thought. *Was it home now?*

"I think we should just use matches," Ella said.

"Whoa, whoa, whoa." Ian had a look of incredulity on his face. "That is definitely *not* going to work." Then there was a brief flash of something else on his face that Ella couldn't make out. Some sort of indecision. Then it was gone.

"Yeah," Ben added. "I don't know if you've ever tried starting something on fire, but you typically need something to get it going if you want it to go fast. You can't just throw matches at it."

"It's true," Ian said. "Ben and I have virtually made a career out of setting things on fire, and I can tell you from experience that a tree, living or dead, is going to need to be drenched in gasoline or lighter fluid if it's going to go up."

"Yeah, remember that time that-"

But Ella had stopped listening. She had built plenty of fires in her time spent back behind her house, and while something told her that the tree would probably burn even if it wasn't drenched in gasoline, that wasn't what she was focused on now. She had just seen something that the other two hadn't, and now she was trying to process what it could mean.

"What do you think of that?" Ian asked as the three of them stopped at the turn-off to Ben's house.

"Of what?" Ella asked, still distracted.

"Awe man, you haven't even been listening have you?" Ben said almost moaning.

"I wanted plausible deniability, for when you two accidentally melt your faces together."

"Those are some big words. What was that?" Ben asked. "Possible deniability?"

"I know things," Ella said. "And it's *plausible* deniability."

"She heard it on an episode of Law and Order last night," Ian muttered.

Ella kicked him in the shin and he gave a brief yelp.

"Whatever," Ben said hastily. "So, we'll do it tonight. We'll pull the old double switcher on them. Ya know, I've got a sleepover at your house, you two have got a sleepover at my house. That old thing."

"Wait a minute," Ella interjected. "How are we even going to find the thing? It's not like we know where any dead bodies are."

Ian looked weirdly uncomfortable again, and for a moment Ella thought that he might actually know where a dead body was, but she dismissed the thought. Over the last few months, she had gotten relatively good at reading him and while she couldn't tell exactly what it was that was bothering him, she thought it was something else—something other than how they were going to find the creature.

"The cemetery," Ben said.

"What?" Ella couldn't believe it. If it were really that simple she was going to shoot herself.

"I mean it's the tree of *death* or something, right?" Ben was obviously sold on his own idea.

Then something visibly clicked behind Ian's eyes. "Hold on." He put a hand out, as if to steady himself. "No, yeah, I think you're right. Remember that time a while back we were passing the cemetery and it felt...off? Or looked off or something?"

Ben nodded, instantly hooked.

"Well, I think we saw something. Or we heard something or —who knows—even smelled something. Whatever it was, I feel like we perceived something was off about that place. I mean, we've been living here our whole lives. We know every inch of this town, so when something's off..." He spread his hands apart. "Maybe it's something that everyone instantly recognizes, but the fact of it doesn't quite make it past their willingness to—I don't know—believe it. Am I making sense here?"

"I'd be more willing to buy that if Poplar hadn't been harboring a serial killer for years," Ella said.

That seemed to stop him in his tracks. Finally, he rolled his eyes and said, "Okay, so it's not a perfect theory, but I'm telling you: I felt *something* there that day. And whatever this thing is, if it's feeding off of *death*, then that seems like a reasonable place for it to hang out. Don't ya think?"

The three of them stood there in silence, then eventually, one-by-one, they were all nodding. Not because it was a particularly good idea, but because it was their only idea.

"Well?" Ian prodded. Then, seeming to think of something

else, he shot a glance at Ella. "What we should really think about is how dangerous this is going to be. Any ideas?"

It seemed a weird question, but then again, they had never actually seen the monster do anything other than rip snakes out of the ground. But that wasn't what Ella was focused on, what she was focused on was the combination of Ian's question and his glance. What was he getting at with all of this? What—

Goddamit.

She knew what was on his mind now. Not for sure, but she thought she had a pretty good idea. At first, it made her angry—really angry—but then another idea came to her. A kind of perfect solution to what Ian was surely going to suggest and what she alone had witnessed just a few minutes before.

"I think it's extremely dangerous," she finally said. "I think it's more dangerous than you could possibly imagine."

26

―――――

It had been less than two whole days since he had killed Rosaline, but the pressure to do the next one was already unbearable. He had cruised the boy's house a few times, and at one point had even caught him going inside wearing some ridiculous hat. Was it some sort of ignorance that drove him to wear such things, or was it a bold acceptance of his personality? Rutledge hoped for the latter.

That was the problem with these quick kills, he didn't get to know the subjects as well. It felt almost like speed-reading to him. *Finished, now onto the next. Finished, now onto the next.* It felt almost wasteful. But then again, time was short. There was a time in his life when he thought he could go on forever, but now he had to come to grips with the fact that there were books he'd never read. Stories he'd never know. People who would never know *him*.

No, that isn't the way it is and you know it. You're the observer of this world. The reader. And when you end, so do they. Your blood will unlock the doors to a brand new world. Your world.

Rutledge tried to convince himself that it was true—that he *was* the be-all, end-all. And when he dug down really deep, he believed it. He knew it. He knew that he would kill the boy and whoever else he could before the time came—the time to end. And then that was that. It was all over. Everything would be gone.

All but the stars.

The stars. His legacy. His immortality. They would keep the pages turning, those heavenly characters, launching this finite world into eternity. They would observe the world after him—the world that tore itself apart in his remembrance. Soon they would all look up to the sky and despair, for his name would be written on it. Constellations of bodies dug up from the ground just to be put back in. Death follows life. But the stories survive.

Yes, Rutledge thought as he cruised past the Whelan residence. Their lives were about to change. Their son was about to die and become immortal.

Like the great stars in the sky, uncountable in their number, their world was about to burn.

———

IAN'S BEDROOM floor looked like it had been a staging ground for a sprawling Lego-metropolis, and then had a bomb dropped on it. The tiny multi-colored pieces lay scattered and heaped in random places throughout the room, acting as a kind of low-stakes obstacle course.

"How do you live like this?" Ella asked. Ian was sitting on the edge of his bed trying to build a helicopter made almost completely out of guns while Ella traced invisible objects on the floor. A river. A swan. A snake. A tree.

"Oh, I just live my life one Lego block at a time just like any other kid."

Kid. Was that what they were? The only time Ella ever felt like a kid was when she wasn't strong enough to defend herself against her father's fists, and if that's what a kid was, then she wanted no part of it.

"I think you wanted to ask me something," Ella said. No point in waiting any longer.

"What?" Ian tried to feign confusion.

"I know you've had something on your mind, why don't you just say it."

Ian carefully set the helicopter down in the middle of his bed, then leaned back alongside it and looked up at the ceiling. "I think you should stay here tonight."

There it was.

Ella didn't respond immediately. What should she say? What *could* she say?

"Why?"

"Because it's going to be dangerous, and well, I care about you."

Ella bit back the words that came to her mouth, swallowed the bitter draft.

"Okay," she said simply.

Ian looked shocked. "Really?"

"Yeah," Ella said. "I don't think I can do much more of this. Not right now at least. Ever since my father. My mom..." She didn't have to work for tears and it surprised her. "This whole thing is just...It's so *fucked up.* I know it probably feels like some adventure to you, but this is my life. And right now it's all but trashed."

The bed made a light groan as Ian got up. He took a few tentative steps toward Ella, but she couldn't tell if his hesitance was because he was nervous or because he was avoiding the Legos. Whatever the reason was, he found his way through the multi-colored maze and sat down next to her on the floor.

"Look," he said. "I'll admit, what we're doing...well, I'd be lying if I didn't say it was exciting. I mean for Ben and me it's just been day-after-day of school and pretending and trying to figure out who we are and where we belong. We've grown up watching all these movies about slaying monsters, but the closest thing to that here is shooting some hapless deer in the woods. Then this thing comes along." Ian exhaled and gazed up to the ceiling. "It's like some sort of *purpose,* you know? It's something we can finally do that isn't-" he waved his hand around in the air, "-math or science or learning or obsessing over what boring job we're going to have when we grow up. This is actually *something*. It might be dangerous, but it's something."

Silence hung in the room. The sun had gone down almost all the way now and artificial light sprang against the bedroom window as one of Ian's parents flipped the backyard light on. It was almost time.

"But you're right," Ian said. "It is different for you. This isn't some game, some adventure. Your family is in shambles. You've been tossed into this new situation with new parents and a new-" The word brother clearly formed on his lips, but he bit it back "-friend. So yeah, maybe you should stay here tonight. Maybe what you need right now isn't to go off and fight some monster. Maybe you've seen enough monsters. Maybe right now what you need is some stability, which is something that we have a lot of. Too much of it, actually."

Ella thought that he might say more, but he didn't. To be honest, she hadn't expected much more than a *"the battlefield's no place for a woman"* speech, but what Ian had said held some pang of truth to it. It might have even touched her if it didn't make her feel so sad. And it wasn't the truth that made her sad, but the fact that it was someone else's truth. It was Ian's truth, or at least how he saw her. As that young boy articulated his feelings and philosophies, Ella endured the slow and sinking realization that Ian didn't actually know her—didn't understand her or what she really needed. In the same way that he had attributed all of the evil in the town to the monster—the Harbinger as it called itself—he had also attributed every piece of every love interest he had seen in movies or read in books to Ella. She was simply a vessel into which he could dump all of the useless knowledge he thought he had about women that—up until he had met her—was just rattling around in his brain, searching for an outlet.

She'd let him have it though. Ella would let him hold onto that fairy-tale version of her for just a little bit longer. She could at least do that for him, and if she was being honest, for herself.

"I'll do it," she said. The tears had dried on her face like wasted rivers. "I'll stay here."

Ian leaned in and kissed her on the cheek.

As soon as the backdoor closed behind him, Ella strode quickly to a singular drawer in the kitchen; slid it open; and withdrew a large, stainless-steel knife. The grip was cool and angled for a bigger hand, but if she held it closer to the tiny hilt, she could still get a decent grip on it. Ella took a second to look at it. If she turned it just right she could see her reflection staring back at her: a solemn girl, too old for her age.

What are you doing? Never before had she asked herself that question. Usually, she just *did* whatever she was about to do. But this scared her. This was big. This was like nothing else she had ever done before. It was planned but planned hastily. She was prepared, but not enough.

Ella wrapped the knife in a kitchen towel she had snatched off the stove handle, carefully slid the blade through her belt—a tiny sword in a fluffy scabbard—and then she strode over to the front door where she had secretly stowed the only other item she'd need.

27

Marshall Rutledge sat in his car with his heart hammering. Ian had just left his house and left it alone for that matter. This made everything easier —made everything *perfect*. At first, Rutledge hadn't known how he was going to get the boy. Pick him up on his way home from school the next day? No, he'd have those two other kids with him. Break in and snatch him out of bed like the boogeyman? Oh lord, nothing could surely go wrong with *that* plan. In truth, he hadn't had a single clue. He had simply planned on cruising the house occasionally and watching it from different angles, which was what he was doing now.

After spying the three children as he drove by the first time, Rutledge took a quick spin around the neighborhood before swinging back and settling down a few blocks up the road from the Whelan residence. He could even see his old house from here, and when he looked at it, he felt a small twinge of home-sickness.

None of that now. You're closing in on the end here, and you're damn lucky to have gotten this far.

And luck was his only explanation for it. By all rights, he would have expected to have been caught by now. There was a national manhunt going on and he was driving around town for God's sake. Sure, he had a new car, but he had stalked Rosaline for *days*. Maybe people just didn't worry as much as he had thought. Though that didn't seem right. He knew that the local stations were already tearing the world apart over his last victim, and the tip hotline had undoubtedly been flooded with hysterical people afraid that the Roadtrip Ripper had just rung them up at the local grocery store.

The Roadtrip Ripper. He liked that. When news had first broken about the far-reaching nature of his slow-burn killing spree across America, it seemed like every news station on the planet was rushing to slap a catchy nickname on him. Over the last few months, he had been called everything from The Pentagram Slayer to the Five Point Killer. Some of them had a sort of cinematic quality to it that he rather liked, but eventually, the name Roadtrip Ripper was the only one of the batch still alive in fresh newsprint. Sure, it lacked any semblance of his philosophy behind his actions, but that philosophy would be made clear soon enough once the seal broke. Then, even if his literal name wasn't remembered, his exploits would be—the very heart of everything he was would be remembered in the shock wave of consequences that rippled out through history and the final gasping breath of reality.

The pressure was building up to something. He couldn't say exactly what it would look like in its completion, but he could feel it in the air. Marshall Rutledge, the Roadtrip Ripper, was about to become the ultimate distillation of meaning itself. Like some giant serpent of old, he was about to swallow the world.

That meant that he didn't need to be careful—didn't need to be diligent. People weren't as observant as they thought they were—weren't as cautious as their desire to sleep at night would let them believe. The world was complex and opaque: containing an unknowable multitude of monsters roiling beneath its murky surface.

The evils of the world could be seen, but remain unseen. Felt, but undiscerned. Strangers could live in close-knit communities—monsters out in the open. And so loud was the world that the sheer noise of it could obscure the sound of approaching footsteps until they were already behind you.

Rutledge had momentum going and the river of current events had gotten so swift and rapid that there was nothing he could do but enjoy the ride. Ian would die and be elevated to the status of an important historical figure and in that power—the prestige of plucking a fresh-young child from the realm of the living—Rutledge would pierce himself so firmly between the ribs of society that it would have no other choice but to limp along until it simply bled to death.

And that would be his legacy. There wouldn't just be one more new star in the sky but billions. Too many to count. Every story would be his story.

Rutledge gripped the handle of his hunting knife so hard that he thought he might break it. He would have to grip it pretty hard indeed for that to happen, but so what if it did? It didn't matter. He would grab the kid. Strangle him. Smash his head against a wall. And who would stop him? Who *could* stop him? His earthly life was sure to end in a hail of gunfire, but who needed guns when knives were so much more intimate; when the police couldn't find their own funding, let alone a killer; and when the town of Poplar was so submerged in its lethargic haze that it could do nothing but quietly offer up its best and brightest for the slaughter.

And now another piece of luck had fallen right into

Rutledge's lap. The boy was leaving the house alone—the boy who never went anywhere alone. He was far off, but with that ridiculous hat on, Rutledge could have spotted him from Mars.

Now! Grab him now!

No, the boy had to get closer first. But *ohhhhh*, Rutledge could almost feel his bones cracking beneath the pressure. Maybe he should just fire up the car and run him down. No, not sweet enough. He wouldn't be nearly close enough to enjoy it. He wanted to *smell* the boy's fear before he did it—wanted him to know it was him, and that yes, he had made the wrong decision when he left his house this final time.

Just a little closer. That's it.

But wait, what was this? The kid was turning down a driveway. It wasn't the Ryewheeler boy's house, that was through the woods. No, this was even better. This was *his* house! This was Rutledge's house! Perfect! All so perfect! Rutledge felt as if he had broken through some ceiling of existence and was literally controlling the world around him like a god.

But why would he be going to my house?

To shoot his fucking birds probably. To shoot his squirrels or maybe poison his bird-feeder. Fucking boys. Fucking goddamn adolescent boys. He'd show him. He'd show that little shit what would happen to disrespectful little shit-stain boys.

And just as he had the thought, he watched Ian pick up a large rock from out of his winter-wilted garden and use it smash Rutledge's living room window.

Enough, Marshall thought as he flung the car door open so hard it almost swung back and hit him in the face. He blew right through it and nearly broke into a run as he watched a bright white sneaker disappear through the vandalized window. *Didn't even need to break the crime scene tape.*

Wait, he hadn't even closed the car door. He had just jumped out and ran.

Fuck it. Kill him. Do it now.

Even with the occasional porch lights, the neighborhood was sparse enough to cloak Rutledge's approach in shadow. He was old, to be sure, but the Roadtrip Ripper could still hustle when he needed to and hustle he did. Before he knew it, he was already walking up the steps to his door.

God, I hope they didn't change the locks, Rutledge thought. He didn't know why they would, but the thought still struck him out of nowhere. *Keys. Keys. Keys. Fuck!* He had left them in the car, right in the goddamn ignition. But wait, he still had the spare in his wallet.

The old man's hands shook as he fumbled the leather billfold out of his back pocket and hastily dug for his spare key. Credit cards, reward cards, and three-year-old receipts fluttered like snowflakes to the ground until he finally found the dull, bronze-colored piece of metal wedged down in one of the card slots. Stifling back a cry of triumph, he quickly jammed the key in the keyhole, twisted it, turned the knob, and threw open the door.

When the time came, surprise was always his strategy, and this time was no different. The heavy door banged off the doorstop and Rutledge reached in and flipped on all the living room lights with a single swipe of the hand and *yes, yes, yes, there he is.*

But no. It wasn't the boy. For a moment frozen in time, Rutledge stared as the intruder standing in the middle of his living room pulled off his hat. No, not *his* hat. *Her* hat. It was the girl. The one he had seen earlier as he drove past. Waves of confusion washed over him and then an extremely brief feeling of panic. *Caught*, it screamed.

Then the feeling passed. Of course, there was no need to panic. This wasn't the victim he had intended, but she would be a victim nonetheless.

"I didn't expect you to be here so early," she said. "I didn't even get to sit down." Her face was hard and humorless, her stance wide for balance. Then Rutledge watched as she reached behind her and pulled out a long and gleaming kitchen knife.

Marshall smiled and reached for his own.

28

"What do you mean she's not coming?" Ben asked.

"I mean we talked it over, and we both decided that it would be best for her to stay out of this one." Ian had left almost immediately after his talk with Ella, and after a brief moment where he was unable to find his hat, he decided he could just steal one of Ben's.

"Ben, are you still here?" Ben's mom called from another room.

"Yes, mom," Ben shouted. "We're just getting ready to leave."

"Who's 'we?'"

Ben sighed so loud it could have almost been a scream. "Me and Ian," he shouted. "We're just grabbing a few things before we head over to his place, that's all."

Ian looked around as Ben and his mother yelled back and forth. The Ryewheeler house was a beautiful two-story home with a stained-pine interior, a wood fire stove to accompany the more modern gas heat, and an enchanting collection of antiques that looked so fragile that Ian didn't even want to breathe around them. He had been there a countless number of times in the last decade or so, but Mr. and Mrs. Ryewheeler's infinite treadmill of antique trading ensured that there was always something new to look at.

Wrapping up, Ben's mom yelled, "Okay, have a good time you two. And make sure you're back home by four tomorrow, Ben. It's pizza night."

"OK mom!" Ben looked as if he had just run two-and-a-half miles. He turned back to Ian. "Let's finish this outside in the shop."

IN STARK CONTRAST to the interior of their house, the Ryewheeler's woodshop was piled high with scrap wood, mounds of sawdust, an infinite assortment of tools, and the things that Ben and Ian were currently in there looking for: matches and a full can of gas. They found the gas can right away, but when Ben hefted it up by its handle a look of uncertainty washed over his face.

"You gonna carry that all the way to the cemetery?" Ian asked.

Ben looked thoughtful for a second. "Well, it is only a few miles away, and if all goes according to plan it should be lighter on the way back."

"I don't know man, that thing looks pretty heavy."

"Yeah, I guess. Let's see if we can find anything smaller we can put the gas in."

As they looked, the two boys talked about Ella.

"So you really think she's okay sitting this one out?" Ben asked as he dug through a box of random tools, pieces of rope, and punctured containers.

"Yeah, we talked it over. I think she understands."

The woodshed was quiet except for the clanking of tools being pushed about by the two boys' searching hands.

"I don't know," Ben said after a bit. "That doesn't sound like her. You sure you two didn't like, get in a fight or something? You didn't accidentally swing a lamp at her head and knock her unconscious, did you?"

"No way, man, she's cool," and after a brief pause, "and conscious."

"If you say so. I just think the whole thing smells weird. If I'm being honest, I think you'd stand a better chance of getting hurt tonight than she would. Just saying."

Ian felt anger flare in his head, but his retort was immediately extinguished when he found what he was looking for. "Hey, will this work?" He held up an empty two-liter soda bottle. The label had been ripped away and the cap didn't fit on quite right, but it looked relatively free of holes or cracks.

"That should do," Ben said. "I found some matches too. Waterproof. There aren't many of them, but they should do the trick.

"Why don't you try one?"

Ben, who never needed to be told twice to set something on fire, pulled a single match out of the little cardboard box and struck it on the side. The tip of the match flared with a bright flame that immediately shrunk and leveled out into an orange burning dot of light. Ben observed it with quiet fascination before furiously shaking it out. He dropped it on the cement floor, snuffed the smoldering end with his tennis shoe, and kicked it for good measure.

"Think we're set?" Ian asked.

"I think we're set."

———

"WHAT DID you think was going to happen here?" Rutledge asked. Ella could see his hand slowly rubbing the handle of some long knife he had sheathed on his hip. Hers was longer, but probably not as sturdy. She hoped it would still do the trick.

"There's a monster that lives in these woods, did you know that?" Ella asked.

Rutledge's face adopted an expression of curiosity. "Why yes. I'm quite aware actually."

"I don't mean you," Ella replied quickly. "An actual monster. A walking tree. A Harbinger of death."

Rutledge laughed. "Well, that sounds awfully...*menacing*. So why aren't you out there hunting it then? Why are you picking fights with killers when you could be out-" he waved his hand in dismissal, "-chopping down some evil tree?"

"Because there's something my friends don't understand yet. I think they will in time—maybe tonight even—but they haven't seen what I've seen."

"And what have you seen, little girl?"

"I've lived on my own for years. I've taken my father's beatings as often as he'd dole them out. I've dug my own mother's body out of the ground and I'm one of the only three people who actually knows she's dead. I've seen where evil comes from. I've seen the thing that lets monsters into the world. And it's not some ancient monster in a cemetery, it's not some snake. They're what follows the real monster. They're the consequence of something else. I think that we're going to be dealing with them for a long time, but they're not what started this. We are."

Rutledge raised his eyebrows as if to appraise her.

"But there's good news."

"And what's that," he said smiling.

"There's going to be one less real monster after tonight."

"I agree," he said.

For what looked like an old man, Ella was shocked to see him move so fast.

———

THE 2-LITER BOTTLE of gasoline fit snuggly into one of Ben's old backpacks, but after an extensive education via video games, Ian felt a little bit like he was walking next to a friend-shaped bomb. Ian had offered to take the matches so as to reduce their risk of accidental immolation, but then Ben said that they would have been like those Russian soldiers in World War II who would receive either an empty gun or a fistful of ammunition, but never both. Ian didn't argue.

The night was cool and wet. The previous day had melted a lot of the leftover snow and now it hung liquid in the air like the ghost of winter. One would expect it to get darker as the cemetery drew near, but the opposite was true. Ben and Ian's neighborhood was actually rather dark, relatively speaking, and Poplar's cemetery was located just on the edge of town. Less than half-way there, streetlights began to light the way. Traffic was light around this time, Poplar being a generally sleepy town, and Ian only saw two or three cars on his way to the cemetery.

"All right," Ben said nervously as they drew alongside a chain-link fence. On the other side, there lay a speckle of gravestones and narrow walkways.

"Yup. Come on."

Feeling somehow criminal (and probably appearing so) the two boys spent the next twenty minutes hunting the cemetery for any sign of movement. But other than a rabbit and a few bats that flitted overhead, there was nothing. Ian's feet were soaked again and he was pretty sure that it was just a matter of time before someone saw them and asked what they were doing.

"Man, I don't know if we're going to find anything like this," Ian said.

Ben looked like he wanted to argue, but seeing as there were no tree monsters jumping out at them, he couldn't really think of anything good to say.

"Hey, you got a knife?" Ian asked.

"A knife? No."

"We came to kill a monster and you didn't even bring a knife?"

"Well, apparently you didn't either," Ben said. "What, are you going to stab a tree with a knife?"

"Yes, actually." Ian bent over and fished around on the ground for a rock. After a minute he found a jagged piece of stone about the length of his palm. "This should work."

"What are you thinking?"

"You know how all of Rutledge's victims had stars carved into them? What if we can call it that way?"

Ben looked skeptical. "I don't know, man. You said that there were holes where Ella's mom was buried right? So it must have been there, and she didn't have a star on her."

"Yeah, I know, I just kind of have a feeling though."

"A feeling? Man, I hope you have more than that."

"Do you remember the words in the book we got from Pastor Carlyle? There was something about the monster being summoned by something burning in the sky. I remember it because it sounded so weird. At first, I thought it was talking about the sun, but what if it's a star? What if a star can summon it?"

"I don't know, but this thing seems to be drawn to things—to dark places. To symbols. To *intent*. And I don't think it's really afraid or even concerned about anything. I think if we make some sort of effort to reach out to it, it'll come." Ian walked over to the nearest tree and started to carve a crooked star into the birch bark. "At least I hope it comes because if it doesn't then I'm just some dick who carved a pentagram onto a tree in a cemetery."

ELLA THOUGHT she had known what she would do when the time came. In her mind's eye she saw herself dodging Rutledge's blow and sinking the knife into his chest. Easy as that. She had so much confidence in it that she didn't even stop to consider what would happen if it didn't work—couldn't stop, actually, because she knew that if she had slowed down for even a second to consider what she was doing, she wouldn't be able to do it at all. But when the time came—when Rutledge finally rushed in, knife snapping up to meet her—her body reacted instead.

RUTLEDGE STOPPED at the last second. He did things quickly and decisively, but when he saw the girl flinch away and swing her arm overhead to protect herself—almost against her will—he knew he had all the time in the world. She had made an impulsive decision, and now she would be regretting it.

He raised his arm and backhanded her, and in the swing, he felt every person he had ever taken in that fashion. He felt a hundred cracking skulls. A hundred stars against the night sky, bursting as they were born. The girl went down, the knife clattering out of her hand. And when she looked up at him from the ground he saw hatred, but not just that. He saw fear. Fear and familiarity. This wasn't her first time being struck to the floor and she knew the drill.

As his hand connected with the side of the girl's head for a second time, Rutledge looked into those eyes, brown like winter grass, dewy with fear and intensity, and he knew that the moment was now. It was too sweet not to.

Who knew spontaneity could be so delicious? If he had known how wonderful it was to kill without the lead-up, then maybe he would have been doing it this way all along. But then again, maybe it was for the best that he hadn't. Maybe some part of him knew that it was, but resisted all the same. How easy would it have been for him to get caught right away in the beginning? How quick and terrible? No stalking. No stars. No stories.

No, he had been doing it right all along. It was worth it, wasn't it? To have such a huge back-catalog of souls tucked away inside of him. But now that the story was drawing to a close, he could have a little fun. Finally, act a little impulsively. Who, after all, would stop him?

He readied the knife in his hand. A silver viper's fang jutting upward out of his fist.

Then the whole house shook as the front door crashed open.

———

AT FIRST, it looked like carving the star into the tree would amount to nothing. The two boys stood silent in the cemetery as rogue gusts of wind blew around them. The air whistled through the branches of the scattered trees, bent trunks moaning along. A wooden choir worshipping the wind.

And maybe that's what it was that made the hair stand up on the back of Ian's neck. He didn't see anything different—the night was still dark around them, the gravestones standing unique in their individual make-up but united through the singular purpose of paying tribute to the dead—but maybe it was the fact that the song of the wind in the trees changed ever so slightly. A new voice in the choir. A new harmony, low and sad. Those swollen major chords, now minor.

Ian turned and looked. It's possible that the tree behind him had simply been there the whole time. It may have been a good idea for the two boys to take stock of every tree in the cemetery upon their arrival, but the thought hadn't occurred to either of them until now.

He felt it though.

After carving the star, a jaggedly off-center little thing, he had tried to call the monster in his head. A prayer, almost. Unlike the forest that bends itself toward the sun, Ian did the opposite, and bent his heart toward the darkness, calling upon it. Reaching out in faith.

And there it was. The more he looked at it the more certain he was.

"We're getting rid of you," Ian said in a shaky voice, feeling a little stupid for talking to a tree. It stood absolutely still.

The wind blew again. Another minor chord. Frigid fingers of wooden strings.

"Uhh, are you sure that's it?" Ben seemed skeptical, but hefted the bottle of gasoline just in case.

"It is," Ian croaked, then more sure of himself, "It is. Do it."

Without a moment's hesitation, Ben ran forward and started jerking the big bottle forward, sending little gouts of gasoline down the side of the tree. As he watched, he thought that the black bark looked less like bark than it did dry skin soaking up water. In the places where the gas landed, the bark looked almost relieved.

"I don't know man, it doesn't seem to be reacting," Ben said, the bottle almost three-quarters empty now.

"It is," Ian repeated. "Look at the bark, it's soaking it up."

"Yeah, it's not the only skin soaking it up. I think I've got about half of this stuff running down my arm," Ben said as he finished off the bottle. It thunked to the ground as Ben reached with his dry hand into his pocket to fish out the matches, his other one held out and dripping. "Ya know, I think you should probably be the one to light this thing. I'd probably go up just as fast."

"Sure thing," Ian said. Never taking his eyes off the tree, he reached out and took the matches from Ben. "Here we go."

There was a scraping sound as Ian swiped the matches against the side of the box. All three ends flared, then instantly shrunk down to fingernail-sized flames that wavered ever so slightly as they began their slow descent down the wooden shafts.

Ian threw them like so many lots.

29

The force of the door exploding inward was so great that it was hard for Ella to tell if Richard Carlyle had turned the knob first or had simply thrown the crushing weight of his fury against it like a human battering ram. Either way, the shock and surprise gave her just enough time to spring away from Rutledge toward the knife she had dropped.

"Oh, no you don't," Rutledge growled as his hand shot out and caught Ella by the hair. The young girl cried in pain as she was yanked backward.

"Drop her," Carlyle yelled.

Rutledge didn't back down however; he pulled Ella back to her feet and drew her in close to his body, pressing the knife to her throat.

Richard raised a small chrome pistol and aimed it directly at Rutledge's face. "I said, 'drop her.'"

At this Rutledge hesitated. Ella could feel his indecision, the fact of his failure slowly dawning on him as he struggled to come to terms with the idea that suddenly, everything had changed.

"What are you going to do pastor, shoot me?"

Ella felt the man's grip tighten around her hair and her already aching scalp sent bolts of lightning through her head. But even as fear and pain and shame raged around inside of her, there was something underneath it all, a kind of desperate hope. And underneath that? Well, as for that feeling it was hard to describe, but it was familiar. Like the feeling that immediately follows plunging one's head underwater in a cold lake. A kind of clarity.

She had been foolish to try and take on Rutledge alone, she knew that now. She should have gone with Ian. Or better yet, she should have made him stay back. Who gave a shit about that monster anyway? What had it really done so far other than shed a bunch of light on all of the dark deeds done by the normal people of Poplar, Wisconsin? How could he possibly focus on that when there were bigger dragons to slay?

Because he doesn't know what monsters look like, Ella thought. *Not yet, at least. But he will. Give it time and he will.*

"Any reason I shouldn't?" the pastor asked. His tone was dead and even, but from where she stood, Ella could tell that he didn't look very good. His complexion was drawn and pallid, his eyes bloodshot. She had seen the look many times in the face of her father, and for one startling second, she forgot who was supposed to be the good guy in the room and who was supposed to be the bad one.

Maybe they were all monsters, wild beasts destined to snap at each other until the end of time. Maybe they all deserved to be put down. Just looking at the way Richard Carlyle stood there, a gun in one hand, his other dangling limply at his side like a dead branch. His posture was lopsided, Ella noticed, and the dangling arm looked bizarrely stronger than the other.

Stronger. Why did she think that?

Because it bulged, that's why. Because even through his long sleeve shirt, Ella could see the tight chords of muscle flexing beneath the thin fabric.

"You won't kill me," Rutledge said, snapping Ella out of her reverie. "You can't. It's not destined."

"And what do you know about destiny," the pastor asked. "What do you know about fate? Do you think yourself God? Do you think yourself the same God that saw fit to save my Lilly at birth just to have her swiped away over two decades later? Are you the God that thought it wise to give my other little girl cancer, and then send it miraculously into submission, just to have her victory smacked away by her dead sister?"

There were no tears in the man's eyes. Ella thought that he had probably cried himself out long ago, but sitting down there in that church basement with nothing to dwell on but his senseless fate, what had this man become? She thought that he had been an ally when he burst in, but now she wasn't so sure.

"If you think of yourself as that God," Richard continued. His face was flush now and spit was flying from his mouth as his words gained steam. "If you are him, then you will die as he should! You'll die as she did! You'll-"

In a split-second of furious motion, Rutledge leaned in and pushed Ella so hard that she half-stumbled, half-flew at Mr. Carlyle. Shocked and caught off-guard, Richard flinched and then reached his free hand out to catch her as she crashed into him. A shot exploded next to her head as the revolver went off, and the noise was so loud it was like sound itself cracking in half.

Richard stopped her fall, but barely, twisting his ankle in the process. "Let go, let go, let go," he said feverishly. His voice was pitched now, and for a second Ella didn't know what he meant.

Then she did.

As she half-hung there in the man's arms, her hands gripping his biceps, she felt revelation wash over her like cold rain.

They had no time. In actuality, less than a second had passed since Rutledge had pushed her, and even as she stood there, horror coursing through her, she knew that he was already moving. Already lunging with knife-in-hand. He was going to kill her—kill them both. But in that singular moment, it didn't seem to really matter.

It didn't matter because Richard Carlyle wasn't strong, he was weak. He had a right to that weakness, sure enough, but suddenly Ella understood that he might now be the weakest man on earth. Because he wasn't filled with justified anger, he was filled with poison. And the thing underneath his shirt wasn't an arm. Or at least, it wasn't just an arm. There was something else under there too. Something wrapped around it.

Something that moved.

———

WHEN IAN THREW the lit matches at the tree, he expected it to light slowly. For years now he had watched his father with fascination as he reached down with a lit match to light a small mound of charcoal, and every time he would watch the flame climb across the lighter fluid in a blossoming orange flower.

This was different.

The matches hadn't even hit the tree yet when the gasoline ignited with a dull *whump*. Heat leaped out at them as it was engulfed, its gnarled branches suddenly wreathed in flame. And if Ian hadn't known better, he could have been convinced that he had not just set a tree on fire but a man.

As soon as the fire caught, the tree began to twist and howl with a sound like that of a hundred whistles, all blowing at once, blending into a cacophony of agony. Ian saw Ben clasp his hands over his ears as he involuntarily did the same. The two boys should have run—*would* have run—but the sight before them was so unworldly that to not bear witness to it would have been something akin to nihilism.

"Stop," someone yelled. To Ian, the voice sounded shrill and full of pain, and for a second he thought it was the tree yelling. But as he heard it again and again, he realized that it was his lips moving—his vocal cords straining beneath the grinding weight of sobs and curses that were now spilling unbidden from his mouth. Tongues and words he didn't understand had gripped him and were coursing out like so much vomit.

Tears flooded Ian's eyes as he looked over at Ben who was now kneeling in the dirt. "Stop it! Stop it! Shut up!" his friend was yelling. He couldn't hear the words but he could feel them. Ben was digging in the ground now, tearing up clumps of grass and rocks and hurling them at the tree. To any onlookers, the whole scene would have appeared nothing short of absolutely bizarre, but Ian felt the same thing. He hated it. As the monstrosity burned before them, Ian felt like it was infecting the air, poisoning it. Every unrealized fear and buried rope of anger came bursting out of his heart in a single tidal wave, and now he was hurling clumps of earth too. At the tree, at the gravestones, even at Ben. He felt like he wanted to tear the whole fucking world down.

"Die!" Ben yelled. "Die! Go back! Go back to Hell you bastard!" And at that final curse, Ian watched as he began clawing at one of the small gravestones next to him.

Surely he didn't intend to pick it up and hurl it, Ian heard a small voice in him saying. But there were other voices now. Loud and terrible ones that wanted it to be so. Anger and irreverence surged through him like hot magma, and later on, Ian would find himself wondering if that was what people in mobs felt like as they hurled bricks through storefront windows or strung people up by their necks.

"Go back!" Ben yelled again as he heaved the stone out of the ground. Leaning back on his right leg like a shot-putter, the young boy hurled this final stone at the dying demon in front of them. But as the projectile left his hand it was suddenly filled with something else.

Fire.

Ian watched in horror as one of the tree's branches shot out and clutched his friend's hand in a death grip. And as soon as those blazing fingers wrapped around Ben's muddy fuel-drenched palm, fire raced up his arm. Ben's eyes were wide and wet now, his arm burning in front of him. And even though it lasted for only a few seconds more—even though the gravestone hit the tree square in the center of the trunk, causing it to explode into a swirl of ember-laden ash—the sight of the tree that grew in the Shadow of the Valley of Death holding the bubbling hand of his best friend would remain branded on Ian's mind for the rest of his life.

There was the sound like that of a burning house collapsing in on itself as Ben's hurled gravestone punched through the tree like a silver bullet. The air around the boys swirled and whooshed upward in a cyclone of smoke and ash and the sickly smell of burning flesh, and the mighty gust quickly blew out the fire that was devouring Ben's arm.

It was over.

EVEN AS IAN scrambled toward his friend who was now shivering violently on the ground, he couldn't help but feel relief that their job was finished. They had succeeded. The monster was dead. It was done.

But as Ian approached his fallen friend, the acrid smell of burnt flesh still wafting up at him, he realized that Ben was mumbling something. He was saying something over and over again with his eyes wide open, his pin-prick pupils staring right through Ian.

"What?" Ian asked as he half-knelt, half-slid to his friend's side. Later he would find that he gouged his knee on an upturned rock as he did this, but in that moment he didn't feel it. All he felt was a chill running up his spine as he bent over to hear the words his friend kept repeating like a chattering wind-up doll.

Over and over again, in a clipped and ragged voice, Ben declared "It is done."

"It is done, it is done, it is done, it is done, it is done..."

And at that very moment, back in an abandoned house on Wilmer Street, it was.

30

Ella was in the air again. A graceful swan with her wings spread, soaring down the stairs. Set free from her father's hands. Set free from everything. She was a bird, bound to nothing but the air around her. Beating her arms like angel wings, she conducted the atmosphere and let it lift her up. Up, up into the sky. Into the stars. She pressed her hand against the glass that separates worlds and...

There was a loud crash as Ella's body slammed into the bookshelf behind her, sending dozens of small paperbacks fluttering down on her head. Rutledge had hit her from behind—had slammed into both of them actually: Ella and Richard Carlyle. Standing off-balance, they had been sent sprawling in two different directions as Rutledge threw a shoulder into the two of them.

Pain throbbed through her back where she had hit the large, wooden shelf. Struggling to her feet, she watched in horror as Rutledge walked over to the spot where Mr. Carlyle now lay and swung a foot into his face. There was a dull smack as it connected, and the pastor went sprawling for a second time.

"You thought you could stop me," Rutledge roared. He reached down and picked up the spent man who was now bleeding profusely from his nose. Lifting him up by the collar, Rutledge held him aloft for a second before throwing him back down to the ground in what Ella could only describe as a wrestling move. She had always thought the overly dramatized wrestling matches as cheesy and impractical, but there was nothing funny about this. Richard's body hit the ground so hard that Ella thought she heard bones break.

"You thought you could kill me? You thought you were the *hero* in this story? Well, I hope it's obvious now that-"

But Ella never found out what was supposed to be so obvious. In the struggle, Carlyle's shirt had ripped and was now hanging off of his body in places. And one of those places was his left arm.

RUTLEDGE STARED IN MUTE HORROR. At first, it had looked like a tattoo, or at least that is what his mind tried to tell him. Just a tattoo. But it wasn't. The snake was long and black and wrapped so tightly around the flesh that Rutledge could only see tiny white marks where the skin was poking through between the coils. But that wasn't the worst part.

The worst part was the eyes.

The serpent had its fangs firmly locked into the middle of the man's bicep, but with its head twisted around to face Rutledge, it pinned him to the ground with its stare. Only it didn't have the narrow slits of serpent eyes, but rather the round and watery eyes of a person, a human being. Rutledge was even close enough to tell that the irises were a deep and earthy brown color.

What was it that people said about eyes? That they were the window to the soul?

If that were the case, then this thing's soul carried more than the dull apathy of a cold reptile. It also carried deep wells of sorrow, and sharp pinpricks of razor-sharp anger. This thing's eyes were more human than most human eyes.

Rutledge wasn't sure what he would have done if more time had passed. Kill it? Cut it in half? Stomp its head into the carpet like the body of a scurrying roach? There was even a small, quiet part of him that wanted the man to hold completely still so they could carefully try and remove the thing, never mind the fact that they had been trying to kill each other just a second before.

But he never got the chance to do any of that; because in one swift motion the snake withdrew its fangs, uncoiled its body, and flew across the floor and into the dark hallway beyond so fast that it looked less like it was slithering and more like it had been fired from a crossbow.

A moment of silence hung in the air. Two grown men and an adolescent girl breathed and tried to come to terms with what they had just seen, but for Rutledge, the experience was already fading into something of a bizarre happenstance rather than a life-altering event. There was even a part of him that was surprised to observe how fast his old-murderous self was pushing away the awe-struck observer of just a few seconds before.

Maybe the girl was telling the truth, he thought. *Maybe there actually are monsters out in these woods.*

For the better part of Rutledge's adult life, he had been out to achieve something. When he had been just a young man in his early twenties, he had been visited by someone. A man. Though now he wasn't so sure.

The man had shown him things—told him things that he

shouldn't have known. He had recounted Rutledge's life in Poplar—recounted his traumatic upbringing, his early departure for a new and different world, the last few years of his bloody and nomadic lifestyle. Then he foretold his return—he talked about how it would all end where it had begun, but first, there was something that needed to be done.

It was called the Seal of Solomon and his destiny would be to break it.

The man was scant on details, but the way he spoke about Marshall's life—as if it were some grand play and he was just now reaching the point where his path was laid out before him —the whole thing was absolutely intoxicating. Like the ghost of Hamlet's father, the man had laid out a course of destruction that Rutledge had followed to a T. The whole thing had added another dimension to the ritual—an added layer of depth and intentionality.

For years after that night, Rutledge had carved his way through state after state, killing and marking his victims. All with a singular purpose in mind—all fulfilling the grand narrative of his life. Sure, there were times that he doubted his purpose—nights where he would lay awake and wonder why he was doing all of this. Not the killing—the killing was something compulsive—something that had to be done. No, what he wondered about was the overarching ritual. The man. The Seal.

Over time, his mind had filled in the gaps: he was engaging in a piece of art. The killings were a tableau of sorts and when he was finished he would be hailed as the ultimate artist. But what if the man he had spoken to swept in and stole the credit? What if this was just some big joke?

In actuality, he didn't have those thoughts all that often. The man had seemed so otherworldly, so—*god*-like, that it wouldn't have made sense for him to do such a thing. Plus, there were things he knew about Rutledge that he shouldn't have known. He didn't just know the events of his past, he knew what he was *thinking* during those events. He knew who Rutledge was at every step of his young life.

Even knowing that—even knowing that the single time he had seen that shadowy figure he had seen something closer to a ghost or a demon, he was wholly unprepared for what he had just witnessed. The thing that had been attached to the pastor's arm had been nothing short of a monster. Was that what this was all about? Was there something waiting on the other side of this plane of existence, and had Rutledge's entire life been devoted to letting those things in?

He thought about that—thought about what it meant to not just be a monster, but to be the monster that lets the other ones in.

The thought made his heart flutter with something like pure elation.

And with that, Marshall Rutledge turned to the man on the carpet who was still trying to recover from what had happened, and with three small steps, he closed the space between them, drew the knife back out of its sheath where he had placed it, and sunk it into Richard Carlyle's chest.

How quickly we return from our caves, he thought, *once the serpents slink back into the darkness.*

Despite what people might think, driving a knife through a person's chest isn't as easy as sinking it into the ground, but with enough force and a strong blade, it's still possible. Richard Carlyle made nothing more than a small gasping sound as the knife went in, and Rutledge got to see the look in the man's eyes as he realized he was going to die.

Another story drawn to a close. *Be with your daughter now.*

"You were never going to stop me, you see," Rutledge said.

"I'm in control here. This is my world. My story. My legacy. And you're just one of my-"

A scuffing noise came from behind him.

The girl. With all of the madness surrounding the snake, I almost forgot about the girl.

"You can't save him, you know," Rutledge said as he turned around and was surprised to see that the girl looked almost as bad as Mr. Carlyle did. Blood ran from scrapes on her face and arms; she stood lopsided, favoring her right leg; and the look on her face was one of absolute detachment. If it wasn't for the knife in her hand—probably the same one she had brought on her ill-advised journey over here—then he might have believed she had given up altogether.

But wait, it wasn't a knife in her hand, was it? It's what she should have had—what the grand narrative of his life demanded. She should have been broken and bleeding but ready to defend herself one last time. She'd lunge forward with the knife and he'd knock it out of her hand and finish her off with a final slash from his. But it wasn't a knife.

It was a gun.

Shit, Rutledge thought to himself, she must have picked it up when he was taking care of the pastor. No matter. She was a child, and a stupid one at that. She had believed she could come over here all by herself and stop him. Which she obviously couldn't. No one could. Not even the man at his feet, the pastor with the demon at his side, a physical manifestation of God and the Devil wrapped into one and *he* couldn't even stop the Road-trip Ripper.

Because this is my story, he thought. *My legacy*. He knew exactly how to play this.

Rutledge dropped the knife and raised his hands into the air. "Okay, you got me," he said. "What now?"

Ella let out a small breath, and then she shot him in the heart.

He didn't even hear the bang—didn't see the flash. Just blackness as it clouded his vision. Legs failing, he fell to the earth, blood blooming in the center of his chest. A ragged hole torn in the fabric of his existence. A hard punctuation mark.

A dark and crimson star.

31

The police showed up to the late Marshall Rutledge's house 30 minutes later. They would have shown up sooner, but Ella hadn't called right away. In fact, she may not have called at all if it weren't for the thought of Ben and Ian.

Upon shooting the Roadtrip Ripper, Ella's first instinct had been to hide the body. The last thing she wanted to do was try and explain to the police why she had pulled the trigger when she didn't need to. And to tell the truth, she didn't really feel like explaining *anything* to the police. Not now, and probably not ever. There were dead men sitting here, and this time, Ben and Ian weren't here to absorb some of the responsibility. It was just her, as it had always been, and in this situation, she knew that she was going to be questioned over and over and over again, and every stumbling word or contradiction would be scrutinized under a microscope. There would never be any peace for her, Ella, the girl who had killed one of the most infamous serial killers in the last decade.

But what if she wasn't? What if she didn't have to be that girl? What if she was simply the girl who had been taken against her will and rescued by the brave pastor who had lost his daughter to that same killer? That was a lie she could sell to the world, and most importantly, one that she wouldn't have to sell to Ben and Ian.

If Ella had hidden the bodies like she wanted to, then she had two choices: tell Ben and Ian and make them carry that secret as well, or refuse to tell them anything. Bury it. Like her mother had been buried.

And that was the thought that did it. Ella had enough buried ghosts and demons, and hadn't it been nice to be able to share something with the two boys, however naive and gung-ho they seemed to be? Did she have to shoulder everything by herself, or could she let some of the weight off? It was still a secret they'd have to bear, to be sure, but a girl who had justly defended herself and stopped a cold-blooded killer was much easier to bear without the addition of, *oh yeah, and I hid the body and no one can ever know what happened to him, Rutledge, the new town boogeyman.*

God, there's no way they could keep a secret that big—that the Roadtrip Ripper was actually dead and buried. They would either blab the first chance they got, or they'd be crushed beneath the weight of it. Before they knew it, that idiot Josh would be telling a story about how Ella was actually a trained CIA sniper and had killed Rutledge and maybe even Richard Carlyle to keep the whole thing quiet. That was the last thing she needed. So why not make it easier? Why not provide a little alternative history, rather than simply bury it?

And that's what she did.

After 25 minutes or so of contemplating her predicament, Ella finally picked up the phone, dialed 9-1-1, and told the operator that there had been a shooting on Wilmer Street. A few short minutes later, there were flashing lights and wailing sirens outside the blood-soaked Rutledge house.

Ella would be in the clear. The boys in blue would ask their questions and she would answer them.

———

UNKNOWN TO HER, Ella wasn't the only child graced by the sound of sirens that night, but in Ben and Ian's case, the circumstances were a little more bittersweet. It wasn't that Ian was sorry to see the flashing lights of the sheriff's cruiser round the corner, followed shortly thereafter by a firetruck and ambulance, but as soon as he realized what the scenario might look like to an outside observer, the edge of his enthusiasm was blunted slightly. What, after all, could he tell them? How could he explain the scene: bits of fire and ash strewn around a quiet cemetery, his friend's arm burned so severely that the smell was making him nauseous.

He found out later that someone in one of the the neighboring houses had called 9-1-1 when they heard Ben screaming, poked their head out the window, and saw the dancing glow of flames coming from the cemetery. Considering the circumstances, Ian couldn't say that he would have done anything different.

In the end, Ian did the only thing he could think of: he took it square in the face. After months of trying to get people to believe that he had seen a hell beast striding across his backyard, Ian had learned that the easiest explanation would always be the best. So as they hauled Ben Ryewheeler away on a stretcher to be raced off toward the nearest ICU, Ian explained to a stone-faced deputy that the two boys had come out to start a campfire in the cemetery, because it seemed like the kind of half-cool, half-creepy thing a couple of young boys would stupidly dare each other into doing, and one thing led to another.

"You didn't think it might be dangerous to use gasoline to start a fire?" the deputy asked. His nameplate said *Kizowski,* and that sounded right to Ian. He was a new guy hired on just this year, if he remembered right. "Isn't all you kids do these days is play video games where you blow up gas cans?"

Harboring a little resentment at the fact that he couldn't admit that that was exactly what he was thinking as they lugged the big bottle of gasoline down the road, Ian guessed that it was probably safe to assume that the young deputy, probably not having video-game-aged kids yet, only knew this because he himself played those very same video games.

"We thought it'd look cool," Ian said. "We dumped a bunch of gasoline on the ground and Ben must have got some on his arm because as soon as he lit the matches, his arm went up like crazy. It was like *whoosh,* and the fire spread, and man, I just freaked out. I think I just stood there and watched it, I was so shocked. Man, I'll feel bad about that forever, I think. Oh gosh, what will his parents think? Do you think they'll ever let us hang out again?"

And on and on he went. Ian realized that he was rambling now. He had originally intended to do this in an attempt to show that he was just a freaked-out kid, and hey, maybe go easy on him? But as soon as he started talking, he learned that he didn't really have to act like he was thoroughly shaken because the truth of it was: he *was* shaken, right to his bones. They had just used fire to kill a monster in a cemetery in the middle of the night and his best friend had been grievously wounded, maybe even beyond repair. The words gushed out of Ian as he divulged all of his fears to Deputy Kizowski.

The deputy eventually held out his hand. "Okay, okay, I get it. I think your friend will be okay. He's hurt pretty bad though, it's no small thing you kids did tonight. There are gonna be consequences, but I think you know that."

Ian nodded, all of the energy gone out of him.

"Now I still have a few more questions for you." The deputy flipped to a new page in his notepad. "Do you know anything about the incident that happened at your neighbor's house tonight?"

"My-what?" Ian hoped his face showed shock, because it *was* shock. What had happened at Ben's house?

"Well, it just seems so unlikely that the biggest serial killer the Northwoods has ever seen would die at the same time you were out here pulling this stunt, don't you think?"

"What?" Ian blurted. "Somebody killed the Roadtrip Ripper at Ben's house?" And even as he said it he knew it was wrong. Of course, it hadn't happened at Ben's house, it had happened at Rutledge's. But thankfully, it was his immediate ignorance that convinced Deputy Kizowski that Ian had nothing to do with the incident. Unfortunately, he refused to give Ian any more information on the subject. He continued his line of questioning, and as he did, Ian began to answer with shorter and shorter answers as his mind began to spin a million tales about what could have happened at the Rutledge house.

ELLA AND IAN were able to visit Ben when he returned home a few days later. Ian had been grounded beyond the very edge of time for the role he had played in his friend's injury, and Ben's parents sounded like they were bound and determined to never let the two boys ever see each other again. But after some time passed and Ben was able to pull himself out of his drug-induced stupor and take some responsibility for his part in the blatantly disobedient and destructive event, Mr. and Mrs. Ryewheeler finally relented and allowed the two kids to see him.

"You look really good," Ian said after they had sat down. Ben was lying propped up in his bed while his parents looked on. A couple of kitchen chairs had been appropriated for guests.

"Yeah, I bet," Ben said quietly, then he looked over at his parents. After a moment of indecision, they finally allowed their son and his friends a moment of privacy. With a stony glance at Ian, Mrs. Ryewheeler quietly closed the door behind her.

"I'm surprised you guys were able to kill it," Ella said once she was sure no one was standing outside the door listening. "Seriously, I expected you to just wander around the cemetery until you got arrested."

"Well, both of those things did kind of happen," Ian said. "Though we didn't get arrested exactly. We both had to pay fines."

"Really?" Ben asked. "Shit."

"Oh yeah, that's a thing. I bet your parents haven't told you yet. You'll be doing chores until your other arm falls off."

"Goddamit," Ben moaned. He tried to lift his right arm which was wrapped in white bandages, then made a small sound of pain and lowered it again. "Yeah, this one's toast I think."

"Literally," Ian said, and his friend snorted a laugh.

The three of them spent some time catching each other up on what had gone on that night. Ella explained everything that had happened at the Rutledge house, right down to the snake that had been wrapped around the pastor's arm like a giant leech, though she may have made the part where she killed Rutledge sound a little more defensive than it had actually been. Ian and Ella had talked the following day between being questioned by the police and yelled at by Mr. and Mrs. Whelan, so most of what took place now was for Ben's benefit. Still though, they all enjoyed telling their stories, knowing full well that those present in the room were the only ones that would probably ever hear them.

"Man, I still can't believe you shot him," Ian said. "You got really lucky there."

"Well, I like to think that my stone-cold bravery had something to do with it," Ella replied. "But in retrospect, I do agree that it could have gone a lot of ways. I think if Pastor Carlyle hadn't have busted in like that, I'd probably be dead."

"I keep forgetting he's dead now," Ben said. "First his wife, then Lilly, then him. What a torn-up family."

"Yeah, I feel sorry for Claire. She's been through a lot for her age." Ian leaned back in his chair and looked at the ceiling. "I guess we all have now."

The bedsprings squeaked as Ben shifted uncomfortably. He winced and it looked to Ian like he might be coming up on his next round of pain medication. A clock on the wall ticked as the three of them thought their own thoughts.

"Guys?" Ben finally said.

"Yeah?" Ian answered.

"What do you think happened to all of those snakes? Like the one Ella saw come off of Mr. Carlyle's arm? Do you think they're still out there?"

They all thought about that for a moment, then Ella said, "I think so. I don't really know how they work, but it seemed to me like it was poisoning Richard's thoughts or something. The Harbinger is gone, but I think they're here to stay, so we should probably all watch our backs from now on. Why do you ask?"

Ben made a face and Ian couldn't tell if it was because he was in pain or because he was thinking.

"I saw something," he finally said in a tentative voice. "When my arm was burning, I saw a lot of things."

Ella and Ian absorbed this quietly for a moment.

"Like what?" Ian asked.

"I saw a river. It was flowing from a huge mountain." Ben's eyes moved rapidly as he spoke. "There were bodies floating in the water, and some of them had our faces, and some had faces I've never seen before. I saw a rabbit that had its throat cut, and I saw a tree at the center of the world with roots like tentacles. I saw a shield lying broken on the ground with a huge spider standing over it. And then I saw-" and at this, he looked confused, "-I saw hundreds of them. Thousands. All blotting out the sky."

"Thousands of what?" Ian asked. "Thousands of spiders?"

"Swans." Ben closed his eyes. "I can see them now. Thousands upon thousands of swans all filling the air like smoke—all of them silent—all of them white."

Ian was confused. He prodded Ben for more but his friend had stopped speaking. Now he was starting to twist in pain.

"Mom," he yelled. "Mom, it hurts." Tears had started running down his cheeks.

Both Ian and Ella got up as Mrs. Ryewheeler entered the room, a glass of water and a bottle of pills in her hands. "Get out, both of you," she croaked. Her eyes were tired and bloodshot.

The two kids didn't need to be told twice.

The front door closed abruptly behind them as they stepped out into the driveway. The day was the first genuinely warm one in a while, but Ian knew that springtime in Wisconsin could be even crueler than winter with its false promises of warmth that could easily be swept away by another surprise blizzard or two following winter like a segmented tail. He thought about taking the road back to his house—Ella's house too, he supposed—but decided to take the quicker route through the woods instead.

The two children walked around the Ryewheeler residence and into the wide-open backyard. They moved quickly, aiming at Ian's house which could be seen through the thick growth of trees. And off to the left, through those same woods was a dull glimmer, the yellow reflection of sunlight off of a windowpane —a windowpane that Rutledge had once watched birds and squirrels through. The house finally standing empty and robbed of all of its secrets.

Ian looked at Ella. She was looking straight ahead, deep in thought. He thought that she looked paler than usual, white even. White like Ben's swans.

He reached down, taking her hand in his. And the two children stepped into the woods together.

EPILOGUE

The vast majority of Rosaline Shuffer's assets were liquidated on a sunny spring day when after most of the snow had melted and the whole of Poplar, Wisconsin lay bare and ready for renewal. Due to Shuffer's distinct lack of close relatives, the role of executor ended up falling to a nephew who lived in Colorado and opted to sell off everything as quickly and easily as he could. The young man knew about his late aunt's rare and valuable book collection of course, but on his single trip up north from Denver, Colorado he was upset to learn that the vast majority of the books had been stolen in a recent break-in.

Being the obvious suspect, Tony Langley had to prove his innocence, which ended up being relatively easy, seeing as the downstairs window was broken and he technically had access via his very own doorway. Add on top of that, the fact that no books were ever found in his apartment, nor did they show up for sale online in the passing days. After a short but thorough investigation, leads dried up and the books never surfaced on the market, thus reducing the nephew's inheritance substantially.

Even though the priceless book collection that Ms. Shuffer had kept in her bedroom had disappeared, the robbers could hardly have taken every book in the house without being prepared to back a dumptruck up to the front door, which even in a sleepy town like Poplar would likely be observed and reported. So it was that only her private collection detailing obscure aspects of the occult and supernatural was stolen, leaving behind her massive accumulation of novels, memoirs, nature writing collections, and pop-history she had collected over the years.

And lumped in with all of those was a nondescript blue hardcover with thinly etched black lines. If someone were to open it, it may have been obvious that this was no ordinary book, but no one did until it had been safely procured along with a dozen or so mystery and fantasy novels for the reasonable price of $17.

The other books that were purchased in the transaction were flipped through a few times over the years, but hardly a day went by that the blue book wasn't cracked open and studied for at least fifteen minutes. The writings were vague and obscure, but their otherworldly quality had a magnetic pull practically refusing to be ignored.

The most tantalizing thing though, Ella thought to herself one day after closing the book and returning it to its spot in her closet, was what *wasn't* in the book. After all, it was unlikely that the entire supernatural world could fit inside of a single volume.

There was a whole world out there that no one even knew existed. Sometimes dark and sometimes magnificent, there were things beneath the ground and beyond the stars that the eyes of humankind had never seen, and Ella Windthrope was determined to see it all.

———

WHEN DEPUTY BRIAN KIZOWSKI got home, he opened his door and flipped on the lights to find a man sitting in his living room. Or at least, he looked like a man. Kizowski knew better though. The age-worn lines and well-kempt hair could probably have fooled most people, but it was the eyes that gave it away. They were—not to put too fine a point on it—totally dead. A few of Kizowski's new *associates* had eyes that were sad and full of sorrow, but not this one. This one was different. These eyes had seen far more.

"I didn't expect to see you so soon," said the deputy. He had in fact been kind of hoping to never see him again. There had been a brief time of dependence when the creature in its snake form had latched onto Kizowski's arm and pumped poison into him for days on end. He had had to call in sick, which wasn't ideal during a national manhunt, but once Anderson came to his house and saw his face, the new sheriff had relented. The problem was that he was then kept out of the loop as far as anything revolving around the Roadtrip Ripper was concerned, and he got stuck with the usual bullshit like domestic disputes and that thing with the two kids in the cemetery.

"Our timeline might be accelerating a bit," said the figure in a smooth voice. They must have looked so much like two regular men in that moment that Brian found himself briefly questioning his own sanity. "Apparently one of the guardians of this town sent out a letter before she died. My little spiders tell me that two men are on their way to Poplar right now."

"So?" Kizowski said. "I thought you said the Magen Society was all but in ruins at this point. What could they possibly do?"

"Well, they can kill us for one. Don't think that you're beyond that sort of thing, because you're not."

"Okay, what do you want me to do about it?"

The man-shaped creature in Kizowski's living room didn't answer immediately. Instead, he reached into his breast pocket and pulled out a hand-rolled cigarette, lit it, and took a drag. He looked up at the ceiling as he exhaled.

"Tell me," he finally said. "What do you think it is we're trying to do here?"

"I don't know, we didn't really talk much about *you* guys. You pretty much just talked about me, so I'm not sure. Are you trying to destroy the world or something?"

The figure nodded and took another drag on his cigarette.

"If we were to-" and at this, he scrunched his face in mild disgust, "-*destroy the world* as you put it. What's in it for you? Why would you want the world to be destroyed?"

"I don't know." The deputy sensed that he had answered wrong by now, but he still followed the line of question. "I took this job because, when I thought about it, I couldn't really come up with anything else. Anderson acts like he's out to protect the community, but that's bullshit. All anyone really wants is power, and that's what I want. I'll say it. I don't care. I've spent a lot of time getting shit on at the bottom, so when it comes right down to it, I just want to climb out. But you already know that. That's pretty much all we've talked about so far."

"Okay, and what good is being on top, if what you're on top of-" and at this, he flicked the cigarette onto the carpet and ground it out with his heel, "-is a heap of ashes?"

Kizowski winced. Burn marks in his brand-new carpeting wasn't exactly what he had hoped to get out of this relationship.

"I've spent enough time dwelling amongst ashes," the thing said. "You have no imagination, Brian. That's why you went with the first job you could think of. That's why you just want to light the world on fire, even if you're standing right in the middle of it.

Did you know that you were so easy to turn I had enough time to turn another one? You know that girl who killed Rutledge? I've got her father now, *not that he was a stone fortress, mind you,* but it took Sawscale almost *four months* to turn the pastor, and even then, he still needed a constant feed."

Kizowski was angry now. But worse: he was scared. His nerves had felt scorched for months on end at this point, his temper red-hot. Without realizing what he was doing, he felt his hand drift down to his gun-belt. He wasn't exactly a quick draw, but the thing in front of him was just sitting there unarmed. It had promised him power—promised him immortality and abilities beyond his own comprehension. That was nearly five months ago now, and all he had to show for it was being kicked down the ladder at work and an endless string of frayed mornings and sleepless nights. He was done. Done with all of it.

The shot was explosive in the tiny living room. Gunsmoke hung thick and heavy in the air, but there was none of the rest. No hollow *thunk* of lead hitting flesh. No smell of scorched skin or misted blood. To Brian Kizowski, the room looked empty now. The chair the thing had been sitting in had a hole the size of a penny in it and pieces of stuffing lay on the floor behind.

For a second, he thought he had lost it. A man standing alone in his living room pumping bullets into an empty chair. Maybe he was having some sort of crack-up, he thought. Maybe he needed to go check-in somewhere and-

"You disappoint me, deputy," said a voice from behind. "I think we might need to take some time for a little re-education. I think you need to try and see things *my* way."

Brian spun on his heel, but not fast enough. All of a sudden, his body was crushed in the powerful grip of something huge and foul-smelling. The young man tried to squirm out, but he might as well have been stuck in dried cement up to his shoulders.

The giant snake held him firmly, but not so hard as to break any bones. A large reptilian face floated in front of Kizowski like some horrible balloon animal lolling on a string. Then Taipan, Prince of Vipers, sunk his fangs into the young man's eyes.

THE END

Ash Above, Snow Below

Violent Wonder

ABOUT THE AUTHOR

Fredrick Niles lives in St. Paul, Minnesota where he writes fiction, bartends, rants about movies, drinks cheap whiskey, lurks in bookstores, and practices introversion with his wife.

facebook.com/fredricknilesauthor
instagram.com/fredrickniles_author